EVERY LAST ONE

A KATE REID NOVEL
BOOK 15

ROBIN MAHLE

HARP HOUSE PUBLISHING

Published by HARP House Publishing
November 2022 (1ˢᵗ edition)

1

The drum-line echoed and the cymbals clashed as the 96th Annual Independence Day Parade officially got underway. Nineteen-year-old Emma Katz looked on while the Jansville High School Marching Band stood in formation on Market Street. The townspeople lined the parade route, forming a sea of red, white, and blue along the storefronts. Flags waved, and snow cones melted in the rising sun. Nestled at the foothills of the Blue Ridge Mountains, this rural Virginia community looked forward to the event every year.

Emma was home from college for the summer. Her red hair that brushed her shoulders glistened in the morning sun as she stood beside her family. A smile raised her freckled cheeks when the Grand Marshal waved from the backseat of a '67 red convertible Ford Mustang.

It was then she spied Brian Keller, her old high school boyfriend, from across the street. The good times they'd shared flooded her thoughts and her cheeks flushed for a moment. Emma had been so busy with her summer job at the grocery store that she'd hardly had a chance to catch up with all her old friends, including Brian. She tapped her father's shoulder. "Hey, Dad."

The middle-aged man with a stocky build and a shaved head turned to his daughter. "Yeah?"

"I forgot my sunglasses. I'm going to run back to the house and grab them. Save my spot?" she asked.

"Sure, hon. Hurry up, though. You don't want to miss seeing the company float. It turned out great this year." Dave Katz was the town's only CPA. He and his small staff built a giant Uncle Sam float every year. And every year, Dave insisted it was better than the last.

"Okay, Dad. I'll hurry." Emma rose onto her tiptoes and kissed his lined cheek. "Mom, I'll be right back," she added.

Sharon Katz was a tiny woman with red hair worn long in a single braid. Her sky-blue eyes lit up. "All right, sweetheart. Don't be long. You know how your dad is about the float."

"I know." Emma searched for Brian again among the crowd, and on catching his gaze, she nodded at him. Brian looked around and then pointed to his chest. "Yes, you," she whispered, before offering a wave of her hand.

Emma carried on to the next block and kept watch of Brian while he waited for the parade to pass.

He soon caught up and nervously pushed his hand through this thick dark hair to move it out of his face. "Hey, Emma. No work today, huh?"

She examined him for a moment. He hadn't changed much since last year. Still kept his hair at his shoulders. Still wore basketball shorts and a graphic tee. Still reminded her a little of that guy Steve from *Stranger Things*. It was probably just the hair. "It's a holiday. Store's closed. I'm glad to have the day off, to be honest. I've been working a lot since I got home last month. My parents like to remind me that I need to earn enough money to take back to school in the fall."

"Sure. Makes sense. I'm sorry we haven't gotten a chance to catch up much. I've seen you at work, but you always looked so busy, I didn't want to bother you." His eyes roamed over her. "It's really good to see you, Emma. You look great."

She glanced away, feeling the heat rise in her cheeks. "Thanks. So do you. Hey, um, walk me back to my house? I forgot my sunglasses and was going to grab them real quick."

"Yeah, sure."

Emma walked beside him, recalling how they'd been close in high school. How all of them had been close. "Hey, have you been back to the clearing?"

"No." He glanced at her. "I don't think anyone goes there anymore. We were the last of the breed, I guess."

"What? This year's seniors don't hang out there?" she asked.

"Not from what I heard, but I don't hang around the high school anymore. They might think I'm a creeper or something." He laughed.

"You're probably right." Her home was just ahead, and Emma walked along the path to the front door of the Craftsman-style cottage. When Brian hadn't followed, she looked back with a curious gaze. "Aren't you coming?"

"Oh, you want me to go inside with you?"

"Of course. It's not like you haven't been here a hundred times before." She unlocked the door and stepped inside, waiting for him to enter. "I think I left them on the kitchen desk." Emma walked into the large kitchen with bright white cabinets and a farmhouse sink. "You want something to drink?"

"No, I'm good." Brian looked around. "So, uh, are you still liking college?"

She snatched her sunglasses from the desk. "It's okay. What about you?"

"It's okay. I mean, I don't go to some big fancy university like you do, but community college is fine."

She headed back toward the door. "It's hardly fancy." As Emma locked up behind her, she turned around and stopped cold. "You know what? I need to run by the store and pick up my paycheck."

Brian stood at the edge of the porch. "I thought you said it was closed."

"It is, but I know Mr. Hardy is there right now. He'll be leaving for the picnic soon, I think, so I can run in and get it. Otherwise, I'll have to wait until Tuesday. Do you want to come with me?"

Brian shrugged. "Why not?"

HARDY'S GROCERY store was on the south end of town, about 4 blocks east of Market Street. Emma had just enough time to run inside and collect her paycheck before she was set to return to the parade for the big float reveal.

She stopped at the entrance and quickly spun back to Brian. "I don't know if Mr. Hardy would be okay letting anyone else inside since he's closed—"

"That's okay. I don't mind waiting out here," Brian replied.

"Great. Be back in a flash." Emma opened the door to a blast of cold air that blew down from the fan above. The owner, Randall Hardy, and his son would probably be leaving soon to join the rest of the town for the festivities and fireworks later tonight.

Emma walked along the white-speckled linoleum floor toward the back office where Mr. Hardy kept the paychecks. Sam Hardy swept the floors at the end of the deli counter, and she caught sight of him. "Hey, Sam. Your dad has you working today?"

"Just for a little while longer, then I can go to the picnic. What are you doing here, Emma?" Sam was the only child of Randall and Carol Hardy, who owned the grocery store. The 22-year-old with short brown hair, and a thick waist, leaned on the broom.

She pulled off her sunglasses and peered at him with bright blue eyes. "Came to pick up my check. Is your dad in his office?"

"Yes, ma'am, as always."

Emma approached Sam and placed her hand on his shoulder. "It's looking good in here. Keep up the good work."

"Thanks, Emma. I will."

She offered a warm smile and kissed his cheek before walking toward the manager's office. "Mr. Hardy?" Emma peeked inside.

He removed his reading glasses and turned around in his chair. "Emma, what are you doing here?"

"Decided to pick up my check, if that's all right."

"Of course it is." Randall Hardy came in at about six feet and a solid 200 pounds. The 48-year-old wore a thick beard, though he kept it trimmed along his jawline. He pulled open his top desk drawer and retrieved several envelopes. "Let me see here. Ah, here it is. A check for one, Emma Katz." He offered it to her, but when she tried to grab it, he wouldn't let go.

"Mr. Hardy," she said, playfully.

"All right, all right. What can I say? I like having you around here, Emma. That beautiful smile of yours. I'll tell you, you brighten up this whole place."

"Thank you, Mr. Hardy. I enjoy being here too. I'm grateful for the job."

"Oh yeah?" His smile waned.

Emma blinked quickly and tried to preserve her smile but

noticed something in his eyes had changed. "Yeah, of course." She reached for the check again, but he still held it between his fingers.

Hardy tilted his head. "I bet those college boys are giving you all sorts of attention. You deserve it too. And I'll bet not a one of them is good enough for you."

She grew uncomfortable and cast down her gaze. "Mr. Hardy, I should really get going. My friend is waiting for me outside."

"Sure, yeah, of course." He finally let go of the envelope. "But you ever need anything, Emma, money, or whatever, you know you can come to me."

"Sure, Mr. Hardy. Thank you." She thumbed back. "I'd better go."

"See you at the fireworks show tonight, yeah?" he said as she turned away.

"Yes, sir." Emma didn't turn back and retreated into the hall for a moment to shake off the icky feeling that crawled up her spine. "Gross." She looked over at Sam, who stared at her. With a knitted brow, she wondered if he'd overheard. "Hey, Sam, you okay?"

His eyes wore disappointment. "Did you get your paycheck?"

"Uh-huh. Sure did." Emma donned an awkward grin. "I should get going before all the food's gone at the picnic. So, hey, I'll see you tonight for the fireworks, okay?"

Sam turned down his lips and nodded. "See ya, Emma."

DAVE KATZ WIPED the ketchup from his lips while he sat with his wife in Town Park. "I can't believe Emma missed it. What is the matter with that kid?"

"She's not a kid anymore, Dave. She's a young woman in

college. I'm sure she caught up with one of her friends and lost track of time." The petite, red-haired woman in her late forties reached for a soda from the cooler. "She won't miss the fireworks later. Now come on, finish your hotdog. I want to go chat with some folks."

No sooner had Sharon demanded that Dave finish eating, had she stood up and snatched his plate. He shoved the last of his hotdog into his mouth. "Guess I'm done eating."

Sharon pointed at a table under the shade of a tall oak. "I see Carol over there. I haven't talked to her since Emma went back to work at the store." She looked at Dave. "Wouldn't mind hearing how she's been doing."

"All right. I'm coming." Dave followed his wife as she hastened her steps toward the woman who, alongside her husband, owned Hardy's Grocery Store. "Maybe we'll ask them if Emma's getting a raise too."

Sharon glared back at him. "Don't you go embarrassing me, now, or Emma for that matter. They were good enough to hire her."

"Good enough? They needed the help. Don't go pretending like they did Emma some big favor. They got Sam working there already but he can't keep up."

Sharon stopped and swung back around. "Be kind, would you?"

He threw up his hands. "I am being kind. Just saying..."

"Well, stop." Sharon put on a smile when they reached Carol Hardy. "Afternoon, Carol. Good to see you."

Carol replaced the lid on her casserole dish and returned a bright smile, accented by full cheeks and soft brown eyes. The 47-year-old was well-put-together and wore most anything from the Macy's Department Store sale rack. "Afternoon, Sharon. What'd y'all think of the parade this morning? Great, wasn't it?"

"As always. A fantastic showing. You and Randall did amazing work on your float."

"Well, thank you. Though I do believe most of the credit belongs to the wonderful workers at the store." Carol surveyed the park, wiping away a bead of sweat from her high forehead. "Speaking of... don't suppose you've seen Randall around, have you?"

Sharon screened her eyes with her hand and peered into the distance. "No, I sure haven't. Then again, I've been stuffing my face with food over there for the past twenty minutes or so. Anyone could've walked on by, and I wouldn't have seen them. I only had eyes for that darn potato salad, isn't that right, Dave?"

"Sure, sure. Darn good potato salad." He rubbed his plump belly. "Where do you suppose ol' Randall is right now?"

"Down at the store, I'll bet," Carol replied. "Must've slipped away before I got everything all set up down here. Course, I haven't seen him, or Sam, come back yet."

"Aren't you closed today?" Dave asked.

Carol set her hands on his hips with palpable indignation. "Of course, but you know Randall, always gotta check in on the store. I'm sure they'll be back soon, if not before this evening's fireworks."

"I'm sure they will. We wouldn't miss that for anything." Sharon raised her chin. "Just out of curiosity, how's my girl doing there at the store for you?"

"Emma?" Carol swatted the air. "She's just been fantastic. You two raised a hard worker. And the way she is with Sam. Just so patient and kind. Been a Godsend, if I'm honest."

"Well, that is so good to hear," Sharon replied.

"And where might she be today? Figured she would've been here," Carol went on.

"Oh, she was. Walked back home a while back to get her

sunglasses. Haven't seen her since, but I imagine she found her friends and started talking."

"I'll bet. I gotta say, this past year's probably been quite an adjustment for you two, huh? What, with Emma being away at school and all," Carol added.

Dave placed his hand on Sharon's shoulder. "It's been tough, but we're just so proud of that kid."

"I have no doubt you are." Carol's attention was drawn to a voice that called out. "Looks like Susan's after something. I better go see what she needs. I promised I'd help clean up after everyone was finished, so I'll see you both tonight for the show?"

Sharon nodded. "You know it. We'll see you tonight."

A LIGHT BREEZE drifted atop the water of the bay and gently rocked the 22-foot Bayliner in its slip. FBI Supervisory Special Agent Kate Reid and her teammates sat in its bow, prepared to watch the fireworks. In the towering building adjacent to the bay was where Kate and her husband, Senior Unit Agent Nick Scarborough, called home. He'd owned the place in the DC suburb of Woodbridge before the two married.

Kate's long brunette hair drifted in the breeze as the sky neared dark and the stars revealed themselves. A slender woman of about five-feet-six, and in her mid-thirties, Kate was recently promoted to her supervisory role. The hard-fought battle to overcome a troubling past and a bout of retribution versus a former staffer had nearly derailed her career.

One person was missing tonight, and that was Kate's husband. A last-minute call saw Nick heading back to the office, which was now at FBI Headquarters in D.C.

Colleague, Levi Walsh, stood along the bow's railing, tipping back his can of beer. He glanced at Kate. "Good idea, watching the fireworks from the boat." The 40-something, stout Southern gentleman, who was also a former Army intelligence officer, licked the foam from his lips. "You say Scarborough's planning on finally selling this thing, huh?"

"We never take it out. In fact, it's hardly ever been used." Kate raised a brow. "Why? Are you in the market?"

"Not a chance." He turned back into the breeze, though his dark crew-cut hair remained oddly unmoved. "I am sorry he's not with us tonight."

"Me, too. It happens. We all know what it's like." Kate reached into the cooler. "Anyone ready for another beer?"

"You don't have to ask me twice." Jonathan Surrey held out his hand. The newest member of the team, he'd transferred out of the Denver field office and worked side-by-side with Kate. He was also the best dressed among them. Even now, he wore tailored shorts and a fitted button-down, while no amount of breeze could penetrate his thick brown, perfectly styled coif.

Kate tossed him a can of lager. "What about you, Eva?"

"Sure. Why not? Thanks." Eva Duncan took the can and side-eyed Walsh. "Hey, don't forget you're my ride."

He held up his meaty hand. "I know. I know. I'll get you home safe. Don't need to worry about me."

Kate opened a beer for herself. "I remember those days, riding to work with Nick. How are you two enjoying the carpools?"

Duncan tilted her head and her caramel-colored hair worn in a high bun shifted a tad. "Honestly, it's been great, don't you think, Levi?" She was the closest thing to a sister Kate had and the two shared a close bond. But there was no mistaking, the beautiful, athletic woman was as hard-nosed as they came.

"Yes, ma'am. It's nice having back up on the next floor above."

"I'm glad it's working out for you guys." It was then Kate felt the eyes of Cameron Fisher fall on her. The Senior Unit Agent, and friend, had broken it off with Duncan shortly after he was promoted. A mutual decision that apparently still stung.

He averted his gaze and made his way to the railing. The 48-year-old unit leader had closed himself off since the breakup. It was clear to Kate he had loved Eva very much. As he stood at the railing, he pushed away the strands of salty hair that blew into his eyes and took a drink from his beer.

"So, Reid, how's, uh—how's Scarborough doing with the task force at HQ?" Surrey asked.

Kate joined Walsh on the bench. "He seems to be handling things. I think it was a good move for him. I know he misses his team in Unit 2, but he was ready for the challenge. I'm proud of him."

"And Myers?" Fisher turned around and placed a toothpick between his lips. "How's all that panning out?"

"Fine. It's working out just fine. She's married now. Has a toddler, too, I hear."

"I'm sorry, who are we talking about?" Surrey asked.

Kate pressed her lips together. "Nick's ex-girlfriend, Georgia Myers, is working with him on the task force. They broke up a long time ago. Long before I started with the team here. It's really no big deal."

"I didn't say it was," Fisher added. "It was just a question—"

Kate shifted her gaze to Surrey. "What about you? You're a single guy. Care to buy a boat?"

AT THE TOP of the hill, overlooking Jansville Town Park, Jason Gatwick stepped away from the fireworks platform to check they had the "all-clear." The 20-year-old firefighter joined the small fire department shortly after high school.

He returned to the control panels, where he assisted local pyrotechnics expert, Hughie Barns, alongside his roommate and fellow firefighter, Chris Pumphrey. Under a dim spotlight, he eyed his partners. "You two ready for the grand finale?"

Hughie keyed in the last of the commands while Chris stepped aside. The fireworks expert donned a wide smile. "Here we go, boys. Let's light her up!"

Jason pushed in his earplugs and stepped away. The heat from those candles was about to get intense. He pulled Chris with him while Hughie started the finale. "Earplugs," he shouted and pointed at his ears.

In an instant, the sky illuminated with a spectacular display. Jason glimpsed down the hill and looked at the people in lawn chairs, camping chairs, and blankets. The entire town had shown up, just like always. And all Jason had to do was be ready to extinguish any fires that might break out. This was his first time assisting with the display and never had there been an incident, so he hadn't expected one now.

"This is it, fellas. Last light!" Hughie prepared to press the button on the control board when Jason yelled out.

"Stop!"

Hughie pulled back. "Jesus, dude, what the—"

Jason whizzed by him toward the tree line that was cast in heavy shadow. "Oh my God. Oh my God." He stopped on a dime when he saw her clearly. "Emma? Emma, is that..." She collapsed onto the ground, and he peered over his shoulder. "Hey, we need help! Get my bag, hurry!"

Chris ran toward him and began to slow down, but Jason waved him on. "Go to the truck, Chris, now!"

Jason returned to Emma, who lay face down on the ground.

When she began to move, he placed his hand on her back. "No, don't. Just hang on." His eyes raked over her. "My God, what happened? You're covered in blood. Emma, your head." When he moved her bloodied red hair from the side of her face, he thrust his hand over his mouth. A dent the size of a baseball concaved the back of her skull. His stomach lurched and he lost his breath.

Emma reached out her hand and clutched at his shoes. Her voice was muddled, and Jason leaned closer. "What are you saying? I can't understand you."

It was then Jason saw her face. Fear caught in his throat, and he rocked back, falling on his butt. "Your mouth. Who did this to you?" Tears spilled down his cheeks and when footfalls sounded behind him, he looked back.

Hughie hovered over them, his eyes seemingly frozen wide. "What the hell happened to her, man?"

Jason's chin quivered as he turned back to her. "Someone cut out her tongue."

2

T own Park had been cleared of all except for those close to Emma. Her friends, family, and those with whom she worked. Everyone else had been told to go home. Lock their doors. Hold onto their children. A quiet dread fell over the town. And except for the deafening wails of a mother and father whose daughter was brutally taken from them, nothing else sounded. Not the crickets, nor the wind through the trees. Nothing.

Emma's parents stood at the bottom of the hill, at the sidewalk entrance to the park. Sharon clutched onto her husband, barely able to stand under her own weight, while Police Lieutenant Howard Irving spoke to them.

Her friends huddled together. Amber Hoffman and Heidi Sumner, had been closest with her all through high school, though had drifted since graduation. Brian Keller, who had seen Emma only hours earlier, walked toward them.

"I can't believe this," he began.

Amber's pale face was stained with salty trails. She tucked her long blond hair behind her ears and regarded him. "Who could do this to her, Brian? I don't understand any of this."

"I know." He set his hand gently on her shoulder.

"They cut out her tongue. My God..." Heidi tried to catch her breath and looked on before Randall Hardy glanced at her.

Amber appeared to notice him. "Why is he still here?"

"I guess because Emma works at the store." Heidi kept her gaze fixed on him when he raised a corner of his lips into a rueful smile. She turned back to Brian. "You were with her, right? I mean, earlier today?"

"Yeah, I told Lieutenant Irving already. I told him I left her when we got back here for the picnic." Brian's voice faltered. "I didn't see her after that. He says I have to go to the police station to make a sworn statement."

The group of friends looked on while Fire Chief Barrows and Chris Pumphrey helped the EMTs load the body onto the ambulance.

Jason Gatwick stood at the top of the hill. Brian turned up his gaze toward him. "I can't imagine what Jason must be thinking right now. He looks in total shock."

"Does anyone know if they were still going out?" Amber asked.

"I don't think so," Heidi replied. "I'm pretty sure Emma broke it off with him before she left in the fall. But I haven't had a chance to talk to her hardly at all since she got home." Her eyes welled again. "Now I'll never talk to her again."

Brian wrapped an arm around Heidi's shoulder and looked up again at Jason. Behind Jason, officers searched the woods, and down into the valley; their shafts of light spun around like a Pink Floyd laser light show.

∿

Jason Gatwick kept his eyes fixed on the scene below when he heard Irving call out to him, but his gaze shifted to Emma's parents, who were prepared to leave for home without their daughter.

"Come on down here, son." Irving narrowed his gaze. "You hear me, son?"

Jason blinked hard and forced himself to take a step. The shock of it all had rendered him motionless. He noticed Mrs. Katz inside the car. Her red hair clung to her tear-drenched cheeks and her eyes were practically swollen shut. He felt the sting of his own tears when he finally walked down the hill and reached the lieutenant.

Irving set his hand on Jason's shoulder. "Why don't you come sit down over here? Come on now." He guided the young man to a nearby bench. "I'm damn sorry about what you saw, son. I'm damn sorry about all of it." He looked away a moment as if doing his best not to break down. "Still can't get my head around this. All my guys, they're all out there trying to find whoever did this, you understand? We will find this person."

Jason looked on. "She tried to speak. And then she was gone."

"I know, son. Listen, here. That poor girl somehow managed to find her way out of the woods, so now we gotta figure out how she got there. That part is my job, all right? Your job, young man, is to tell me everything you know about the last time you saw Emma."

Jason reflected on the question for a moment. "I hadn't seen her since a few days ago, I guess. Saw her at the store where she works."

"I understand you two had been going out for a while."

Jason closed his eyes. "We broke up when she left for school, but we were still friends."

Lieutenant Irving removed his hat and rubbed the sweat from

his bald head. He licked his full lips and set his eyes on Jason. "It was amicable, then?"

"Yes, sir."

"And did she break it off because she was leaving for school, or had she decided to go out with someone else?" Irving pressed on.

"Emma told me it was because of school, but I don't know, I think it might've been something else," Jason replied.

"Like what, son? Now, I need you to be completely up-front with me. Whatever you have to say could help me with finding out who did this, you understand?"

Jason raised his shoulder. "I'm not really sure, but I think she didn't like that I was a fireman. She didn't like coming over to my apartment. I really don't know, but we broke up, and now she's dead."

Irving patted his back. "I know, son. I know." He let out a heavy sigh. "You didn't see her at all today?"

"No, sir." Jason cleared the emotion from his throat as he blinked away his tears. "She might've been with Amber or Heidi."

Irving nodded. "We're talking with all her friends, trust me on that. But according to Emma's folks, she'd left the parade to go pick up something from her house. They hadn't seen her since. Young Brian, over there, was with her for a while, but they parted ways, and he came back to the picnic. I am hopeful we'll find her cell phone out there in the woods and that will give us more information." He leaned back on the bench and peered out over Market Street. "Go on home now, son. Do the best you can to get some rest. When you're up to it, I'll need to get a statement from you."

"Yes, sir." Jason slowly stood from the bench and turned to the lieutenant. "Who could do that to someone? To my friend?"

Irving looked down and shook his head. "I don't know, son, but I'm damn well gonna find out."

Along the single-lane road, near the entrance to the highway, lay the five-acre property owned by the Hardys. They'd been married for 24 years, and Sam was the product of that marriage.

When the knock came on the front door, Carol wiped her hands on the dishtowel. Sam had been with her in the kitchen and had just calmed down enough to drink a glass of water while he sat at the table. As she made her way to the door, she noticed him tremble still as he wiped his nose with the back of his hand. "I need to see who's at the door, Sam. I'll be right back." Carol walked on and peeked through the side window before opening the door.

Lieutenant Irving removed his hat and tucked it under his arm. "Evening, Mrs. Hardy. How y'all holding up?"

"Well, it's just been such a shock, Howard. I'm scared out of my mind if I'm being honest. Sam's finally settled down. But not a one of us is going to be all right for some time, let alone Sharon and Dave."

"I know. May I come in?"

"Of course." She stepped aside as Irving entered. Can I get you a cup of coffee or a bite to eat?"

"No, ma'am, but I do thank you."

"Well, come on into the kitchen." She turned to the living room. "Randall, Howard's here. He wants to talk to us." When he didn't turn, she called out again. "Randall?"

"What?"

"Uh, hello, Mr. Hardy," Irving cut in. "I came to finish our conversation from earlier if that's all right with you. Now that you got the rest of your family here, figured it best to get it out of the way."

Randall got up from his chair and walked toward them. "Howard, while I appreciate you got a job to do, we only just got Sam calmed down. He's beside himself with grief over Emma, you see."

"I have no doubt, as is much of the town. But like you said, I got a job to do. And I know we spoke briefly at the park, but there's a few more things I need to ask you."

Carol glanced back into the kitchen. "Maybe it's best we talk in the living room. I just can't get Sam upset again."

"I understand." Irving followed her and sat down on the sofa.

The old farmhouse was sparsely decorated with only a few wall hangings and overstuffed brown sofas in the living room. A large flat-screen television was mounted above the brick fireplace that seemed to harness Randall Hardy's attention.

"Are you sure I can't get you something to drink, Howard?" Carol asked.

"It's a kind offer, but no." He fiddled with the rim of his beige hat. "You mentioned that Emma came into the store earlier today to collect her paycheck, isn't that right, Mr. Hardy?"

"Yes, sir," Randall replied. "Was there just a few minutes, is all. Said she was heading back out to the picnic, and that a friend of hers was waiting for her outside the store."

"Brian Keller. I've spoken with the boy." Irving took out a small notepad. "And about what time do you reckon that was?"

Randall peered up at the ceiling. "Oh, I suppose around ten o'clock. I want to say it was just before the picnic was fixin' to get started."

"Why were you at the store? Thought you'd be closed today," Irving continued.

"Just cleaning house, so to speak. Had Sam with me there, too, but I let him go on and enjoy the end of the parade."

"You got yourself those cameras outside your store, don't you?" Irving continued.

"No, sir. Just inside, but I'm happy to let you take a look. Maybe you'll see something helpful to you."

Irving nodded. "I know it's been a hell of a day, but would you mind accompanying me down to the store so I can take a look now? Best to figure out if someone was lingering, keeping watch of Emma, things like that."

Randall eyed Carol before continuing, "I don't see why not. If I can help you find the son of a bitch responsible for..." he trailed off.

"I'll let you gather your things and meet you outside." Irving walked to the door and stepped out onto the porch.

After he left, Carol turned to her husband. "Thank you for doing this, Randall."

He brushed past her and walked into the kitchen. "Sam, you talk to Emma today? When she came into the store, you say anything to her?"

Carol touched Randall's arm. "He's been through enough right now, Randall. Leave him be."

"Answer my question, boy. Did you talk to Emma today?"

Sam had his back to his father and peered over his shoulder. "She said hello to me and that's all, sir."

"Nothing else?" Randall asked.

"Honey, now, come on." Carol pressed her hand on him again.

Randall brushed it off. "Carol, that's enough. I'm only asking him a goddam question." He looked at Sam again. "That's all she said to you? Nothing else?"

Sam remained silent.

"Damn it." Randall started into the hall and snatched his keys. "I'll be back soon."

Lieutenant Irving rolled to a stop outside the store and cut the engine. "Why don't you go unlock the door, Mr. Hardy? I need to get an update from my officers."

"Yes, sir." Randall stepped out and walked toward the entrance.

Irving looked on while he picked up his radio. "Abrams, you copy?"

"Yes, sir."

"I'm at the Hardy's store here to check out Brian Keller's story about when he and Emma left here today. What's happening there?"

"It'd be better to do this in the daylight, sir. I've got lights rigged up, but it's getting tough to see deeper in the woods."

"You see where her trail started?" Irving asked.

"We reached about 100 yards and then lost sight of any blood trail, or footprints."

"What are you saying? She just showed up 100 yards away and walked out of the trees from there?"

"I'm saying, sir, that it's too damn dark to get a sense of anything out here. I still have Baker and Conroe taking statements from Emma's friends."

"All right." Irving noticed Randall had entered the store. "Secure the scene. We'll have to get back at it at first light. Have the guys finish the statements. They can do the reports in the morning."

"Copy that, sir," Abrams replied.

Irving opened his car door and stepped out under the clear dark sky. Tonight was supposed to be a celebration. Instead, he was investigating a horrific murder. The only one he'd had since running the department here. And the whole thing made no damn sense at all. Whoever did that to Emma left her alive to find her way out of the woods, only to die moments later. Why?

He reached the entrance. The glass doors slid open, and he walked inside. "Mr. Hardy?"

"Back here, Lieutenant."

A moment later, lights above flickered on, and he could see his path. "All right. I'm headed your way." He continued until reaching the back of the store, where he spotted Randall. "This your office here?"

"Yes, sir. Come on in. I'll show you what I have." Randall sat at his desk and turned on his computer. "I don't think you'll get a good look at the outside, but you'll see her on here."

"I appreciate you doing this," Irving replied.

"Emma was a good person. Had a damn good heart. Didn't deserve any of this."

"No, sir, she did not," Irving replied. "I hear Sam took a liking to her. The two of them got on well, according to your wife."

"They did. It's going to be real hard for him for quite a while, I suspect." Randall opened the files. "Here you are. Go on and take a look. Take my chair." He stood from his seat.

Irving sat down at the computer and sifted through the footage. After several minutes, he spotted her. "There she is."

Randall looked over Irving's shoulder as the video played. "You see she came in here, like I said. I don't keep cameras in this office, but only moments later, she walked out."

"Carrying an envelope," Irving replied.

"Yes, sir. That was her paycheck." Randall folded his arms. "Don't know what happened..."

Irving leaned in a moment. "She stopped to talk to Sam, looks like."

"Uh, yeah, that's right. He mentioned she'd said hello."

"Huh," Irving rubbed his chin.

"What is it?"

"Nothing. Just kind of looks like she was upset at something." He noted the timestamp.

"Probably upset from seeing what was left of her check after the government got its hands on it," Randall quipped.

"Maybe so. She's walking out of the store now."

"Check camera 2. That's the main one at the front," Randall continued.

"Got it." Irving opened the camera file and played the video. "Now, hang on here. I think I do see a little something." He leaned closer and narrowed his gaze. "That's Brian Keller, just as he said." Irving glanced at Randall. "This all jibes with what's been said so far. I thank you for your time, sir."

The lieutenant returned to his car and slipped behind the wheel. With his radio in hand, he pressed the button. "Abrams, come in."

"Yes, sir."

"Brian's story checks out, but we still need to find someone who will corroborate that Brian was alone at the picnic and exactly what time that was." The lieutenant drew in his brow as he peered at the store.

"Yes, sir, we're working on that," Abrams replied.

Irving fixed his sights on Hardy as he appeared to be on his phone engaged in a heated discussion.

"Sir, you copy?" Abrams continued.

"Uh, yes, I copy," he replied. "I'm headed into the station now."

NEARLY A MONTH HAD PASSED since Senior Unit Agent Nick Scarborough moved out of his Unit 2 office at Quantico and into

FBI Headquarters in D.C. The joint task force on foreign cyber threats had been assembled and Nick stood at the helm.

And now, as they sat at dinner, Kate missed discussing with him their caseloads. Bouncing ideas off one another. His new job required Top Secret security clearance, and she didn't have it. Their lives revolved around work, so mealtime conversation now had been somewhat lacking.

Kate studied him a moment. Nick's hair was a little bit grayer these days. Still in his early forties, he was just as handsome as the day she met him. Of course, back then, she hadn't taken much notice of him in that way. To the best of her recollection, Nick had been the poster boy for the FBI. He stood at 6 feet and looked every bit the corn-fed Nebraskan. But time on the job had worn him down, which was at least part of the reason he'd moved to HQ. The other part, Kate was certain, was a sense that his star might shine once again.

Maybe a part of her did feel a twinge of jealousy regarding Georgia Myers, a fact Cam had pointed out last night. Whether it had been an innocent inquiry, she didn't know. Although Cameron Fisher wasn't one to beat around the bush. The former NYPD detective was nothing if not matter-of-fact.

It was time to break this silence that lingered between them, even if it would be only to ask the mundane. "Is dinner okay?" she asked.

Nick glanced at her as though he'd been a thousand miles away. "What's that?"

"I asked if dinner was okay. You look like you're on another planet." Kate reached for her glass of water.

"Oh, I'm sorry. No, everything's fine. Dinner's great." Wrinkles formed at the corners of his brown eyes as he grinned. "Well, that's not entirely true. Not about dinner, about work. I had a meeting with Morgan this morning."

"Remind me about her again," Kate replied.

"CIA. Information Ops. She's part of their Critical Infrastructure Protection Group," Nick said.

"That's right. She worked with you on the Amtrak thing." Kate sawed off a piece of chicken. "What happened in the meeting?"

"She shared information about a potential attack on the grid. This is exactly why the task force was created, and I get that—"

"And it's the reason you were asked to head it up," Kate cut in.

"You're right." Nick poked at his food. "And I'm honored to be in this position."

"You earned it."

He shrugged. "Thank you, but I think what I'm getting at is that this isn't a situation where we're looking for a bad guy, a serial killer. Not that it's any less critical to saving lives, but this is more like if I miss something, an entire city could be plunged into darkness, into chaos. It's so much bigger than I expected. The country could be turned into Venezuela overnight if I screw up."

"It's a big deal. That's why you were chosen and not someone else." Kate reached for his hand. "Nick, everyone is looking to you. Honestly, that must be overwhelming at times, given what's at stake. But you will find your footing, just like you did in Unit 2. Just like you did in our unit."

He squeezed her hand. "You always know what to say."

"I don't know about that." She pulled her hand away and reached for her glass again. "I think it's just a situation where I feel a lot of the same things you do. I'm not in the same position, but it's a position where people look to me for answers. So, yeah, I understand."

"I know you do." He prepared to take a bite. "Hey, I am sorry I missed the fireworks show last night. It would've been nice to sit out on the boat together."

"I had a nice time with everyone." She raised her finger. "I did ask if anyone was interested in buying the boat."

"What?" He smiled. "I'm not selling her, Kate. Not a chance. One day, you and I are going to cruise on down to the Keys and just stay there."

"You promise?" she asked.

"Absolutely." Nick's phone buzzed in his pocket, and he picked it up to answer. "Sorry, I need to take this." He pushed back in his chair and made his way to the sliding glass door that led to the balcony. "Scarborough here." He stepped outside.

Kate dabbed her napkin on her lips and dropped it onto the plate. Dinner was officially over. She cleared the table and prepared to load the dishwasher when an alert sounded on her phone.

She reached for it on the breakfast bar and swiped open the screen. The alert was from the FBI's national database, and she received the ones that had been entered into ViCAP, the Violent Criminal Apprehension Program. The implementation of the alert system was fairly recent, and it helped identify violent crimes that often led Kate to calls for consultations around the country. Or, on occasion, her team's investigations, when required.

As she read the alert, Nick opened the slider and returned inside. Her attention was drawn to him.

He seemed to notice the look on her face. "What is it?"

"Uh, I just got a ViCAP alert. A murder in Jansville, Virginia."

Nick continued toward her. "What about it?"

"The killer is at large, and the victim." Kate regarded him with a furrowed brow. "Her tongue was cut out."

3

Sharon Katz marched into the Jansville Police Station with her husband trailing. Her fair and freckled face now appeared heated. Her soft blue eyes appeared dark as night. "I need to speak with Lieutenant Irving."

The man behind the front desk stood in protest. "Now, just hang on Mrs. Katz. I'm going to need you to take a breath and step back for me a minute, would you?"

Dave gently took her by the shoulders. "Come on, darlin'. No point in getting angry at the officer."

She spun around. "And why not? Emma's been dead going on three days and none of these people are doing a damn thing about it."

"That's not true, now." Dave turned his attention to the officer. "Please understand that my wife is grieving, we both are, and we just want to talk to the lieutenant figuring that he might have some updates for us."

"Let me call back to him," the officer replied.

Dave turned to her. "See? There you go. He's going to call and check for us."

"I just don't understand. Why is it taking so long to find who did this to my baby?"

"Darlin, if I knew that, I sure as hell wouldn't be standing here right now."

"Mr. and Mrs. Katz?" the officer called out. "The lieutenant's coming up right now."

"Thank you, sir," Dave said. "Thank you."

A moment later, Irving appeared. "Dave. Sharon. Why don't you both come on back? I'll catch you up on what's been happening." He turned on his heel.

They followed him to his office and walked inside.

"Take a seat." Irving returned to his desk. "Now, you know I've been following up with everyone Emma knew. Already talked to damn near half the town. And I talked to Brian Keller, who was with her at the store."

"And?" Sharon pleaded.

"Well, he says they returned to Town Park and parted ways after that. We are still looking for anyone who'd seen him so we can confirm that detail. My next step is to talk to some of her college friends. See if she had a boyfriend there she didn't mention to y'all about. Maybe other folks who she might've known. My team's still processing the scene and I'm holding out hope—" His cell phone rang. "Excuse me a minute, would you? I'd better take this." Irving stepped out of his office.

Sharon's head grew light, and her stomach turned with rising nausea. "I just can't take this anymore, Dave. I just can't. I need to know who did this to my baby girl. Why doesn't he understand that?"

Dave placed his hand on her back and gently rubbed between her shoulder blades. He blinked hard as he appeared to try to rein in his own emotions. "I know, sweetheart. But you know Howard. He's doing everything he can to give Emma the justice she deserves."

Irving opened the door and stepped inside. "Mr. and Mrs. Katz, that was one of my team. He says they found something at the park where Emma—"

"What?" Sharon leaped from her chair. "What did they find, Howard?"

It was the longest 5-minute drive the lieutenant had ever taken. He'd come from a city where this sort of thing happened with relative frequency, but here in Jansville, it was as foreign to the people here as the French language.

He'd arrived at the park, where only days earlier the town had gathered to watch the fireworks. It turned out to be Emma Katz's final day on this earth.

Irving cut the engine and turned his attention to Dave Katz, who sat in the front passenger seat. "All right. We're going to get out, but I'm gonna ask you folks to do the impossible. You're gonna have to hang back until I say so. You must hear me on this because evidence exists all around here and we can't afford for any of it to be destroyed by not taking every precaution." He glanced back at Sharon. "Do you both understand what it is I'm telling you?"

"I understand," Sharon replied.

Irving opened his door and stepped out into the dusky light. The grounds were empty, and a patrol unit parked alongside the curb. Beyond the park lay the hill where the fireworks had been set off on the evening of the Fourth and where Emma had been found. He spotted his officer ahead and started on. The parents slowly caught up to him. "Just sit tight for a minute. I'm going to talk to Officer Abrams, then, I'll come back here and give you an update."

Dave clutched his wife's arm and they both nodded.

"Okay. I'll be right back." Irving walked on. "Abrams."

"Sir." He peered over Irving's shoulder. "You brought them here?"

"They were in my office when you called. They got a right to know what you found."

He released a heavy sigh. "Trust me when I tell you it would've been best had they not come here."

Irving set his hands on his hips. "What'd you find?"

Abrams waved him on. "Come take a gander up the hill. You'll see." He was a big guy. Tall and wide. Not quite 30. Had been with the force for about seven years.

Abrams stopped at the top of the hill. Trees as far as the eye could see. A few grassy rolling hills nearby. "Go on and take a look for yourself."

Irving stepped into the woods and continued toward the location marked with plastic yellow tags. He peered down. "Dear God." When he reemerged, he rubbed his forehead in disbelief.

"You see why those parents shouldn't be here?" Abrams continued.

"That all you found so far?" Irving asked. "According to the ME's preliminary report, the girl was hit in the head with a large blunt object, likely a rock, and then, her tongue was severed. God only knows how she survived long enough to make it out of the woods.

"We gathered the blood samples, but if that it isn't hers, then we have ourselves a whole 'nother problem."

Irving scoffed. "Then let's get it over to the medical examiner ASAP. How soon before her labs are back, and the final report is issued?"

I'll get an update, sir," Abrams replied.

"Thank you." Irving returned to his patrol car, eyeing the parents as he drew near. His heartbeat echoed in his ears as he considered just what to say to them. "Damn it. This is why I left Ashville in the first place." He recognized the look on the parents' faces as he returned to them. Anticipation, dread, grief. Irving regretted bringing them along. "Mr. and Mrs. Katz, my officers have collected some evidence as it relates to Emma's murder."

"What did they find, Howard?" Sharon asked.

Irving looked down and wiped a finger under his nose. "Her tongue. They found her tongue."

KATE OPENED the door to her condo and stepped inside to the soft glow of a television that flickered in the background. The side table lamp burned a soft amber. She searched for Nick when he emerged from the hallway dressed in gym shorts and a t-shirt. His smile when he noticed her arrival reminded her of how lucky she was.

"You're home," he said. "I just got back, myself, not too long ago. Thought I'd catch the news, then have an early night."

"Sounds good to me. I'll go change first. Be out in a minute." Kate approached him and kissed his lips before heading to the bedroom. She secured her weapon in the safe and changed into shorts and an oversized t-shirt. On her return, she glanced at Nick. "Do you need anything? I'm going to grab a bottle of water."

"I'll take one. Thanks." Nick propped his feet on the coffee table and when Kate returned, she handed him the bottle. "Thank you. How was your day?"

She moved in next to him on the gray sofa sectional. "Busy. I might have to go to Chicago tomorrow. Just a consult."

"Oh. Who's going with you?" Nick asked.

"Jonathan. Maybe Eva, but I don't think she needs to be there. Then again, she knows the guys at that field office, so maybe it's wise to bring her."

"Might be." He tossed back a sip of water.

"What about you, huh?" she asked. "How was your day?"

"We're all still trying to find our space. Trying to come together as a cohesive team. It's hard, but we're moving in the right direction," Nick replied.

Kate hesitated a moment and chewed on her bottom lip. "And Georgia?"

"She's doing okay." Nick tilted his head and raised a brow. "I hate to state the obvious, but you know my feelings for her are long since over, right?" He took Kate's hand. "Not in my wildest dreams did I ever think I'd be so lucky as to marry a woman like you. Don't forget that."

Kate shrugged. "No, it's—I understand that. I didn't mean to suggest..." She stopped and closed her eyes, searching for the words that eluded her. "I'm just happy you've found a home. A place inside the Bureau where you belong and where your talents will be put to good use without leaving a mark."

"Is that what you think is happening to you?" he asked. "Is the job beginning to leave a mark? You think I don't notice these things because we don't work together anymore, but I do."

"I suppose it never stopped and it didn't really bother me before, but now..." She hesitated. "Now I'm not so sure. I'm starting to understand the decisions you made earlier in your career."

"The decisions I made almost destroyed my career." Nick placed the crook of his index finger under her chin and turned her gently to face him. "You are stronger than I ever was. I know what happened in Texas left a mark. I can still see it. But after all you've been through; years of fighting to become the person you are today; I know you won't go down the path that I traveled."

Her heart caught in her throat. "How can you be so sure?"

"Because I'm here, and I won't let you."

Kate's phone rang in her pocket. She closed her eyes and sighed. "Figures."

Nick smiled and raised his shoulders. "If that's Cam..."

She grabbed the phone and checked the caller ID. "You gotta be kidding me."

"It's Cam?"

Kate stood from the sofa. "Nailed it. I'd better see what he wants." She started into the kitchen and answered the call. "Hey, Cam. Nick and I were just talking about you."

"Do I want to know why?" he asked.

"Not really. What's up?" She set down her bottle of water on the kitchen counter.

"I got a call from an agent in the Roanoke Field Office. Actually, he's retired now, but I've known him for a while. Good guy."

"Okay. What'd he want? Does he have a case?"

"Not exactly," Fisher replied. "He called because he has a relative who lives in Jansville. Are you familiar with it? Central Virginia, not far from Lynchburg."

"Jansville. Where did I recently see that name?" She raised her gaze a moment. "Oh, I remember, an alert came through."

"Yeah, I saw that a few days ago," Fisher added. "Apparently, there was a pretty gruesome murder over the Fourth of July. Local girl. Half dead when they found her, died on-scene."

Kate leaned back on the kitchen cabinets. "Her tongue was cut out. That much, I remember. How does this involve us? Is the local field office looking for assistance?"

"This is more a situation where this relative called and asked for a favor. This isn't coming directly from Roanoke," Fisher replied.

"There's no denying the case is distinctive," Kate added. "And your friend—the former agent—he thinks there's something else to it? Something that would require a once-over by the BAU? I'm happy to consult if that's what they need. Not sure I could develop a comprehensive profile at this stage of the game, but I can take a look."

"I'd appreciate it if you could. It's a couple hours' drive, but it does raise the hairs on my neck."

"Cutting out a victim's tongue could be a sign of a few things. A liar, someone with a secret. It's not your typical murder," she replied.

"Which is why I'd like you to check it out. Now, the local PD hasn't asked for this, so I'm not entirely sure how receptive they'll be," Fisher added.

Kate walked back into the living room. "I can be persuasive when I need to be."

At this, Nick eyed her and smiled.

"I know you can," Fisher continued. "So, let's talk more about it in the morning. In the meantime, get some rest and tell your husband I said hello and to stop talking shit about me."

"Will do. Goodnight, Cam." Kate ended the call.

"A case?" Nick asked.

"Maybe. Sounds like it could be interesting."

As THE SUN set behind the mountain, 17-year-old Anson Voss rode his bike along the gravel path toward the chicken coops on his family's farm. It had taken a lot to convince his mom the chore still needed to be done because if the foxes were there, well, that would be it. Anson tried not to think about what happened to Emma Katz, even if the entire town talked about it. He just wanted everything to go back to normal. This was supposed to be his summer vacation.

Anson hit the brakes and skidded to a stop, kicking up dust that floated in the dim evening light. The chicken houses were cast in the shadow of the mountains. He climbed off his bike and flicked the kickstand, holding there a moment. "It's quiet. Why aren't y'all talking?" Usually, the chickens squawked nonstop when they were locked inside, but all he heard were the cicadas in the trees.

The young kid shook his sandy blond hair out of his eyes and started toward the first coop. "Door's closed." Relief swelled in his chest knowing he hadn't left it open. And when he unlocked the door, he peeked inside. "All here." Anson secured the door and moved on to the next coop. All three had been secured, just like he'd left them.

He returned to his bike and stopped a moment at the noise in the distance. It came from beyond the wire fence and Anson proceeded to investigate. "There it is again." He'd reached the property line and craned his neck left, then right. The farm bordered the foothills and ahead of him was the forest. Several paths had been carved out that led to the main trailheads deeper into the mountains. People often hiked those trails, but near his house was mainly a local route hardly anyone traveled.

Anson carefully stepped over the barbed wire and walked out a few feet. He set his hands on his hips and peered in both directions as he reached the narrow path. A branch cracked underfoot and drew his attention to his left. He noticed a few swinging branches, their leaves rattled by something that passed through.

His nerves got the better of him. "Go back. Go back." Anson spun on his heel and ran toward the fence. He jumped over and caught his hand on one of the barbs. As he tumbled onto the other side, the pain shot through his arm. The gouge on his palm spilled blood down his wrist and forearm. "Damn it." He reached for his bike and jumped on. With a glance back into the woods at whatever had made that sound, Anson peddled up the path back to his home.

THE TOWN MOURNED the death of Emma Katz, and while nearly a week had gone by, shock still prevailed, especially since no suspects had been found. Doors that had once been rarely locked were now anxiously secured. Stores shut down by dark. And community events had been canceled for the foreseeable future. So when the teenage son of Bruce and Helen Voss hadn't returned home as the sun descended in the sky, Helen's hackles rose.

From her kitchen window, she peered out over the grounds. The small 10-acre farm had been in the Voss family for generations. Corn, hay, and soybean crops were just enough to keep the family's income afloat. Helen had sent 17-year-old Anson to check on the chicken coops to make sure they were secured for the night.

She turned at the footfalls behind her. "Bruce, would you mind checking on Anson? He hasn't come back from the coops. It's been almost an hour."

Bruce was a towering man. Full-waisted, full-bearded, and a full head of brown hair he kept just a little long. "I just got back from the shop. Been working on the tractor all day. Can I get a glass of water first?"

"I'm worried about him, Bruce. With what happened to the Katz' girl. . ."

He closed the cabinet door and set down the glass that he'd retrieved. "Did you call him on his phone?"

"Went straight to voicemail," she replied. "Tried texting him too. No reply."

All right. I'll go find him and whip his backside for causing his momma worry."

Helen cracked a tender smile. "Boy's damn near as tall as you, now, so good luck with that." She glanced away a moment while her smile faded. "Just bring him home for me, please."

"I will." Bruce kissed her cheek and returned outside into the evening light.

From the kitchen window, Helen watched Bruce head out to his truck, wiping away the sweat from his neck with a red bandana. When he stopped cold a moment, peering out into the darkness, she tried to see what it was that caught his attention. A figure appeared. And when that figure turned into her son, her shoulders dropped in relief. "Oh, thank the Lord." Helen set down the dish towel and opened the kitchen door to step outside. "Boy, where have you been? You got any idea how scared I was?"

"I'm okay," he said.

She glanced at Bruce and then back to Anson. "You are not okay. Look at you. What on earth happened to your hand? Bruce, do you see this?"

"I see it." He carried on toward his boy. "Get off the bike. Let's have a look-see, shall we?"

Anson held out his hand. "I'm okay."

Helen looked at him with a raised brow. "You get into a fight with the barbed wire fence?"

"Something like that."

"What happened?" Bruce asked. "How'd you catch yourself on the fence?"

Anson looked at his feet and swallowed hard. "I jumped over to the other side."

"Why?" Helen asked. "Why would you do that?"

He returned his gaze to his dad. "I heard something out beyond the fence. Like a person, or something."

"Well, did you see anyone?" Bruce asked.

"No, sir. But I knew it had to be a person. The way the branches and stuff moved when they disappeared—"

"What do you mean 'when they disappeared'?" Helen asked. "Did you see someone or not?"

"No, ma'am. I-I came right back over the fence. I knew with all that's happened—"

"Bruce, call the police," Helen insisted. "Right now. You call the police, you hear me?"

He raised his hands. "Calm down, Helen. The boy didn't see anything. Only thought he did."

"I don't care, Bruce. Someone's out there near our property. No, I'm not taking any chances. Now, call the police, or I will."

4

For some, leaving the town where they grew up was an easy choice. Others, like Heidi Sumner, had a harder time. So, rather than go off to some big college like her friend Emma had done, Heidi chose to get an apartment and, along with her part-time job at the convenience store, attend the nearby community college to figure out what it was she wanted to do with the rest of her life.

Now, as she stood behind the cashier's counter at the store, she mourned the death of her old high school friend, Emma. Heidi considered that maybe working here in the store wasn't the smartest idea in light of the fact that whoever killed Emma still roamed the streets. But it wasn't like the entire town could roll up into a ball and turn out its lights. People had to work, had to pay their bills. And Heidi was no different. The silver lining—for tonight, at least, was that it was almost time to clock out. Hardly anyone came by. Most of the town remained shuttered in their homes. Who could blame them? In fact, Heidi looked forward to going home, locking her door, and pulling the covers over her head tonight. Pretending none of this was happening seemed the best course of action.

Heidi made the final cash count and walked the bundle of money to the safe. She entered the code and the door popped open. The owner of the store would arrive first thing in the morning and remove the cash to make his daily deposit. Heidi set the bundle inside and closed the safe door, securing it again.

She rose from behind the counter and walked to the slushy machines. "I hate cleaning these things." They were practically full since so few people came by today, so she dumped out the machine's contents and wiped them clean. Funny how this wasn't really where she thought she would be right now. In high school, she was popular, like Emma and their friend Amber. Of course, in a small town, it was easy to be with the popular crowd. But Heidi thought she would be onto bigger and better things. However, when it came right down to it, she was afraid to leave Jansville. Afraid to leave her parents. Probably more so now.

Heidi continued with closing the store, emptying the coffee pots, and turning off the hot dog heaters. So gross. She knew how long the owner left those things in there and would never dare tell their customers.

When all was finished, Heidi checked the time. "12:45, not bad." It took all her energy to keep from thinking about Emma and the awful thing that happened to her. To do the routine tasks, like closing for the night. She walked to the back room to clock out and after checking one last time that the front door was locked, Heidi exited through the rear, opening the door to the warm and muggy night.

The crickets chirped and a light breeze ruffled the leaves on the tall oaks and pines that surrounded the store. A single light hung on the exterior and helped her to see as she locked the back door. She turned toward the small, paved lot behind the store while sweat beaded at her hairline from the sticky air. Heidi pulled the hair tie from her jet-black locks, unleashing a wave of curls down her back. She walked to her car under the moonlight that illuminated her way.

The shuffle of feet atop the chip-sealed pavement made her stop in her tracks. Her pulse elevated and her senses heightened. Heidi took another step and another footfall sounded behind her. She tried to swallow the lump caught in her throat, but her mouth dried in an instant.

"This is your fault, Heidi."

The man's voice was unrecognizable to her. Deep-throated, gruff, angry sounding. Before she could move, a hand slammed down over her mouth from behind. Adrenaline surged in her as she attempted to pry away the man's fingers. Heidi tried to turn around to see who attacked her, but his squeeze was tight, and he pulled her back. She lost her footing and the heels of her shoes scraped along the pavement as he dragged her toward the tree line. She cried out but the words muffled under his hand. Tears streamed down her cheeks while she thrashed to break free.

"Stop fighting me."

Stars filled her eyes at the blow against her head. Blood oozed down her temple and Heidi cried out in agony, though hardly a sound filtered through the hand that still covered her mouth. Her head grew light, and nausea spun in her gut. Consciousness barely held on as the blurred tree line approached. Heidi was losing the fight and grew weaker by the moment. "No."

"You did this to yourself."

She squirmed beneath him as he removed his hand. Barely alert, she felt him throttle her neck before she slammed against the soft earth.

Mud covered her face while blood spilled down her temple.

The pressure in her eyes unleashed a wave of fresh pain in her head.

She saw a hunting knife draw near before blackness closed in on her. Heidi was gone.

Dusk was a good time for fishing, or so Phil Thomas believed. But as the light diminished and he could scarcely see to bait his hook, the time had come to pack up and head home. At the river's edge, Phil opened his tackle box and returned his lures to their rightful spots. The two rainbow trout he'd managed to reel in flip-flopped in the water as they hung on a line to keep them alive. With the net, he raised them out of the water and laid them on the ground. A quick blow to the head and they were ready to place into his cooler.

The camping chair fell over from a brief gust of wind and Phil walked to pick it up again. He folded the chair and returned it to the nylon cover before tossing it higher on the banks while he finished gathering his gear.

Another gust of wind pushed through the canyon and blew his empty bottle of water several feet downstream. "Damn it." Phil traversed the slippery rocks and mossy bank to retrieve the litter. With his feet positioned on the river rocks, he bent down to snatch the bottle just as the current picked it up and took it farther down-stream. "Really?" He walked several more feet and when he reached for it again, he noticed something drifting toward him. In the dark waters, he couldn't make it out. "The hell?" He squinted for a better look, and as it floated near, his lips parted, and he gasped. Phil shot up straight, nearly losing his footing. "Oh, merciful God in heaven."

FLASHLIGHTS SHONE through the trees as Phil stood fixed at the edge of the riverbank where he'd pulled out the body. "Over here!" he called out. Several officers emerged from behind those beams of light. "I'm over here. To your right."

Lieutenant Irving carefully navigated the rugged terrain until he reached the river. "Mr. Thomas, are you okay?"

"I'm fine. I'm fine. This here's your problem." He pointed down at the body. "I had to move her up onto the banks or else the current would've carried her right on down. Haven't touched her since, I swear it."

Irving aimed his light at the body. "I believe you, Mr. Thomas. Now, why don't you go on over there? One of my officers can get you some water. I'll need you to stick around for a while, you understand?"

"Yes, sir. Tell me that ain't the Sumner's girl 'cause it sure as hell looks like her. And after poor Emma—"

"Mr. Thomas, please," Irving insisted.

Phil walked up the bank toward the officers. "What the hell's going on in this town?"

Irving trained his flashlight on the victim. "God Almighty. How the hell did you end up here?"

"Lieutenant?" A voice called out.

He peered back. "What is it, Erin?"

The officer hurried to meet him and nearly slipped on a moss-covered stone. Almost out of breath, she continued, "The station just got a call about a missing woman. Heidi Sumner. Her folks said she was supposed to come over for dinner this evening and with everything going on, they didn't want to wait to make the call."

Irving turned back to the body, and his shoulders dropped. "Damn it."

"You think that's her, sir?" she asked. "I don't know her."

"I believe it is, yes. Works at the convenience store."

The young officer looked down at the body. "Sir, why does her mouth look like that?"

He turned his light onto her again. "Because whoever did this cut out her tongue."

She shot a look at him. "Just like Emma Katz?"

He closed his eyes. "Just like Emma Katz."

KATE ARRIVED at the office in the early hours to get a jump on this new investigation Fisher mentioned. At her desk, she searched online for news articles to see how they compared to what had been input into the FBI's database. What signatures had been intentionally left out of the press. From the corner of her eye, movement caught her attention.

Surrey walked into her office with his hands in his pockets. "Where have you been?"

She regarded him. "Uh, right here."

"Not from where I stand. You look like you're a million miles away." He sat down across from her and crossed his legs, clasping his hands on his thigh. "You okay?"

"Yeah, I'm fine. I was just looking for information on the Jansville murder."

He tilted his head. "What's that?"

"Cam called me last night and we talked briefly about it. Jansville, in central Virginia. He got a call from a former agent with a family member who lives there. Long story short, he's asked me to contact the local authorities and offer assistance."

"On one local murder?" Surrey asked.

"One local murder, where the victim had her tongue cut out. The girl was still alive when she found help. Unfortunately, it was too late."

He shifted in the chair. "Okay, so, not your average shooting."

"No." Kate closed the lid of her laptop. "I plan on calling whoever's running the investigation and see what I can do to help. It's a 2-hour drive from D.C. It's practically in our backyard. Someone who cuts out the tongue of their victim isn't your everyday run-of-the-mill murderer. It takes a special kind of hate for your fellow man to do something like that."

WHATEVER AWKWARDNESS LINGERED between Eva Duncan and Cameron Fisher since their breakup months ago had mostly diminished. They remained professional and never let their personal feelings get in the way. Not around the rest of the team, anyway.

As Duncan walked through the halls, she caught sight of Fisher stepping out of his office. There was no denying her feelings for him, but the choice was made. To look at him now; his lightly stubbled face, his broad shoulders, and the slight catch in his gait... She stopped in the hall when he approached. "Good morning."

"Morning."

The silence hung in the air a moment before Duncan continued, "I was off to see Reid. Did you need me for anything?"

He shoved his hands in his pockets. "No, uh, I'll catch up with you later."

She waited for him to pass before the smile on her lips faded. Duncan carried on, arriving outside Kate's office. "I have that information you were looking for."

Kate set down her phone. "That was quick. Come in. Thanks for doing that. I appreciate it."

Duncan walked inside. The Chicago native was in her late thirties with a muscular build that could rival a professional athlete. "No problem. Can I ask why you're looking into a local murder investigation?"

Kate reached for the file as Duncan handed it over. "It was at Cam's request. Well, a friend of his who used to be an agent at the Roanoke field office asked if he could put someone on it, so he asked me. I'm still waiting for a call back from the lieutenant handling the investigation."

"That's why you wanted me to run a check on the signature." Duncan sat down across from her.

"It's an interesting one, don't you think? It's not every day a killer cuts out his victim's tongue. Not sure it's the only signature, but we have to start somewhere. So how many did you find?" Kate thumbed through the file.

"I picked up on 2,290 nationwide since 2019," Duncan replied.

"That's more than I would've expected." Kate continued to read the file. "And it looks like in Virginia since that time, there were three."

"Yep. Only three, and they occurred in late 2019 and early 2020. Unrelated," Duncan added. "Not sure if that helps you."

"It reinforces the idea this is a unique signature. Could be a fetish killing." Kate's desk phone rang. "Hang on. Let me grab this a second." She answered the line. "SSA Reid."

Duncan grabbed the file she'd given Kate and scanned through it again.

"Thank you for calling me back, Lieutenant," Kate replied. "I was interested in the case you're working on currently. Emma Katz."

Duncan drew her gaze to Kate while she spoke.

"Yes, sir, that's right. I'm with the FBI's Behavioral Analysis Unit. Yes, sir, we deal with violent crimes."

A text arrived on Duncan's phone, and she glanced at it before Kate captured her attention again with a tap of her fingers on her desk.

"Another one? I see. And the tongue was severed. Okay. Well, Lieutenant Irving, listen, I'd like to offer my resources. I do know this isn't a federal investigation, but I have a great deal of experience with profiling. I think I can help."

Duncan replied to the message and set her sights on Kate again.

"I can be there in a couple of hours. Thank you, sir. I look forward to meeting you as well. Goodbye." She ended the call. "They found another body. A 19-year-old girl."

"And the first victim was female also?" Duncan asked.

"That's right. Same age. Female. Now I just need to know if the victims knew each other."

"Sounds like this is already turning out to be more than you bargained for. Two killings," Duncan replied.

Kate raised a brow. "The second in just over a week in a town that hasn't had a murder in years."

THE SMALL VALLEY tucked in between the hills was cast in shadow even while the sun neared its peak. The tall trees, full of green leaves, helped shade the grassy floor where moss grew from lack of sun and what had been a wet summer. Trails bypassed the area nearby. So when the Voss family dog ventured into the grounds, his blond fur turned damp and quickly became dirty.

The dog had gone missing after Anson Voss was certain he'd seen something in the woods the other night.

The Labrador sniffed the ground, appearing to hunt for food. He must've been hungry and scared. And when it seemed as though he'd picked up a scent, he carried on deeper into the valley until he reached the source of the smell.

Dead squirrels swung from ropes that wrapped around low branches. Two rabbits lay on the forest floor, their guts sliced open down the middle. Vultures pulled flesh from the carcasses of dead cats, whose mouths hung open with nothing left inside.

The dog whimpered and slowly backed away from the scene. Dogs were smart enough to know when danger lurked. He reached the ridgeline of the valley and turned around, sprinting from the smell of death and decay.

He slowed down when he seemed to spot people several yards away. His tail wagged at his apparent recognition. He looked back from where he came and then walked on toward them.

Anson Voss and his dad were on the trail and noticed the dog. Anson ran to meet him. "Felix! There you are. Oh my gosh, I thought were gone for good." He peered back at Bruce. "Dad! Dad, over here! He's okay. Felix is okay."

The dog's ears drooped, and his tail wagged fiercely.

"You're safe now, buddy." Bruce peered out into the woods. "Good Lord, how did you get all the way out here?" He squatted to examine him. "You're filthy and you must be starving and thirsty." He looked at Anson. "Get him some water, son."

"Okay," Anson reached into his backpack and retrieved a bottle. He poured water into his cupped hand and held it out. "Here you go, Felix. Come on, buddy, drink some water."

The dog lapped up what he could and looked at him, appearing to want more.

Anson offered more and then grabbed a granola bar from his

bag and broke it off into pieces. "Here, eat some of this too." He set the food on the ground and returned upright again. "Let's get him home, Dad."

INSIDE HER FORD EXPLORER, Kate headed southwest to a town with a population of about 800. Jansville was just north of Lynchburg. Kate had never spent any time in this part of the state. Her life existed inside the D.C. metro area unless she worked a case, which saw her traveling, well, the world, in some cases.

It was the first time in a while she'd gone out on her own, even for consultations. Surrey was her partner and the two had gotten along well together. She appreciated how different he was from her. He brought a fresh perspective. But she was glad to see to this alone for now. Call it a test to prove to herself this was still what she wanted, despite it all.

Late afternoon arrived by the time she reached Jansville. She stepped out of her SUV and noticed heat rising from the parking lot of the police station. She grabbed her laptop bag and tossed it over her shoulder before walking toward the entrance.

A man held open the door for her. "You must be Agent Reid."

"How'd you know?" she walked inside.

"Because no one around here wears a suit, especially not in the middle of summer." He smiled and offered his hand. "I'm Lieutenant Howard Irving. We spoke on the phone."

"Lieutenant, pleasure to meet you. Sorry it has to be under these conditions." She continued inside. "Glad to see your air conditioning works."

"Oh yeah. We got all the comforts you big city folks have." He chuckled. "Come on back. Let's talk."

Kate followed him to his office. "I appreciate you allowing me to offer some insight, Lieutenant."

"Call me Irving," he replied. "And it's I who should be thanking you. Never in all my years have I had the pleasure of working with the FBI, let alone the folks at Quantico." He gestured to the chair. "Please, take a seat."

"Thank you. I will tell you working with the Bureau has its challenges. Fortunately, I'm here strictly as a consultant."

"Which means what, exactly?" he asked.

"That I have zero jurisdiction. This is and will remain, your investigation. I'm just here to help where it's needed."

"All right." Irving leaned back in his chair and clasped his hands over his chest. "Maybe you can start by telling me who on God's green earth would murder two young people in this small town of mine, cut out their tongues, and leave them for dead? Who would do that, Agent Reid?"

"That's what I'm here to help you find out."

THE ROANOKE COUNTY MEDICAL EXAMINER's Office had received the two victims from Jansville since the town hadn't the resources to perform autopsies, with only a small hospital and a funeral home. Kate had hitched a ride with Lieutenant Irving to view the bodies and begin the process of learning just what happened to these young people from the small town.

Two dead in just over a week set a dangerous precedent and it was time for Kate to get a handle on the situation, if she hoped to help these people at all. She looked through the passenger window of Irving's patrol car. The two-lane highway was lined with dense woodland on both sides, which made it tough to decipher her location. "How long have you been with the Jansville PD?"

Irving kept his eyes on the road ahead. "About 10 years. Lived in Ashville, North Carolina before that. Was a cop there too." Irving glanced at her. "I thought the grass would be greener here. Turned out, it was greener but only because of all the bullshit."

Kate snickered. "I understand that more than you know."

"I'll bet you do," Irving replied. "But I will say this, I never had one single murder investigation in this town. Not a damn one. Not that folks haven't died here, but you know, car accidents, heart attacks. Had a gentleman keel over once in his tractor in the middle of his field. But this, Agent Reid? This scares me. And you deal with this kind of thing on the regular?"

"Sadly, yes, I do," she replied.

"Well, God bless you, ma'am. I don't think I'd have the stomach."

Picking at that scab was a bad idea. Given Kate's recent introspection, it was best to move on to another topic. "What can you tell me about the families of the two victims?"

"You know, just hard-working families. The Katz' have the one daughter—had. The husband works in town as a CPA. The Sumner family, well, Heidi had her own apartment and went to community college in the next town over. So, if you're looking for a connection between the two, I already went down that road and I can tell you, both girls were friends back in high school. Course, the families knew each other. Wouldn't say they were close, more like acquaintances. Most everyone knows everyone else in town, so that's no surprise." He glanced at her. "Does that help you much?"

She raised the corner of her lip. "Two friends killed within a week of each other? Yeah, I'd say that helps. And I do think that the person we're looking for most likely isn't a transient."

"You believe whoever did these things lives in our town?" Irving asked.

"Given the nature of the murders, the locations of the bodies;

it's someone familiar with Jansville and the people in it. I pulled up a map and noticed the river where your second victim was found isn't anywhere near a major road or highway. Anyone who would travel that road would only do so if they were local. And the first young woman, she was found near the town's main park up along the ridge during a July Fourth celebration."

"That's right."

Kate peered through the windshield again. "She was left for dead someplace the killer knew she would be found, nevertheless, I don't think she was supposed to survive long enough to make it clear of those woods. I'm not sure it's the same for the river where Sumner was found, but either way, this is someone who knows this town."

"Well, hell. I can't argue with your logic." Irving exited the highway. "The ME's office is just ahead. I'm interested to see what else you come up with."

THE JANSVILLE FIRE DEPARTMENT consisted of three full-time firefighters and two volunteers. Jason Gatwick, the 20-year-old, whose family had moved to Jansville when he entered high school, was one of the full-time guys. He'd volunteered during his senior year and loved it enough to make a career from it. He noticed a police officer approaching the garage as he wiped down the firetruck. "Afternoon." The brawny young man with short dark hair and a square jaw stepped down from the truck. "I expected Lieutenant Irving."

"He's otherwise engaged." A middle-aged corpulent officer with a crew cut retrieved his notebook.

"What can I do for you, Officer Abrams?" In a town with only a handful of officers, and being in his line of work, Jason knew each one.

"Well, first off, I'd like to say just how sorry I am about you being the one to find Miss. Katz."

Jason cast down his gaze. "Thank you."

"And you knew her well, did you?" Abrams asked.

"We went out for a very short time last summer before she left for school. We were still friends, though."

"Fair enough." He jotted something in his notebook. "Uh, there was one thing I wanted to ask you. When you gave your statement to the lieutenant, you said you'd spoken with Emma a few days before when she was at work. What did y'all talk about?"

Jason felt a knot tighten in his stomach. "I don't remember. Does it matter?"

"It's just a question, son. Sometimes, in the heat of the moment, fear sets in. Folks don't always think straight, so it's best to come back and double-check what we have is correct." Abrams paused a moment. "Am I correct? You did speak to Emma at the store on or about July Second?"

"Yes, sir. I had to buy a few things and saw her there. I mean, we were still friends. It wasn't like we had any bad feelings toward each other or anything. I think I just asked her about her plans for the parade. That was all."

Abrams closed his notebook and returned it to his shirt pocket. "And she didn't say anything about hanging out with any friends on that day of the parade?"

"Not that I remember, sir. No," Jason replied.

He kept his eyes fixed on Jason and turned down his lips. "And you know about Miss. Sumner now too, don't you?"

"Yes, sir." Jason felt his eyes sting again and wiped a tear from his cheek. "Can't figure out why anyone would do that to my friends."

"No, sir. I can't either. It does seem strange that it was those two girls, though."

"Strange in that they were murdered? Yes, sir. Very strange."

Abrams cocked his head. "I mean strange in that you dated both of them for a time. Miss Sumner, more recently."

Jason's face deadpanned. "That ended months ago."

"Why was that?"

"We just didn't gel as a couple. It was better to stay friends," he replied.

"I see." Abrams flipped through his notes again. "And where did you say you were the night before last? The night Miss Sumner was found?"

"Uh, I don't think I've talked to Lieutenant Irving about that yet."

"No, that's right. He's had his hands full trying to get everyone's stories straight. So, let me be the one to ask the question. Where were you when Miss Sumner was killed, Jason?"

5

E mma Katz lay on the steel table covered in a white sheet. She was number 35. The other one, Heidi Sumner, she was 36. That was the number of bodies Kate had examined, hovered over, or stood near since she started with the Bureau. The morbid notion of keeping count was more than that. It reminded her that each of the victims she witnessed demanded justice. They screamed for it in her dreams.

To look at Emma Katz was to see a promising young woman. A woman with faith and love to spare. But with her slack jaw and hollow mouth, Kate also saw something else. Emma looked as though she had cried out, begged—more like, for mercy from a killer who had none to spare.

"Agent Reid, what do you think about the ligature marks?" Irving asked.

"They encircle the neck below the thyroid cartilage. Slight indentations indicative of pressure from thumbs," she began. "He got her by surprise. An attack from behind and he tried to get her to lose consciousness." Kate stepped closer to the victim. "You mentioned cause of death hadn't yet been determined, but by the look of this wound, it's fair to say it was the blow to the head. She likely fell unconscious from that point, then he cut out her tongue. From there, he must've believed she was dead or about to be and fled the scene. It's also possible he saw someone draw near and didn't have time to finish the job."

"So she stumbled out of the woods and died in front of her ex-boyfriend," Irving added.

Kate clasped her hands behind her back and eyed the lieutenant. "The killer isn't a big guy. I'm thinking average or slightly below average in build and stature. He had to rely on catching her off guard to take her down."

"He?" Irving asked.

"In general, it's usually a male, but I do tend to use that by default. I'll know more when I analyze the autopsy reports."

"But why the tongue?" Irving asked.

"It could symbolize the killer wanting the victim to keep quiet about something. To keep quiet in general. To stop the spread of lies. Historically, it's been known as a way to punish gossipers. Teach them a lesson, so to speak. Hard to say at the moment." She carried on toward Heidi Sumner. "And then you have this young woman. You said the two were friends."

"Back in high school, yes, ma'am," Irving replied.

"Removing the tongue suggests both victims could've known something their killer hadn't wanted to get out, which also suggests they knew their killer, even if they hadn't seen him, as I'm sure was the case with Emma Katz." Kate glanced upward to consider her theory. "Heidi's body was found in a river. Any chance that river runs through where Emma was found?"

"I'm not certain, to be honest," Irving replied. "You of the belief they were murdered in the same location?"

"The river could've been where the killer had intended to

leave Emma's body as well. It was a busy holiday. The entire town was out, so it's possible he was interrupted."

"And then he got his chance with Heidi." Irving nodded. "He's not going to great lengths to hide his victims."

Kate pulled the sheet over Heidi Sumner's face. "That's intentional."

"How so?" Irving asked.

"If this was a case where these two women knew something secret about their killer, then it's possible he's delivering a message to anyone else who may know what these two girls knew."

BRIAN KELLER WAS the last person to have seen Emma Katz alive. Technically, it had been Jason Gatwick, but technicalities weren't going to sway anyone's opinion. Everyone in town knew Emma had been with him only hours before her death. Emma's parents knew it, too. He'd sat through hours of police questioning. And then, when Heidi Sumner was found in the river only two days ago, the police knocked on his door again.

Now, as nightfall set in, Brian snatched his keys from the kitchen table of his parents' home. "I have to go to the store. We're out of milk."

His mother and father had hardly spoken a word about what happened. Brian was pretty sure they thought he killed Emma, maybe Heidi too. After all, they had all been friends once.

He waited for their response, but on glancing into the living room, he saw the backs of their heads as they stared at the television. Brian walked out to his car. The 19-year-old tinkered with his old Jeep just enough so that it continued to run. He started it up and drove toward Second Avenue where Hardy's was located. It was the only grocery store in town, and if folks wanted something better, they'd have to drive to Lynchburg for the Walmart or Kroger's. Milk was his excuse to leave the house. The silence from his parents was unbearable.

The store was due to close in 30 minutes and as he arrived, he parked near the front. A few other cars were parked nearby. Mostly, the entire town had shut down since all this happened. People were afraid to leave their homes. Two murders in about ten days. That sort of thing didn't happen in Jansville. Brian had never known anyone who'd been murdered before. Now, two of his friends had. One, with whom he had still been in love.

He opened the door and stepped into a blast of cold air. The fluorescent lights cast a sickly glow down the aisles. The store was in need of an update, but they still had the best prices in town. In fact, they had the only prices in town.

As he continued inside, the cashier glanced at him and quickly looked away. The milk was down the second aisle near the back of the store. He felt eyes on him coming from every direction. While there weren't that many people inside, their hateful glares bore into the back of his head.

Brian made it to the refrigerated section and opened the glass door to grab a gallon jug when he felt a tap on his right shoulder. He flinched at the touch and glanced back. Sam Hardy, the son of Carol and Randall Hardy, stood before him. "Hey, Sam."

"Do you miss her?" Sam asked.

Brian squared up to him. "Emma? Of course I do. She was my friend."

"She was my friend too." Sam turned on his heel and shuffled toward the front of the store.

Brian cocked his head as he watched Sam walk away. It appeared even Sam thought Brian had killed Emma.

As he returned to the check out, the cashier gave him that look again. She waited for him to set down the milk and then pressed her little button to make it move down the conveyor belt.

"That'll be $3.79."

"All right." Brian reached into his pocket and retrieved his wallet. He handed her a five-dollar bill.

She returned his change, and as he grabbed the milk and started toward the doors, she called out. "We all know what you did, Brian."

The other customers joined her in glaring at him. Brian eyed each one and knew that was exactly what they all believed. And when he looked at Sam, Sam turned his back and pretended to straighten the cigarette cartons behind the counter.

"You all go on and believe what you want. I don't give a shit. She was my friend. They both were."

INSIDE THE LOCAL DINER, steam rose from Kate's coffee cup. A plate of fried eggs and toast sat on the table in front of her. Muffled chatter sounded in the background while she stared at her wedding ring, turning it between her index finger and thumb. It was a single gold band with a diamond engagement ring in front of it. Kate recalled the moment Nick proposed, in his office, of course. But it had been sweet and beautiful, and it seemed the answer to her prayers.

Her eyes were drawn to Lieutenant Irving while he slipped into the booth across from her. "Good morning."

"How was your commute from D.C.?" he asked.

"Not bad. I left before the rush."

"Good. I see you ordered the special." Irving turned his coffee mug right-side up as he settled in. "Best fried eggs in town. Better eat 'em before they turn cold."

She cut into the yolk. "Yes, sir. So, I've started putting together a profile to home in on a suspect."

Irving garnered the waitress's attention. "Cup of coffee and a blueberry muffin, Cheryl, if you don't mind."

"Coming right up, Howard." She retreated behind the counter.

Irving turned to Kate. "Thing is, Agent Reid, we don't have time to make assumptions and guess whether the person who did these things has mommy or daddy issues, or whether he was cruel to animals. Now, I'm aware you were alerted to this case through a former agent who has family here. So I understand why you were contacted, and I absolutely appreciate the help. But right now, I need to be getting after clues and leads. Figuring out if anyone saw anything, or heard anything. That's what I could use help with. We don't have time for psychological mumbo jumbo. No offense."

Kate returned a crooked smile. "You know I wasn't always a federal agent. I worked for San Diego PD a long time ago."

"Is that a fact?" Irving tore off a bite of his blueberry muffin that had just arrived.

"Yes, sir. I used to collect evidence, so I understand where you're coming from." Kate sipped on her coffee. "And maybe you're right. I'm approaching this as though it was a federal investigation and I have time, resources, and a team. While I do have resources, we don't have time. If someone out there is looking to keep something quiet or take revenge for something that might've been said, that person's going to move quickly because we're left to assume something happened. A catalyst that set off this chain of events. That said, I do believe my insight could still be useful. I've confronted more killers than I care to think about, and I do know them. Probably better than I should. So, how about this? How about I follow your lead? I'll use whatever clues surface and continue to look for patterns of behavior. Meanwhile, we won't waste a moment's time."

Irving tipped his coffee mug to his lips. "I like it, Agent Reid. And I have a plan in mind."

~

THE TREE LINE at the top of the hill above Town Park was where Emma Katz had been found. Kate now stood there with Irving at her side. She scanned the area with a close eye. "Have you had any rain in the last few days?"

Irving turned down his lips. "Nope. Been dry as a bone."

She took a few steps toward the wooded area. "How or why would Emma have come up here, and had she done so alone? I don't see any all-terrain vehicle tracks in this area. Looks like a light truck was over there, but that would make sense considering the fireworks display was set off up here. And I suppose you and your team had a thorough search of the area." Kate turned to the lieutenant. "She could've come here willingly, which suggests her killer brought her up here to talk about something and then turned violent on her. The other scenario would be that her killer met her somewhere, knocked her out cold, and then brought her here."

"And we have no idea where she went after Brian Keller left her," Irving added. "According to him, Emma said she was going straight to the picnic. Well, we all know that didn't happen. So somewhere between the time she returned to Market Street from the Hardy's store, and the time she was found right here, someone else had been with her."

Kate kept her eyes fixed on the grassy hillside and walked around. "Do you have any red light cameras or other surveillance around here? Even an ATM that would have footage that might have captured her."

"I did think about that, Agent Reid. Only bank we have is the next block over. Nothing on Market Street. Brian said they parted ways just as they reached Market Street."

So she was in this area." Kate peered back into the trees. "And then you have her friend, Heidi Sumner." She turned back to Irving. "Any paths back there accessible with an ATV?"

Irving started toward her. "We did a thorough search of the area. Oh, I'd say a good 2-block radius. Found the tongue, of course. But going back to your question, it's possible a 4-wheeler could've navigated through the trees farther down." He looked back at Kate, who caught up to him in the shadow of the woods. "It would make more sense had she met someone up this way. It'd take an awful lot to carry an unconscious woman up the hill—unseen, no less."

"I agree. What's on the other side?" Kate asked. "If someone was to cut through this area, where would there be access?"

Irving rubbed his smooth shin and puckered his lips. "Well, down that way, toward the west, is the high school. And you got a few homes on a couple of acres down east."

"Whose homes?" Kate asked.

"Off the top of my head, I believe the Andersons. You got the Bunns next to them. Uh, I believe the Hardys, then you got the Dickersons. A few of the locals got some land."

Kate walked through the trees again. "The river is where Heidi was found." She pulled up the map on her phone. "We talked about this earlier, but I'll bet my map will show if it runs through this area. We could see where it leads." She opened her phone and pinned her location on the map. Zooming out, she noticed several tributaries from the main river. "There's where Heidi was found." Kate moved the map to their current location. "Look right there."

Irving leaned closer to view her screen. "Well, all be. That stream there runs down on through the valley and up through here, continuing out east." He looked at her. "What do you make of that?"

"It's good, but it still doesn't answer the question as to whether Emma came up here on her own or whether her killer carried her here. And if that was the case, my guess is, he intended to leave her in the stream and wait for the water to carry her. Just like Heidi Sumner."

JASON GATWICK RETURNED HOME after a 36-hour shift. Now, he would have 36 hours of rest. His roommate, Chris Pumphrey, just started his shift and Jason had the apartment to himself. The alternating work hours made for a good arrangement for the young men.

He shed his work clothes for a t-shirt and basketball shorts before heading into the kitchen to make lunch as the clock struck noon. A ham and cheese sandwich with chips on the side would do the trick. Throw in a Coke for good measure.

With the plate in hand, Jason sat down at the kitchen table and retrieved his laptop. He opened Facebook and clicked on Emma's page. A post appeared at the top. Jason thought it must've been from her parents.

"This page will no longer be monitored. Our beloved daughter, Emma Katz, has passed on."

"That's it? That's all you have to say?" Jason typed a comment below, but quickly deleted it. "No. Don't."

When Emma returned home for the summer, she had gone to work right away at the grocery store. Jason had stopped in during those first few days she'd been home, not realizing she was back in town.

He had approached her while she stocked bread on the shelf.

"Emma, you're home?"

She looked at him, wearing the same beautiful smile she always had. *"Hey, Jas, I only got home a few days ago. Hardly anyone knows I'm back. I got a job here and, well, here I am. It's so good to see you."*

Their breakup was amicable enough, he supposed. But then he'd gone and asked her out again.

"That'd be great. I'd love to hang out with you. I'm off tomorrow night. How about we meet at Gino's for some pizza? I haven't had a good slice of pie since I left for school."

"I'd like that. Okay, great. I'll see you around seven at Gino's," he had replied.

"All right, then."

He'd been so excited to go out with her that he'd completely forgotten why he was at the store in the first place. It wasn't until he returned home that Chris had asked him about the bread.

"Oh, man. I completely forgot. I saw Emma and we're meeting up tomorrow night for pizza."

"Emma? Your ex-girlfriend from last summer?" Chris had asked.

"The same one. Look, I know you didn't think much of her—"

Chris had shrugged it off. *"It's not that. She didn't like me. That was pretty obvious. But it doesn't matter to me who you go out with."*

Jason peered again at the Facebook page and clicked "unfriend" before closing the lid on his laptop. And as he returned his dirty plate to the kitchen, a knock came on his front door. He opened it to find an unexpected arrival. "Oh, Lieutenant Irving."

"Jason." Irving removed his hat. "This is FBI Agent Reid. She's helping us out with getting to the bottom of all that's happened."

"FBI?" he asked.

"Jason, nice to meet you. I'm only here to offer support," Kate replied.

"Officer Abrams came to the station earlier today to ask me the same stuff you did," Jason continued. "Can I ask why you're here now? I told him I was on shift when Heidi..."

Irving raised his hand. "I know this has been beyond difficult for you, son. But we're here to learn whatever else it is that you might know about Heidi. Now, you and she were friends, too, is that right?"

"Yes, sir. Just like I told Officer Abrams." Jason closed the door after they walked inside. "We all used to hang out last summer. I didn't go to school with Emma and all them, but since we'd gone out a few times before she left for college, I got to know her friends."

"You're, what, a year or so older than the others?" Irving asked.

"I am, yes." He stood in the center of his small living room. "Um, I didn't really know Heidi all that well, then, sir, but you may already know that we went out a few times earlier in the year. It didn't pan out."

"So I gathered," Irving began. "I'm here to ask if there was anything that you and your friends, particularly Emma and Heidi, had discussed in the days leading up to, well—what's happened."

He raised his eyes as he pondered the question. "I'm sorry, but no. Nothing that comes to mind. Last I talked to Emma was shortly after she got back into town. We grabbed dinner at Gino's. It was no big deal. Uh, I saw her again a few days before the parade. As far as Heidi, I haven't talked to her probably since spring shortly after we called it quits."

"And what about Brian Keller?" Kate cut in. "Are you two good friends?"

"I wouldn't say 'good', but we're friends."

Kate tilted her head "And when was the last time you two spoke?"

Jason clasped his hands behind his back. "I don't really remember. I keep pretty busy with work."

"If you were to guess," she continued. "When do you think you talked to him last?"

"Come to think of it, I guess it was on the Fourth," he began. "I was helping set up for the fireworks show. I think I saw him at the park or walking out of the park. I wasn't paying much attention. Said 'hi', I think was all."

"Any idea what time that was?" Kate asked.

Jason raised a shoulder. "An hour or so before the show started. Yeah, that's right. I remember I was at the truck getting my things, ready to hike up the hill. I saw Brian come out of the park."

"He say what he was doing there?" Irving asked.

"No, sir. He didn't."

6

H eidi Sumner's body lay face up on the riverbank. Her mouth, open. Her eyes, bulging. Her skin, blue and waterlogged. Her black hair wet and matted over her shoulders. These were the images Kate examined as they lay scattered on the lieutenant's table in his office. Emma Katz was only slightly different. She'd collapsed onto her stomach. But her eyes still bulged, and her mouth hung open. Her shiny red hair, knotted with blood from her skull.

Based on the photos, Heidi probably hadn't survived the blow to the head. Kate already knew Emma had survived only moments. Long enough to bring the young firefighter who found her to his knees with overwhelming anguish.

Kate believed the autopsy would disclose that Heidi went quickly, which would bring a small measure of comfort to her family. Emma's family would get no such reprieve. Their daughter's tragic death caused her great pain before the end. She turned her gaze from the heart-wrenching crime scene photos and looked at Irving. "What else do we know about Brian Keller?"

"He's a good kid, by all accounts. Lives with his folks, goes to community college."

"But you still can't account for his exact whereabouts after he and Emma parted ways?" Kate pressed on.

"Unfortunately, no. His folks had some trouble recalling an exact time, but they had seen him."

She glanced at the image of Heidi on the riverbank once again. "And where was Heidi last spotted?"

"At work. She worked at the convenience store near the edge of town," Irving replied. "She'd finished her shift and locked up for the night." He paused a moment. "Never made it home."

"And you mentioned you'd found her car at work?"

"That's right. So whoever did it, knew she was working that night and must've waited for her to clock out. I've spoken to the store owner. He recalled when the alarm on the store was set, and it agreed with the time Heidi clocked out. It wasn't until the next evening, when her folks expected her for dinner, that the call came in."

Kate moved the pictures on the table as though they were puzzle pieces. "Do we know whether these two girls spent time together recently?"

"I have spoken with a young woman by the name of Amber. She was part of their group of friends back in high school. According to her, the two had seen each other in passing, but both worked and lived on opposite ends of town." Irving cocked his head. "What are you thinking, Agent Reid?"

"So these girls, who we assume hadn't hung out recently, but used to be friends in high school—they're murdered within a matter of days from each other. Same M.O. mostly, except Emma survived a short time after the attack." Kate ran the scenario through her head. "Did Brian have a relationship with Heidi Sumner?"

"No, ma'am. Although, he was part of their circle of friends," Irving replied.

Kate examined the photos again. "I understand you've gotten statements from these friends. But now with a second member gone, it's time to revisit their connections. When each one last saw the other. How close they were. Because here's where I'm at right now, Lieutenant." Kate raised her index finger. "A common thread exists between these kids besides their friendship, and whatever that is, I believe, has made them targets."

THE TWO-HOUR DRIVE back to D.C. put Kate in town by 9 pm. She'd promised the lieutenant to return as soon as possible in the morning. Unfortunately, her input had done little to move the case forward. Irving was right. They needed clues and leads and right now, they had neither.

Kate arrived at Quantico and displayed her badge at the guard gate.

"Thank you, SSA Reid." The military guard returned her ID and opened the gate.

She drove through and navigated the roadway that led to the FBI's BAU buildings inside the massive Quantico military compound. As she neared the parking garage, Kate called Nick on his cell. When the call went to voicemail, she left a message. "Hey, it's me. I'm back in town but wanted to stop by the office before heading home. Sounds like you might still be working anyway. I'll catch up with you later. Love you. Bye."

While she parked inside the garage, she noticed Surrey's SUV. "Glad to see I'm not the only one working late." Kate reached the elevators and when the doors opened on her floor, she headed inside, stopping by Surrey's office first. "Look who's working late."

He glanced at her from his desk. "I'm not the only one. How'd it go in Jansville?"

Kate walked inside and sat down. "We didn't get as far as I would've hoped. It was more of me wasting the lieutenant's time catching me up on the case."

"Are you planning on going back?" he asked.

"I'd like to." Kate crossed her legs and let her arms rest on her lap. "This signature is unique enough that I feel almost certain more victims will surface. And I'm not sure the lieutenant is ready for what that means for his town."

"Do you have your sights on any potential suspects?" Surrey asked.

"Couple of young men I'd probably consider persons of interest. No real suspects yet. One of the men doesn't appear to have a solid alibi. The other was the lucky one to see the victim in the moments before her death. But unless he could've been in two places at once, I don't see how he could've murdered the first girl. Now, the second, I'm not so sure. What's interesting is that the girls were part of a group of friends that also included the two guys."

Surrey closed the lid of his laptop and captured her gaze. "What's your next move? If you want to help this investigator, you'd better come up with a viable plan."

Kate looked on as she pondered his question. "For now, I'm going to my office to stand in front of my whiteboard and stare at it until something comes to me."

"Sounds like you've figured it all out." He cracked a smile. "I'm happy to offer my two cents. I've got nothing better to do at 9 p.m. on a Wednesday."

Kate pushed off the chair. "Great. I'll put on some coffee."

NICK SLIPPED his phone into his pocket and returned to the conference table, where two other members of his task force convened.

Georgia Myers looked up from her notes. "Everything okay?" She shook away a strand of red hair that fell into her eyes. It was shorter now—above her shoulders. A few fine lines creased at her eyes when she spoke. She was still fit, of course, it was a requirement in this line of work. Her voice wasn't as soft as it once was, and the job seemed to have worn her down. Although, she did have a toddler at home, which could also explain it.

Nick pulled out his chair and sat once again. "Yeah, it was just a voicemail. Sorry for the interruption. Where were we?"

CIA Special Ops Case Officer Candice Morgan stood from the table and approached the wall monitor. The slender, short-haired blond aimed her index finger at the screen. "This map, here. It's the most recent we have of Kyiv's power grid."

"Which Russian forces have attempted to cut off," Myers said.

"Correct. And should they succeed in bringing down their system, it'll mean they've fully developed their current technology and it would only be a matter of time before they either sell it to the highest bidder or—"

"Use it against us," Nick cut in. "So now the time's come to see just how close they are to completing it." He turned to DHS Agent Jake Benson. "What are we doing to prevent private industry's intellectual property from being stolen and used to help the Russians finish their project?"

While the agent retrieved the latest reports, Nick eyed Georgia for a moment. She'd kept checking her phone. "Is everything okay?" he whispered.

"Yeah, fine. My babysitter will need to leave soon. Just watching the clock."

It was still strange to think of Georgia as a mother. She'd been so different when they were together. A hard worker, determined, always stood her ground. It was part of the reason he'd loved her. And he had loved her—for a time. That time ended when she'd crawled into bed with an agent they both knew; someone he had once considered a friend. Of course, she'd blamed it on the notion that Nick had feelings for Kate and she had felt helpless to compete against that. He had denied his feelings for Kate for too long and it took Georgia's betrayal and confrontation to convince him that Kate had been the one. And now, here they were, working side-by-side once again, even if in a different environment. They no longer hunted serial killers. They hunted those who sought to destroy the country. To wipe out towns and cities with a keystroke.

He missed Kate right now. Hearing her voice message suddenly felt more important than ever before.

Myers raised her index finger. "Excuse me, Jake, I need to head out. I just got a message from my sitter. She has to leave, so I need to get home. I'm so sorry, but I'll review the report still tonight and be prepared with comments tomorrow."

Jake looked up at her. "Oh, yeah, sure. It's no problem. Hey, we all have a life outside this place, even if we don't spend much time at it. "Say hello to your husband."

She smirked. "I will if I see him."

HAVING BEEN a cop in a previous life, local Jansville lieutenant, Howard Irving knew his way around a murder investigation. But he'd never come across anything like this. Two young people bludgeoned with their tongues cut out? No, never in a million years had he ever believed he would work a case like this. The federal agent's involvement was a Godsend as far as he was concerned.

Her level of expertise was sorely needed, but even she seemed stumped—for now.

He'd insisted she return home to D.C. After they'd questioned a few more folks, there wasn't a whole hell of a lot left for her to do. Now, they awaited forensics results. Were any drugs in the victims' systems? What weapon had been used to knock them unconscious? They already knew a serrated hunting knife had been used to sever the tongues, but far too many people in this town used knives like that. Irving needed more if he hoped to find their unsub, as the agent had put it.

As he drove along the streets, not a single soul walked among them. It was nine o'clock on a Wednesday night, but during the summer, this was unusual. The local movie theater parking lot was nearly empty. The Dairy Queen looked abandoned. Darkness had only just settled over the town and yet it appeared shut down. "They're afraid."

With his hand resting on top of the wheel, Irving continued along Market Street where, only days before, the town's people packed in for the local parade. As he gazed out among the mom-and-pop shops and restaurants, he spotted a man walking with his back to him. Irving narrowed his gaze and slowly came up to him. "Sam?" He rolled down his window and called out. "Sam, hey, bud, are you okay?"

Sam Hardy looked over at him. "I'm okay."

"The hell you are," he whispered as he pulled to the curb and stopped. He stepped out and approached the young man. "What are you doing out here by yourself?" Everyone looked after Sam, it was just how things were, but for him to be out here alone was out of the ordinary and Irving feared for his safety. "You drive here, son? Where's your car?"

"I walked, sir."

Irving grunted. "You walked? Your folks know you're out here?"

"Yes, sir. I wasn't doing anything wrong," Sam replied. "I'm just sad is all."

"Hold up, son. Just stand still a moment, would you?" Irving gently took Sam by the shoulders and that was when he noticed the marks on his face. Sam clearly had tried to hide the swelling and bruising with his overgrown brown hair. "Did you get into a fight or something?"

Sam turned down his gaze. "No, sir."

Irving took a step back and examined him. "Your daddy do that to you? Is that why you're sad?"

Sam kept his eyes on his feet. "I'm sad 'cause Emma's gone. She's not coming back, either."

"No, Sam, she's not. I know you two were close. She is gone and that's part of the reason why I don't think you should be out here alone. You understand what I'm telling you?" Irving pressed on. "Now, why don't you hop on into my car and I'll drive you back home. Unless you want to go to a friend's house or something like that."

"I don't have any friends."

"Course you do, son. Plenty of folks around here enjoy your company."

Sam returned his sights to Irving. His eyes had welled with tears. "Emma was my friend. My dad's mad because she's gone. He didn't mean to hurt me."

Irving pursed his lips. "No. He never does, does he?" He placed his arm around Sam's rounded shoulders. "Come on now. Let's get you home. But promise me something?"

"Yes, sir?"

"You come to me if you need help. Any sort of help, you understand?"

Sam nodded. "I do."

Two EMPTY COFFEE mugs sat on Kate's desk while she and her partner, Surrey, stood in front of a whiteboard, staring at it as though it might spontaneously produce the results they desired.

"You mentioned the victims were connected to the two persons of interest," Surrey began. "But even so, what you're lacking is motive."

"If I knew the motive, I'd have the killer." Kate approached the board and grabbed a marker. "Emma dated Brian Keller in high school." She drew a line between Emma's and Brian's names. "Then she went out with the slightly older guy, firefighter, Jason Gatwick, last summer." She drew another line between them. "And then you have Heidi Sumner. She was friends with Emma and Brian. And Jason went out with her too."

"So who was she currently dating?" Surrey asked.

"No one, according to her parents."

Surrey approached the board and held out his hand. "May I?"

"Be my guest." Kate placed the marker in his hand.

"Heidi Sumner was found in a river about, what, half a mile from where your other victim was found?" Surrey drew a circle on the map. "And that was right here."

"Give or take a few yards, yes," she replied.

"And then over here is where Emma was found." He circled her location.

"Yes, I'm aware of all this." She eyed the map and knitted her brow. "Wait, hang on a second."

He glanced at her. "What is it?"

"I need to measure the distance here. Grab me a ruler, would you?"

Surrey eyed her desk. "Do you have one here?"

"In my top drawer."

He opened the drawer. "Got it."

Kate held out her hand. "Thanks. Okay, so the distance from the river to the center of town is..." She laid the ruler on the map and compared the distance to the legend below. "1.75 miles."

"And that means what, exactly?" Surrey looked on.

"Give me a second and I'll tell you." Kate proceeded to measure the distance between the nearby hillside adjacent to the park and the stream that led out to the river where Heidi had been discovered. She turned to Surrey. "Is it possible for a body to float that far down a narrow stream in a day, and without anyone seeing it? We don't know exactly when she died yet, but she was last seen at her job, then her parents expected her to come over for dinner the next night. That was when they called it in."

"It seems pretty unlikely unless there had been a storm and winds picked up the current. Remember, there would've been obstructions along the way. Fallen branches, boulders, even bends in the river." He turned to her. "What are you getting at?"

Kate studied the map again and chewed on her lower lip. "If we're to assume the body couldn't have traveled that distance in that amount of time, then they couldn't have been killed in the same location. Heidi was either killed elsewhere or moved after the fact. And according to the lieutenant, he didn't believe she'd been killed at the store where she worked." Kate walked to her desk and grabbed the file on top of it. She flipped it open. "These are the preliminary autopsy reports. Take a look here. This is Emma Katz. The diagram shows she was hit with a blunt object here, at the back of her head."

"The killer came up from behind her," Surrey replied.

"That's how it appears, which I think is because the unsub isn't a large man. He's someone who would need to take someone by surprise. And look here." She flipped over to the other report. "This is Heidi Sumner. No summary as of yet, but we know based on the diagram, that she was struck with a blunt object." Kate flipped over the photo. "If you look closely, they don't appear to have the same marks."

"Suggesting the weapon used was different. Maybe the killer got his hands on whatever he could find at the moment?" Surrey added.

"But he still had a hunting knife. At first glance, the severing of the tongues appears to have been done by the same instrument," Kate replied.

"So he used a similar technique," Surrey added. "Blunt force trauma. A blow to the head, but not with the same object."

"And we initially noted ligature marks on Emma's neck, but not on Heidi's." She turned to him. "Are we looking at a different M.O.?"

"Maybe Heidi didn't give him a chance to lay hands on her and he just used whatever object he could find to hit her in the head and knock her out." Surrey rubbed his cheek. "Do you have forensics back on any foreign matter left on the body? Soil, plant material, obviously DNA, but also anything that might have been embedded in Sumner's body that could offer some idea as to where she was when she was killed."

Kate set down the file on her desk. "Not yet. They only just got her transported. Both victims are in at the M.E.'s office. Labs were sent to the county for analysis."

"We should be the ones doing that analysis," he replied.

"I'd agree with you except that this isn't our case. This isn't our jurisdiction," Kate replied. "I asked if I could offer advice. I wanted to help, but this case belongs to local and county officials." She turned back to the whiteboard. "But I get what you're saying. If it can be determined, based on foreign material found on the bodies, a possible location, would go a long way in helping to narrow down a suspect. Narrow down the timing as well. Then we could compare alibis. But I don't want to dismiss the obvious differences in these murders."

"Agreed. You're planning on heading over there again tomorrow?"

"I am."

Surrey nodded. "Mind if I join you?"

IRVING ROLLED to a stop in front of the Hardys' home. "I can walk you up, if you'd like, son."

Sam opened his door. "No thanks, I got it. Thank you for the drive home." He closed his door and carried on along the gravel driveway that was set far back from the road. After a moment, he turned back to watch Irving pull away, before walking inside.

Carol jumped from the sofa. "There you are. Sam, you can't just leave like that. Not right now."

He kept his eyes on the floor. "Sorry, Mom."

Randall pushed down the footstool on his recliner and marched toward him. "Where'd you go, boy? How'd you get home?"

"Lieutenant Irving drove me home. He said I shouldn't be walking around at night right now."

"Well, at least he's got that right." Randall grabbed his arm and pulled him into the hall. "You can go on straight to your room."

Carol trailed after them. "That's enough now, Randall."

He stopped and turned back, glowering at his wife. "What did you say to me, Carol?"

She shrunk away. "He's been through a lot. That's all I'm saying."

Randall turned back and opened the door to Sam's bedroom. "Get inside. Back away, Carol, unless you want to be next." He slammed the door in her face.

Sam stood in the middle of his room.

"Look here," Randall lunged toward him. "You go out looking like that and the cops will come here. Is that what you want, son?"

"No, sir," he whispered.

Randall crossed his arms. "You know she's dead because of you, right? The girl would still be here if you hadn't gotten her all upset that day."

Sam's face was masked in confusion. "I didn't get her upset. She came out of your office. I heard what you said to her."

Randall raised his arm and backhanded Sam squarely across his cheek. "You think this is my fault?"

Sam's head bobbed backward, but he kept his feet firmly on the floor. The young man wasn't as tall as his father, but he was sturdy. "I didn't say that."

Randall stepped within inches of Sam. "Emma didn't love you, boy, you know that right? She wanted nothing to do with you. She just wanted to be with all her friends. Always asking for time off to hang out with them. They were the ones who took her from you. Just like I told you when it happened. Now someone's gone and taken Heidi too." He stepped back again and regarded Sam. "There it is." His lips curled into a smile. "I know that look all too well. You want to take a swing? Try me."

AT THE HEAD of the table, Fisher opened the meeting to comments. "Reid, what's on your mind?"

She tapped her pen on the table. "This case out in Jansville, you know I was out there yesterday and the day before. Surrey and

I started looking at the facts. Long story short, the local authorities are happy to have our help, so I'd like to bring in Surrey to lend a hand."

Levi Walsh had been away on a consultation with the Chicago field office when he raised a finger to garner attention. "I'm just hearing about this, but based on what you know right now, is this going to get any bigger?"

Kate raised a brow. "They have two dead already. Both, young women. Friends. Both had their tongues severed..."

"So that would be a yes," Walsh replied.

She nodded. "In my opinion, we're a long way from this being over. Given the set of criteria, the primary marker, we're dealing with someone who may have a personal vendetta. I don't believe this is a random killer traveling through town."

"Why not ask the locals to put in an official request for our help?" Duncan asked.

"Nothing in this case makes it federal, but yeah, they could officially request federal assistance," Kate replied. "I'm not sure the man heading up the investigation finds that necessary at the moment. That could change."

"I'd almost prefer it go that route, Reid, especially if Surrey wants in," Fisher replied. "We start guiding the investigation and it's not our jurisdiction, you could be opening the door to a tainted conviction."

"Let me ask you this," Walsh cut in. "What's your next move, assuming you think this unsub isn't finished? What had you and Surrey planned for today?"

"Of course, the lieutenant is awaiting forensics reports back from the county. Doesn't help us now, but it'll still be important to move forward," Kate began. "And I'd like to review the witness statements with Surrey. We could find details the lieutenant over-looked or hadn't believed were relevant."

"The intimate nature of the crimes suggests a message was being delivered," Walsh added. "I agree this doesn't appear to be an unknown person to the victims." He looked at Fisher. "Kate has an eye for this sort of thing, Cam. If her gut tells her the unsub isn't finished, I'd suggest we prepare for this to find its way into our territory. Maybe we can start laying some groundwork in that event." He surveyed the team. "I know I've got some time to spare. Not much, but enough to get a jump on things. This is a small town and the people, if they aren't already afraid, they will be. We've all dealt with this scenario before."

"Back in Kentucky," Kate added.

"Yes, ma'am," Walsh replied. "And that got ugly real fast."

"Well, look," Fisher cut in. "If Reid and Surrey want to head that way again and get a better handle on the situation, I don't have a problem with that. This is practically in our backyard, so if we can keep it contained, so much the better." He stood from the table. "Keep me updated and we'll go from there."

IN THE EARLY MORNING LIGHT, Lieutenant Irving stood along the riverbank where the body of Heidi Sumner had been found floating downstream only days before. Had the fisherman not been there, the girl would likely still have been considered missing, and it would've been much more difficult to put together that the two cases were clearly linked.

What happened last night with Sam Hardy still bothered him. Randall Hardy had a temper. Everyone knew that, and so it wasn't entirely surprising he'd laid a hand on his son. Unacceptable, but not surprising. And since Sam was an adult, he'd have to press charges against his father and Irving knew he stood a better chance at winning the lottery than convincing Sam to levy a charge against his father. The young man hardly knew better, which was the real shame of it.

Still, Irving was left with two dead bodies in his town. He'd known both the victims and felt compelled to bring them much-deserved justice. Getting the help of the federal agent was a blessing, but as of yet, nothing had come of her expertise, save for a few suggestions here and there. What Irving needed was proof.

And after several more moments, he knew he wasn't going to see that proof here. Too much time had passed. Mother nature and the elements had taken care of whatever might've remained the day Heidi was found. So, the lieutenant started back to his patrol car. Agent Reid was slated to return this morning, and he hoped a good night's rest offered her a fresh perspective and a new direction.

Irving slipped behind the wheel when his radio sounded. He picked up the receiver and pressed the button. "I'm here, Dispatch. Whatcha got for me?"

"Yeah, Howard, uh, we need you to run over to the Quick Mart on Lanier Drive."

"What's going on over there?" he asked.

"Uh, something's been found over there, Howard. You need to get there before people start congregating and contaminating the scene."

Irving dropped his head. "Son of a bitch. I'm on my way."

7

In the early morning light, Kate slipped on her sunglasses from behind the wheel of her SUV. Surrey was in the passenger seat and had been occupied with the contents of his phone. They headed back to Jansville with the blessing of Senior Unit Agent Fisher.

She hadn't said much on the two-hour drive and neither had Surrey. He still kept those on the team mostly at arm's length and maybe Kate was going to have to be okay with that.

The silence finally broke when her phone rang through the speaker, and she pressed the button to answer. "Agent Reid here."

"Agent Reid, this is Howard Irving. I assume you're headed my way this morning?"

"We are." At this, Kate noticed Surrey's attention return.

"We?" he asked.

"I have Agent Jonathan Surrey with me. He's my partner. I apologize I didn't run this by you first—"

"Agent Reid, sorry to cut you off, but I'm standing behind the

Quick Mart here in town. A call came in a short while ago. We, uh, well, it looks like we've found the other one."

The agents traded glances when Kate continued, "The other what?"

"Tongue, Agent Reid. Heidi Sumner's, I believe. How far out are you?" Irving asked.

"About thirty to forty-five minutes."

"I'll drop a pin on my location. Do me a favor, you and your partner get over here just as fast as you're able. I'm going to hold off touching anything until you get here."

"We'll be there as soon as we can." Kate ended the call.

THE BRICK-CLAD convenience store with a shaker roof was ahead on the right. Kate noticed a patrol car parked out front, beyond the two gas pumps that faced the road. She turned into the parking lot that contained several small potholes and crumbling asphalt.

Kate rolled to a stop near the entrance and stepped out of her Ford Explorer. She turned back to see Surrey climb out and close his passenger door.

Irving stood outside under the awning with a paper cup in his hand. He raised it to his lips before crumpling it and tossing it into the nearby trash can. "You brought company."

Kate offered him a handshake. "I did. Lieutenant Irving, this is Special Agent Jonathan Surrey. He and I work closely together. I thought he would bring a fresh pair of eyes."

Irving outstretched his hand. "Your timing couldn't be better Agent Surrey. Good to meet you. Well, let me show you what we got." He started around to the back of the store that had been cordoned off. "Course, after Heidi was found, I came here to sweep the scene. We found her car and had it towed to the impound lot, where it now remains. However, during the course of searching the scene, I found only minor evidence of blood. Not as much as you'd expect under the circumstances, which was why I believed she'd been killed elsewhere. Probably at the river where she was eventually found. That said, I never did find the tongue." He turned back to them. "Until now. I've been holding off sending this to the coroner this morning, figuring it best to keep everything as is till you folks could lay eyes on it. I've had a look around. Haven't seen anything else that might help with the investigation."

"When did the call come in?" Kate asked as she walked alongside Irving.

"Shortly before I reached out to you. Luckily, you were already headed this way. It was the owner of the store who called. He was set to open and was throwing out some boxes around back. Came up on it near the dumpsters. I'm stumped as to how this is here now. It most certainly wasn't during my sweep."

As they reached the back of the store, an overturned box lay in front of the garbage bins. Irving squatted low. "I didn't know what else to use to keep the critters and bugs away. Seems crude, I know." He wiped his sweaty brow and lifted the box from the ground.

Kate approached the tissue that had already begun to decompose. "It's been out in the elements a while. Looks like something's gotten to it. It is strange that it turned up now."

"Why would the unsub come back?" Surrey asked.

"That's a good question," Kate replied. "We'll get it to the M.E. and see what he can do. Lieutenant, you'd mentioned she clocked out, according to the owner."

"Yes, ma'am. The time clock is digital, and it notifies the owner's computer program when someone clocks in or out."

Kate noticed Surrey had already begun to survey the exterior of the building and turned back to Irving. "Don't suppose the owner has any cameras installed?"

"Not outside. Just inside. I've operated on the assumption young Heidi was taken before she died. Just not enough evidence here to suggest otherwise. Then left in the river for dead." Irving headed toward the entrance.

Surrey waited for the lieutenant to step inside and gently took hold of Kate's arm. "He didn't check surveillance around here? Are you kidding me? That should've been done first thing."

"The man's had two murders in a matter of days. I get he's in over his head, but that's exactly why we're here."

"What concerns me more is that the cameras inside might just be for show," Surrey added. "Irving hasn't looked yet, so who knows?"

"If that's the case, we're right back at Square One." Kate peered out over the road ahead. "Let me see if I can get my bearings straight." She pointed to the left. "That's the high school that way." She turned to her right. "That way leads you to Market Street. It doesn't look like Heidi Sumner died here, so how did she end up in the river?"

Irving stepped outside. "You two coming in?"

"Yes, sir." Kate started on.

Irving held the door for her. "Well, I just got a call from Mrs. Hardy. She's concerned about her boy, Sam. He's agitated. I saw the young man last night, roaming around Market Street by himself."

"Is he a minor?" Surrey asked.

"No, sir, but we all look out for him. Thing is, he was close to Emma Katz. Good friends. Knew Heidi as well. I imagine he's having some difficulty coming to terms with all that's been happening. Hell, I'm having difficulty. Point being, I have to help see to him. Make sure he's not gonna harm himself. Can I ask you two to stick around here and have a chat inside with the owner? Look at the CCTV. Have a walk around. Maybe you'll find something I missed. I'll try not to be long, regardless, and I'll keep in touch."

"Of course. No problem." Kate watched Irving step into his patrol car and drive away.

Surrey cocked his head. "That's odd."

"What is?" she asked.

"Well, if this kid, or young man, was roaming the streets late at night—last night when the victim's tongue magically appeared—where were his folks? And can we account for his location when this woman was killed?"

"Irving seems to be close with the family. He might not take that into consideration," Kate replied.

"He might not, but we sure as hell should." Surrey stepped inside. "Let's go talk to the owner. See if we can figure out who was here the night Sumner died."

Kate noticed the water stains on the ceiling. The vinyl floors were scuffed, and a nearby stand contained paper maps. "Wow."

Surrey regarded her. "What?"

"I just haven't seen paper maps in a while." She pointed to the stand.

Surrey glanced at it. "I doubt they're a top seller."

An elderly man, possibly in his sixties, stood behind the counter as Kate reached for her credentials. "Excuse me, we're working with Lieutenant Irving—"

"You're the FBI, aren't you?" the man interjected.

"Yes, sir. I'm Agent Reid. This is Agent Surrey."

"Howard said y'all were coming. So, you see outside, did you?" he asked.

"We did," Kate said. "We understand Ms. Sumner closed up for you the other night."

He wiped his heavily lined eyes with the back of his hand. "She was a good kid. Helluva hard worker. Never did show up late. Not once." The old man grabbed a tissue from his shirt pocket and wiped his nose. "Can't imagine why anyone would do that kind of thing to her. To either of them, for that matter. I was having a hard enough time as it was with all this nonsense going on. I went out this morning and damn near stepped on..." His lips trembled.

Kate pointed to the ceiling. "We noticed you have cameras inside."

"Yes, ma'am. Nothing outside, though I wish I did now."

Surrey took a step forward. "May we see the video from her last night here? Have you had a chance to look at it?"

"I did, sir, yes. Didn't see anything out of the ordinary, but by all means, have a look and see what you think." He walked around the counter and headed into the corridor. "Come on back. I keep it in the storage room. Got no other place for it."

They followed him into the narrow hall lined with cases of bottled water and motor oil that led to a backroom where excess inventory had been stacked along the walls.

"How long have you owned this store?" Kate asked.

"I opened the place back in eighty-seven." He pulled out a chair behind a small desk and turned on the desktop computer. "This is nothing fancy. Black and white. No audio. I keep the footage stored on my hard drive and delete it every Monday morning. 'Less, of course, something happened."

"You get much trouble here?" Surrey asked him.

"Nah. Teenagers boosting a tallboy now and then. Maybe a candy bar. Never once in all these years have I had something as awful as this happen. That girl, though, she was just the sweetest thing to ever walk the planet."

"How long had she worked here?" Kate asked.

"Since high school. I believe she started somewhere around when she was sixteen or seventeen, I suppose. She works part-time even now while she attends the community college in the next town over." He paused a moment. "Guess she don't attend there now." He cleared his throat and eyed Kate. "From her last shift, huh?"

"Yes, sir. Please." She stood at the desk next to Surrey and elbowed him. "And you didn't think he had any footage."

Surrey shrugged. "Glad I was wrong."

"All right." The old man peered over his computer. "You want to come see what I got?"

Kate walked behind him and both she and Surrey peered over the man's shoulders.

"This is from that night about seven pm. We close at midnight, so I reckon Heidi would've started closing out the register shortly before then. We don't tend to get too many folks here after about ten, especially lately, but I keep the place open in the summer till the movie theater lets out around eleven, just in case kids want to come by for snacks. Course, after what happened to Emma, I made Heidi promise to not mess around. Close up, lock up, get in her car, and go on home." He choked back his emotions. "I wasn't gonna let her work that shift, given what happened to her friend, but she insisted. Said she couldn't just sit around at home and be sad. Still shouldn't have let her."

"I understand," Kate said. "You don't think it'll happen again. That it was just an awful thing, and you still have a livelihood to consider. I'm sure that's what Heidi thought too. You can't blame yourself."

"That's kind of you to say." He pressed the play button.

Kate waited for the video to load. As it began, she glanced at Surrey, and he mirrored her expression. The grainy black-and-white video was going to make it hard to identify anyone.

"Can you speed up the playback until we see something?" Surrey asked.

"Yes, sir." He fast-forwarded the video.

Kate looked at the screen as the victim, Heidi, appeared to scroll through her phone from behind the counter. "She's not talking to anyone on the phone."

"Could be texting," Surrey replied. "I'm sure Irving will request phone records, but let's make a note to follow up on that."

"Hang on. Stop the video right there." Kate aimed a finger at the screen. "Who is that?"

The old man squinted at the image. "Can't quite tell. Let me see if he comes in a little clearer." While he pressed play again, he slowed down the video.

"What time was this?" Kate asked.

"9:45," he replied. "Don't look like he's much interested in buying anything."

"No, and he walked straight to the counter," Surrey added. "There's no volume here?"

"Like I said, this system's older than dirt."

Kate focused on the man who approached the counter. She had only talked to a few people in town with Irving and the guy there hadn't looked like one of them. "She's off her phone. She's talking to him."

"Smiling. Doesn't look scared," Surrey replied. "She must know him."

"Most everyone knows everyone here in town, sir," the old man replied. "But I sure can't tell head nor tales who that man is." He leaned in closer. "Although..."

"What is it?" Kate asked.

"You see that on his forearm?"

"The tattoo?" she continued.

"Yes, ma'am. I seen that before. I think that's Randall Hardy.

Fact, yeah, I'd bet my left arm that's Randall right there." He looked back at Kate. "Man served a while back. Iraq, I believe. He was in the Army. Talks about it often."

"He's the owner of the grocery store, isn't he?" Surrey asked.

"That's right. Which makes it kinda odd he'd be stopping by my place. Figured if he wanted something, he could go to his own store, you know?"

"Maybe so." Kate looked on. "Regardless, I don't see any unusual behavior. This was after Emma, so since they both knew her, it would make sense they'd be talking about it."

Surrey glanced at her. "But to make the trip there just to talk about it? Is there another person that connects these two? He clearly didn't need anything because he's standing at the counter with nothing in his hands. He only seems interested in her."

IRVING KNOCKED on the door of the Hardy home. "It's Lieutenant Irving. Mrs. Hardy, you mind opening the door for me?" He stepped back and stood with his hand on the butt of his sidearm. Force of habit, and one he learned while working in Asheville. Standard procedure was to be prepared for anything on a domestic call. Guess it stuck with him.

Carol Hardy opened the door and stood on the other side. "Howard, come in. I'm so sorry. Sam's just been so difficult. Thank you for coming over."

He walked inside. "It's no problem at all. Is Mr. Hardy here?"

"He's at the store, of course. Follow me. Sam's in his room now. Think I have to take a breath for a moment." She started toward the hall. "I just can't figure out what's got him so upset. Of course, I realize the loss of Emma has hit him hard, but this just sort of came out from nowhere."

She opened the door to Sam's room. The young man sat on the edge of his bed. His hair covered most of his face.

Irving turned to her. "May I go in?"

"Please."

He walked inside. "Hey, Sam. What's going on?"

Sam regarded him. "What are you doing here?"

He was careful to keep his distance. "Well, your momma asked me to stop by. She said you were pretty upset there for a while. You want to tell me what's going on?"

Sam's chin quivered. "My friend's dead."

Irving pursed his lips and nodded. "I know that, Sam, and I'm real sorry about that. Believe me. Is that what's got you upset again? Thinking about Emma? Is that why you were out last night wandering around?"

"We talked to him about that, Howard," Carol began. "Sam, you know you shouldn't be out there alone."

"I'm a grown man, momma," he replied. "I can do as I please."

Irving noticed the fresh bruise on his cheek. "I'm gonna have to agree with your momma on this one. So, you're just trying to get through all these emotions about Emma?"

"It's all my fault." He wiped his eyes and kept his head low.

Irving turned stone-faced. "What's your fault, son?"

"That Emma's dead."

8

The sun burned through the morning clouds and as Kate glanced through the window of the lieutenant's office, she could see the green mountaintops amid the blue skies. "It's quiet out there. Beautiful and quiet."

Irving was at his desk. "People are scared. They don't want to leave their homes and I don't blame them."

She stepped away from the window and set her eyes on Surrey, who'd continued to review the crime scene photos. "We have Randall Hardy showing up at the convenience store a couple of hours before it closed. The man buys nothing and just talks to Heidi Sumner, about what, we don't know. And then you have Sam Hardy, who was out roaming the streets."

"Where I picked him up," Irving cut in. "I just left the Hardy house, Randall wasn't there, but Sam and his mother, Carol were. Apparently, Sam had gotten upset and thought Emma was dead because of something he did. It was his damn father who convinced him of that." He shook his head. "Son of a bitch tried to knock it into him too."

"Have you confirmed his whereabouts when Heidi was killed?" Kate asked.

Irving returned a sideways glance. "I do know he was with his folks when Emma was killed. So, to suggest he had anything to do with Heidi..." He rubbed his bald head. "Even if he did, and I'm sure as hell not saying that, but the kid doesn't have the mental acuity to keep that hidden. He broke down right in front of me just a while ago, saying how he missed Emma and was friends with Heidi. I didn't even know the two were friends. Brian and Jason never mentioned he was part of their circle."

"Maybe he wasn't. And maybe that is the problem," Kate began. "Lieutenant, I don't think we can rule out Sam Hardy as a suspect."

Irving leaned back in his chair. "Brian Keller makes a better suspect, I'll tell you what. He knew both girls. Had seen one on the day she died. Still can't get a confirmation on his whereabouts except that he was at the picnic."

Kate caught sight of Surrey and it seemed the two were on the same page. "It may be time to say something to the people around here. They must be beside themselves with fear. You also might want to consider asking the county to help with additional patrols. Please don't take offense, Lieutenant, but your department isn't equipped to handle something like this."

Irving raised his hands. "I'll be the first to admit that. And You're right. I'll talk with the county. Still need to light a fire under the good doctor's butt. We need those labs back and quick."

"We'll enlist the help of our team at Quantico," Kate said. "Start running checks on the Sumner family, the Hardys, and anyone else you think is a person of interest. Right now, the safety of the people in this town is the priority."

～

THE RELATIONSHIP LEVI WALSH had with Kate had been that of both brother and friend. The friend pushed her to her limits when it came to investigations, knowing her talents were well beyond his own. The brother remained protective of her. She'd been under attack on several fronts during her short career with the Bureau, and that was mostly due to her skillset and those around her who had been envious of it.

Now that Kate led the profiling aspect of the team, Walsh felt somewhat displaced. She had come into her own and she neither needed a brother nor a friend. But perhaps, still wanted those things from him to a degree.

So while she worked this case with local authorities, he couldn't help but feel redundant. And speculation swirled as to what he could do for her. The first thing to come to mind was to gather support from the rest of the team.

"Given our extensive resources, we can do more from here." Walsh paced the floor of Fisher's office with his hands in his pockets, while Duncan peered through the window. He called the impromptu meeting after the brief update Kate provided earlier. "This is a small town, that, according to Kate, hasn't seen a homicide in years. Now there's two in less than two weeks? Gotta be someone on the outside."

"Reid doesn't believe the unsub is transient," Duncan replied.

"Fair point. Then we should consider the unsub could be a recent arrival. A person who'd only just moved there. I know you ran a search for similar signatures, but let's run new parameters. See if anything hits. We can do a lot from here to help them out."

"I agree." Fisher rolled a toothpick between his index finger and thumb. "And Reid said there are a couple of persons of interest. Let's get names and we'll run background. Find out where they work, how long they've lived in Jansville—all of it."

Duncan raised her index finger. "Another thing to consider. I don't know if the local authorities checked for shoe prints or tire tracks, but if they haven't, and if it isn't too late, Reid should make sure that gets done. They have a killer who's moving around. He has to have left prints somewhere near the scenes, near the convenience store. It's worth a look."

"Anything we can do to help expedite the evidence side of this," Fisher continued.

"I could join them to coordinate with the county authorities," Walsh said. "Kate mentioned she'd recommended extra patrols. If I can take that off her plate, I'm happy to do so."

"If the lieutenant there wants you to do that, then I don't have a problem," Fisher replied. "We need to remember this isn't a federal case and unless that changes, all we can do is offer assistance." He placed the toothpick between his lips. "Do either of you have anything pressing that should be handled first?"

"I have a few irons in the fire," Walsh replied. "But I'd like to throw in my hat and see what I can do to help. It's a short drive. Like you said, this is in our backyard."

Fisher glanced at Duncan. "And you?"

"Not sure how much I can help from there. If Reid wants to send evidence here for processing, that'll go a hell of a lot quicker than sending it to the county. And I can still make the drive if need be."

Walsh grabbed his phone. "I'll get back on the horn with Kate. Ask about tire tracks and then I'll hit the ground running on their persons of interest."

WITH ACCESS TO VICAP, Kate could examine the case files that matched her criteria. Irving had set them up in his office while he worked with the county to step up area patrols.

"Eva ran this for me already," Kate began. "But I had only focused on the cases in Virginia, of which, there weren't any recently. Now that we have two more, the net needs to widen."

"And have we obtained phone records of either victim yet?" Surrey asked. "Computers, laptops? It's no coincidence these girls were friends. And if we don't learn soon who they may have been in contact with, chances are too great that more of these girls' friends could be in danger."

Kate raised a brow. "Which was why I mentioned to Irving the need to get in touch with their friends again. We had spoken with one of them a second time already, but I think he's overlooking the need for this."

"You can only tell him so much, Reid. Irving's in charge. Not you and me."

She turned her laptop toward him. "Hey, look at this. ViCAP returned this case out of Pennsylvania. It happened in 2018 in Woodard."

He browsed the file a moment. "What are we looking at, here?"

"The killer was a man named Lawrence Mabrey. He was 28 at the time of the murder."

"Just the one murder?" Surrey asked.

"Just the one. The victim was known to him through social media. Female, 24 years of age. He tracked her down, stalked her for a few months, then kidnapped her. After days of torture, he severed her tongue. When the authorities caught up to him, he claimed the reason he did so was because she refused to acknowledge the one true God."

"Religious beliefs," Surrey replied.

"In this case, it appears that way," Kate added. "The act itself, cutting out a tongue, goes back to ancient Greece."

"Are you suggesting this could be a ritual of some sort or just some guy with a God complex?" Surrey asked.

"I don't know. It's important to add to the profile whether we believe the unsub could be a religious zealot or uses his knowledge of historical torture methods to kill his victims."

"I wouldn't discount the social media aspect of that first case," he added. "And let's not forget, Emma had been away at college. Should we consider the possibility someone there had an unhealthy attraction to her? Maybe followed her home."

"How would that explain Heidi's death?" Kate asked.

Surrey raised his shoulder. "They were friends. I don't know, but this started not long after Emma Katz returned home from school. If her killer, whether at her university or someone she randomly met online, was able to track her down, then maybe that could be a focal point for us."

IRVING RETURNED to his car after walking out of the County Sheriff's office when his phone rang. "Irving here."

"Lieutenant, we need you back at the station," the officer said.

"What's going on?"

"It appears as though everyone's heard about Heidi now, too. People are coming here in droves. I don't know what to tell them," the officer replied.

He stepped into his patrol unit. "I'll be there in ten." As he drove away, Irving picked up his phone again. "Agent Reid, It's Irving. I'm heading back to the station. I hear folks are turning up left and right asking questions."

"We're in the back," Kate began. "I have no idea what's going on. If they're coming here, they're wanting answers."

"Answers I don't have, Agent Reid. And I was sort of hoping you did," he replied.

"We're working on it. I reached out to the others on our team and asked them to pitch in. Right now, we're considering the possibility that the killings are ritualistic in nature. Could be tied to religious beliefs."

"And how does that help me find the killer?" Irving pressed on.

"Do you know anyone in town like that? Someone who seems a little extreme where his beliefs are concerned?" she asked.

"No one who's been obvious about it. Course, what folks do behind closed doors is a whole other situation." Irving drew in a breath. "If that's where y'all's head is at, then we can try to work that angle."

"It's a working theory."

Irving glanced at the passing landscape through the windshield. "Hang on a second, Agent Reid. Let me call you right back." He ended the call and pulled onto the dirt road ahead.

Irving continued down that road about a quarter of a mile and rolled to a stop. He stepped out in the midday sun and slipped on his shades. In the distance, toward the east, he spotted the Voss farmhouse. Their land stretched out over 10 acres. Irving walked along the dirt lane, peering at the ground. He soon reached the gate to one of the farm's entrances. It was a simple A-frame with a cattle guard. When he stepped toward it, he narrowed his gaze. "What in the hell?" Irving turned back and walked to his car again.

On his arrival, he opened the trunk and retrieved his forensics kit. He started again back toward the gate. His shirt was soaked through with sweat and his armpits felt like a swamp before he reached the gate again. This time, he opened his kit. And while he saw no tire tracks, too much time and weather had passed, what remained might have been even better. Blood on the top bar of the gate. Irving took a photo of the dried blood and swabbed the spot.

One final trip back to his car, he slipped behind the wheel, grabbing his phone once again. "Agent Reid, sorry about that. The Voss' had us come out the other night before Heidi was killed. Their boy thought he saw someone in the woods off their property. Anyway, I was headed down the road and turned off on a dirt lane that I know heads up to their land. Thought I'd take another look around, figuring if someone had been there, maybe they came out this way. I found dried blood on the cattle gate. So, uh, you folks have the ability to run samples quickly, don't you?"

Silence persisted on the other end of the line until Kate answered, "We do. Whose is it?"

Irving examined the tube where he'd placed the swab. "If I were a betting man, I'd say it could be the blood of our killer."

9

L iving in a small town sometimes made the world feel small too. That was surely the case for Emma Katz, whose only desire was to leave Jansville and move on to bigger and better things. But during high school, Emma was a flame, and those around her huddled near for warmth. Where she went, they followed, and Emma had found a place to hide out in this stifling town. A place where adults wouldn't bother to look.

Tucked deep into the woods lay a small clearing. Logs on the ground were used as seating. A few stumps from where the forest service had cleared the area long ago formed a semi-circle. And in the center was a well-constructed fire pit. Designated solely for upperclassmen, it was their only respite from the real world of school, homework, and adults who demanded perfection.

It had been almost exactly one year ago when Sam Hardy happened upon that spot. He hadn't been alone. It was the last summer he'd shared with Emma before she was to leave for college. Emma had been Sam's friend since she started part-time at the store during her junior year in high school. Just a summer job for her. For Sam, it was his life for the foreseeable future.

Emma wrapped her arm over Sam's shoulder as she led him to the spot. "So, what do you think?"

He adored her and his smile expressed that admiration. "I think it's great. How come I never knew about this place?"

"Well, maybe when you were in school, kids didn't come here," she replied.

"I bet they did. They just didn't want me with them. I didn't have many friends when I was in high school."

Emma squared up to him. "Well, you do now. Come on. Everyone will be here soon. We need to get the pit ready." Her blue eyes lit up and the freckles that dotted her cheeks grew prominent in the summer sun.

Sam followed her to a pile of wood under a small tarp. Emma pulled off the tarp and handed him the chopped logs.

"Here, take these and drop them in the pit. Stack them so they'll burn evenly."

"I know." Sam took several of them to the pit and arranged them neatly inside. He turned to see Emma, who now stood behind him.

"That's awesome, Sam. Great job."

"Thanks. I used to help the Voss' a few summers ago with some jobs like chopping wood. I did a lot of that stuff for a lot of people. My dad said it was good for me to do the hard work sometimes and get out of the store once in a while."

"Your dad's a smart guy, and I'll bet you helped out a lot of people in town." Her attention was drawn behind her to the sound of voices. "Hey, there you guys are!" She jogged back toward the group of friends who'd just arrived. "Me and Sam were just getting everything set up. Come on."

A teenage girl with long bleached-blond hair blinked quickly and wore a fake smile. "What's he doing here, Emma?"

"He's my friend, Amber. He's a good guy and doesn't have a lot of friends his own age. You'll like him once you get to know him."

Heidi Sumner planted her hand on Amber's back. "Emma's right. Sam's a super sweet guy. You'll love him. Don't be snobby."

Amber tsked. "I'm totally not. And I'd like him more if he brought weed."

Emma laughed while she reached into her pocket. "He didn't, but I did."

"Then let's get this party started." Amber followed her back to the clearing. "Hey, Sam. I'm Amber. I've seen you in the store a few times. How are you?"

Sam had overheard what she'd said, but he was here for Emma, and it hadn't mattered what anyone else thought of him. "Fine." He shook her hand.

She laughed. "No need to be so formal. We're about to have some fun."

"Hey, did I miss anything?"

Emma turned her attention to the voice behind her. "Jason! Come over. Everyone just got here." She noticed Brian behind him. "Oh, hey, Brian."

"Hey." He shoved his hands in his pockets. "So are we getting high or what?"

"I told him we were all getting together. Chris is here, too," Jason cut in. "Hope that's cool."

Sam watched Emma's smile change, as though she forced herself to wear it.

Emma glanced over at Chris. "Sure. The more the merrier. There's enough to go around."

Sam tugged on her shirt.

"What is it?" she asked.

"I don't think they want me here," he whispered.

"Of course they do. They just don't know you yet." She patted his back. "Trust me, once they get to know you, they'll love you as much as I do."

His cheeks turned pink. "You love me?"

"Of course I do."

"I love you too, Emma," Sam replied.

She kissed his cheek. "Aw, that's so sweet."

FROM THE EDGE of his bed, Sam stared at the picture in his hand. The photo was taken at the pizza place on First Street when he'd had dinner with Emma. They had one of those photo booths where he got to act silly and make funny faces. A month later, Emma was gone; off to college, and he was alone again with no friends. All those kids he'd gotten to know last summer had gone and done other things with their lives. Some got jobs in town. Others went off to college, too. But not Sam. Sam would sit here in this bedroom for the rest of his life, he was certain.

As he stared at that picture, he recalled how Emma changed when she came back home this summer. She hadn't seemed to like goofing around. She hadn't had much time for him anymore, but she was still kind. The kindest person he'd ever met. Emma still cracked jokes with him at the store, but they didn't hang out after work. He hadn't seen her outside work in the month that she'd been home. Emma had gotten on with her life, just like all the others.

Sam flinched when his door flew open, and his father stood on the other side. The picture slipped from his fingers and fell to the floor. "Dad, what's wrong?"

"I heard Lieutenant Irving came to talk to you this morning."

"Yeah." His tone was barely above a whisper.

"What'd you tell him, huh?" Randall lumbered inside and closed Sam's bedroom door. "What did he ask you, son? And don't you dare lie to me."

Sam cast down his gaze. "Nothing. He didn't ask me nothing."

"I told you not to lie to me, boy." Randall stepped closer and kicked Sam's leg with his boot. "What'd he want from you, huh? Something about Emma? About Heidi?"

"No."

Randall's brow knitted tightly, and his cheeks reddened. "I'm not sure what game you're playing, son, but Howard wouldn't come here without a reason. You must've given him one."

Sam looked at his father and knew that if he pushed, Randall would push right back—harder. But he'd heard what his dad said to Emma that day. And he knew about Heidi. "You said this was my fault. That Emma was dead because of me." His stomach knotted. "You're the one who upset Emma at the store that day. You tried to get her to like you."

Randall walked over to Sam as he remained seated on the bed. "What's that now? Is that what you told Howard?"

This was going to be bad if he kept on, but he couldn't stop himself. "I know about Heidi."

Randall crossed his arms. "What is it you think you know? You think I killed that girl? You think I killed Emma?"

Sam trembled and his eyes stung with welling tears. He provoked Randall and prepared for what would come next.

"Answer me." Randall slammed his open palm against Sam's shoulder.

He winced but didn't cry out. "She was my best friend." The musky scent of Randall's cologne made Sam's stomach turn. Another slap connected with the side of his head. His shaggy brown hair fell in his face, but he refused to budge, refused to acknowledge the blow.

"You gonna tell me what you think you know, or do I have to hit you harder?" Randall gripped Sam's t-shirt and yanked on it, but the young man stood before it was torn from his body.

Fear took hold of him, and he relented. "I don't know. I don't know, Dad." The hot stench of green chili Randall must've had for lunch lingered on his breath and turned Sam's stomach sour.

A moment later, his father's closed fist struck his jaw and Sam rocked back on his heels. He placed his hand over his throbbing cheek while tears streamed down his face.

Randall walked to the door. "You keep your mouth shut now, you hear? No one would believe an idiot like you anyway."

WALSH ARRIVED at the Jansville Police Station to find throngs of people standing outside, looking to have spilled out of the building. "What is going on here?" He stepped out of his SUV and made his way through the people; grateful they didn't know he was a fed. Had they figured it out, he might not have made it inside completely intact. The fear was real. People were scared and he'd seen it plenty of times in plenty of towns just like this one.

Inside, he approached the front desk and displayed his badge. "Afternoon. Special Agent Levi Walsh. My team is here, I believe."

"Yes, sir. Agents Reid and Surrey. They're in with the lieutenant." The officer stepped out from behind the desk. "I'll take you back."

Walsh glanced at the crowd inside. "You sure you want to leave the front desk?"

"If I don't look like I'm doing something, they'll have my head on a platter. Come on." She started into the hall and made her way to Irving's office. On opening the door, she peeked in. "Lieutenant, there's an FBI Agent Walsh here to see Agents Reid and Surrey."

Kate spun around in the chair before getting to her feet. "Levi."

Irving nodded his permission.

"Thank you." Walsh entered the office. "Looks like there's a situation brewing outside."

"You got that right, Agent Walsh, was it?" Irving stood with an outstretched hand. "Lieutenant Irving. Pleased to meet you, although I don't think I was expecting more of you to arrive." He looked at Kate. "Anyone else heading this way?"

"Not right now." She turned to Walsh. "Thanks for coming down."

"Surrey." Walsh shook his hand.

"Good to see you, man. Take a seat. We were catching up with the lieutenant, who just returned from the county," Surrey replied.

"Listen, I'm happy as hell to have you folks here," Irving continued. "But I feel like we're losing control of this thing. Take a look at all those folks outside. What the hell am I supposed to do about that?"

"Try to calm their fears by reminding them you're doing everything in your power to find the culprit," Kate said. "If you don't address this with them soon, they'll turn to social media, if they haven't already. Trust me when I say, this thing will go viral. When that happens, you'll have local, state, and national media swarming these halls. It'll make our jobs that much harder."

Irving peered through the window again. "All right. I'll come up with something to tell these folks." He turned back to the agents. "In the meantime, that blood I got off the Voss' gate, that has to mean something, right? Especially after their son claimed to hear someone on their property only days after Emma was murdered."

Walsh stepped in. "I can take back that sample you retrieved, Lieutenant, and have our labs run it. We can push it to the top of the pile and try to get you some answers."

"If anyone can get it expedited, it's Walsh," Surrey replied. "While all this was happening, Reid and I viewed the interior security footage from the convenience store where Heidi Sumner worked. Randall Hardy was the last one to see her before the store closed. What are we planning on doing with that information? Seems to me, the man has a few things to answer for."

"I agree, Agent Surrey," Irving replied. "While I already know the family was at the park together when Emma was killed, he does need to answer for that particular situation. Everyone knows Randall Hardy isn't kind to his boy. Never has been, and I'd venture to say it's gotten slightly worse over the past couple years. Now, is he a killer? I don't know and I sure as hell got no idea why he'd go after Heidi Sumner."

"We have the father, who had seen Heidi Sumner the night she was killed," Kate began. "And his son, who was seen wandering the streets the night before a tongue was found at the convenience store. The tissue was sent to the county, and it most likely belonged to Heidi." Kate raised her gaze as she considered a plan. "Maybe we can get Levi to run recon for us."

Walsh cocked his head. "In what regard?"

"No one knows who you are or why you're here, except us inside this room," she continued.

"And the officer at the front desk," Walsh added.

"Okay. What if you were to visit the Hardy's grocery store and talk to a few of the workers? I don't want to alert Randall Hardy because I'd rather be armed with information before he's approached again. I'd like to hear from the people who know him."

"What's the goal here, Agent Reid?" Irving asked. "I know Randall Hardy well enough."

"You do, but you don't work for him. And you're an officer of the law. My guess is he would always be on his best behavior around you. Let Agent Walsh poke his nose around that store a little. Let's find out his schedule. Did he leave at certain times of the day? Had anyone noticed a change in his behavior? How had he treated Emma? Look, I don't want to delay speaking with him because he is absolutely at the top of my list of suspects, given what we saw on the video. But we'll only get one shot at this, so we have to come at him hard. If he's our guy, we have to see how hard he's working to keep a secret big enough to murder for."

"Because why else cut out the tongue if not to make a point," Surrey added.

"Yes, sir. And maybe someone at the store saw something. Heard something." Kate raised her index finger. "And one other thing—I want to be there when he's questioned."

"All right." Irving nodded. "I can get on board with that. In the meantime, I better calm the masses."

"Something I'd consider, Lieutenant," Surrey began. "We probably don't want to make it widely known that we're here. I'm not sure it'll help our cause."

10

The lieutenant looked out among the citizens he had sworn to protect. He stood at the back of the lobby while people jockeyed for position. The door remained open, and others listened from outside as the heat of a late afternoon took hold.

Fear gripped the small town of Jansville. Irving saw it in their faces. "Okay, if y'all will settle down a minute." He raised his hands to garner attention from the restless crowd. "If you'll give me a chance, I can say a few things..."

"Why haven't you found whoever's doing this?"

Irving's attention was drawn to a man near the back. "Mr. Gladstone, we are doing everything in our power to—"

"To what?" another man called out. "We haven't seen anything happening. You'd think it was just another day around here. But it isn't, is it, Lieutenant?"

"As I said, we are all working to find answers for you. I know y'all are scared. Nothing like this has ever happened in our town before."

"Yes, it has."

Irving drew his gaze to the man in the middle of the crowd. "What's that now?"

"It's happened before, but not in many, many years." He looked around. "You all know me, Scott Anderson. I teach history at the high school. This very thing has happened, and it is shocking to me that the lieutenant has no idea."

"Pardon, Mr. Anderson," Irving cut in. "I will respect your authority as the history teacher for our high school, but I ask the same courtesy from you. Now, I haven't been here as long as some of you folks, so if I'm missing something, please feel free to enlighten me when we're finished."

"He's talking about 1835," another man chimed in. "I remember learning about it back in school."

"A man murdered four of the townspeople and cut out their tongues," Anderson continued.

Irving picked up on the whispers that spread throughout the crowd. "Again, feel free to come talk to me after we're done here. For the time being, I will institute a nightly curfew of eleven o'clock." He raised his hands while they voiced their displeasure. "This is for the safety of your families. I realize this is harsh, but we are in unprecedented times, and I will do what is necessary to keep this town safe. Now, go home to your families."

"What about our jobs?" Randall Hardy called out.

Irving set his sights on him. "Again, this is just a nightly curfew. In the meantime, I have asked the Roanoke County Sheriff's Department to step in for additional patrols, additional eyes on the town to help keep everyone safe. And I promise you, we will find whoever has brought this terror to our fine town, and who has harmed the young people in it. Thank you."

When he stepped away, he motioned for the schoolteacher to

approach. "Mr. Anderson, would you come back with me? I have some folks I'd like you to meet."

"Yes, sir." Anderson followed him to his office.

Inside, the agents waited. "Apologies for the delay, folks." Irving ushered in Anderson. "This gentleman teaches history at the high school. He just made us all aware of something you folks need to know about." He turned to the man. "I know you don't think I'm doing enough, but these folks are FBI. They're helping us find the person responsible. So, go on and tell them what you said out there."

"Uh, yeah, okay. My name's Scott Anderson." The 35-year-old teacher pushed up the bridge of his eyeglasses and tucked his hands into the pockets of his khaki shorts. "As the lieutenant mentioned, I teach history at the high school. Back in the early 1800s, around 1835, Jansville experienced a slew of murders. The killer had severed the tongues of his victims. He was eventually discovered and hanged for his crimes."

Kate regarded him. "Is there a complete record of this that still exists? Do we know who the victims were, what exactly happened to them?"

"Yes, ma'am," Anderson replied. "In the library archives."

She turned to Irving. "We need to see those files ASAP."

"I can arrange that," he replied.

"What else do you know about it, Mr. Anderson," Kate asked.

"The curriculum doesn't spend much time on the event," he began, "but I am somewhat familiar with it. This was, of course, several years before the Civil War. Tobacco was the driving force of the economy here, and it had taken a severe downturn. People feared for their livelihoods.

"A man by the name of Grimes had lost much of his land and fortunes when this happened. He grew desperate and had begun to intentionally destroy the crops of his neighbors by setting fire to them in an effort to force them out of business so that he could recoup his own. The son of one such neighbor had witnessed the act. He went to his father. Days later, all three of the man's sons and his daughter were found in the woods when a hunting dog picked up a scent. They'd all been murdered and had their tongues cut out."

"How did anyone know it was Grimes who did it?" Kate asked.

"The neighbor suspected it, of course, but it was Grimes's own wife who said her husband confessed to her," Anderson replied. "A trial ensued, and Grimes was found guilty of murder and sentenced to hang."

Walsh set his sights on Kate. "Is it possible the unsub knows this history or may be a part of it?"

"What do mean?" Kate asked.

"Could it be a relative of Grimes?" Walsh continued.

"Lots of older people around here know the story," Anderson cut in. "The younger generation, not so much. As far as lineage?" He shrugged. "I have no idea if any of Grimes' ancestors live here. If they do, they would be far removed. He and his wife had no children, but Grimes did have brothers, who possibly had kids."

Kate tapped her fingers on the arm of her chair and considered the notion. "Whether there's a relation, that's hard to say and we can look into it. But more importantly, it points us in the direction of someone who knows this history well, studied it, maybe paid homage to it."

Anderson turned to Irving. "If there's nothing else, may I go now?"

"Yes, sir. I can access the library's records. I appreciate your help, sir."

After the man walked out, Walsh stepped away from the window overlooking the corridor. "While you're working on that, I can stop by the Hardy's grocery store and get a feel for things there. I'll be discreet. Then, I'll head back to Quantico and hand over the sample to the lab. It'll be at least 24 hours, even with having it expedited, but it's all you have as far as hard evidence right now, at least until forensics reports come back on the victims."

"Thank you." Kate stood from the chair and looked at Surrey. "The history lesson could prove vital. Given that, maybe it's time to take a pass at the victim's homes, bearing in mind a possible connection to the town's history." She glanced at Irving. "With your permission."

"I've inspected the victim's homes, Agent Reid," Irving replied. "What are you hoping to find?"

"In light of this new information, including what we've learned about a possible connection between Randall Hardy and Heidi Sumner, we'll be looking for signs that point to a secret. Signs that point to an affair, or even a plot against Emma. And now, a correlation to the past. I'm not ruling out anything, and I don't think you should either."

IRVING STEPPED into the one-bedroom apartment that belonged to Heidi Sumner and flipped the switch at the entrance. Recessed lights in the ceiling flickered on and illuminated the small living room. "All right. This is the place."

Kate entered the unit and immediately noticed how clean it had been. "I don't think I've ever seen a nineteen-year-old's apartment this clean, even for a girl."

Surrey grunted. "Makes me wonder who else has a key to this place."

"Her folks do," Irving cut in. "They let me in earlier. Place was spotless then too."

"Did her parents say that was unusual?" Kate continued.

"Honestly, it didn't come up. I was too busy collecting the girl's belongings to enter into Evidence."

"Did you sweep the place for prints?" Surrey asked.

"No, sir. The county has a CSI team. That was planned for tomorrow. I didn't let the parents move around if that's what you're thinking. I do know a few things, Agent Surrey."

He raised his hands. "I didn't mean to imply anything, Lieutenant."

Kate moved into the kitchen. "Not a single dish in the sink." She pulled on latex gloves and opened the cabinet doors and drawers. "She was organized. Almost to a fault, by the look of things in here." She opened the refrigerator door. "Wow."

"What is it?" Surrey made his way toward her.

"This is more like what I expected," Kate continued. "Everything in this fridge looks like she brought it home from her work. Junk food, soda. This is what a college kid eats." Her lips raised into a mournful smile as she closed the door again and Irving's voice sounded in the hall. "Maybe he found something."

They headed toward the bedroom when Kate spotted the lieutenant canvassing the room. "Did you find something?"

Irving turned to her. "When I was here with the parents, I had a cursory look around. I knew County would come and do their thing."

"Okay." Kate walked inside the bedroom.

"So I didn't look in the nightstand drawer." With his gloved hand, Irving pulled out a watch. "This look like a man's watch to you?"

Kate approached him and examined it. "It does. Thing is, not many men her age wear watches unless it's from Apple."

"Her folks said they didn't believe Heidi had been dating anyone," Irving added.

Surrey peered at the watch. "Sounds like a secret to me."

AMBER HOFFMAN MOURNED the loss of her friends, Emma and Heidi. While they'd drifted apart since high school, the friendship was still there, even as Emma had returned home from college and Heidi was busy with work and school. It was surreal to think both were gone now. So when Brian wanted to meet up, Amber wasn't so sure it was a good idea. After all, a killer remained on the loose. Everyone was afraid, including her. Thinking that two of her friends were targeted, and the notion she could be next, lingered in her mind.

Brian insisted he had nothing to do with Emma's or Heidi's deaths. He wanted an ally, and she knew that. It never occurred to her he could do anything to hurt them, so she agreed to meet at their old spot. Nightfall had arrived and she hadn't been back to that clearing in almost a year. Not since they'd all been there together. But it was the only place that would ensure their privacy and avoid being harassed if they stayed past the new curfew.

Amber arrived at the parking lot near the bottom of the hill and hiked up to the clearing. In the dimming light, she used her phone to guide her way. The memories came flooding back as she arrived. Laughter, smoking, drinking. Senior year had been the best. All that was gone now, right along with the people with whom she'd shared those times.

"Hey."

Amber spun around and pressed her hand against her chest. "Oh, my God, Brian. You scared the shit out of me."

"Sorry. I thought you heard me coming," he replied. "You just get here?"

"Yeah. I was just thinking about all the fun we had senior year."

He smiled. "It was a blast."

"What'd you want to meet me for? I don't like being out here with everything that's happening. It's not safe."

"No one knows about this place." He laid his hand on her back. "Come on. Let's sit down."

She let him usher her to the tree stumps, where they used to gather around the fire pit. "Guess this year's seniors don't know about this place, huh?"

"I don't think any of us ever said a thing at school about it. Well, I know I didn't."

"Kind of makes it special then, doesn't it?" She sat down and peered up at what little light remained in the sky. "I'm sorry about what's happening to you, Brian. I know you'd never hurt Emma. I know you loved her."

"Yeah well, since I was the last to see her, everyone seems to have forgotten all that. I mean, she dated Jason Gatwick after me and no one thinks he's the killer. And I wasn't anywhere near Heidi."

"Seems insane that we're even saying all this." She regarded him a moment. "What did you and Emma do that day, the day of the parade?"

He looked out into the trees. "I knew she was in town, of course. I'd seen her at Hardy's a couple of times. We couldn't really talk then, though, so when she waved at me at the parade, I thought, well, maybe I'd catch up with her. I met her across the street. We walked and talked until she reached her house. She asked if I wanted something to drink, so I followed her inside. We talked for a few more minutes and she mentioned needing to pick up her check at the grocery store. I tagged along. After that, we started back toward Town Park, and she said she wanted to go back home and change. Something about it being too hot. She told me she'd catch up with me at the picnic." He shrugged. "So I left. I went home for a little while to get out of the heat and then I went back to town. The parade was over at that point, and I didn't see Emma, so I figured she was just hanging out with her parents, and we'd catch up later, like she said. And that was it. That was the last time I saw her."

"Do the cops really think you killed her?" Amber asked.

"I don't know. They look at me like I did. When I went home, no one else was there, so I have no one who can vouch for me. I saw my folks later and that was what they told the cops."

"What about your phone's GPS? Why didn't you just show them your location?"

Brian fidgeted with his hands. "I'd dropped my phone in the river a few days before."

Amber knitted her brow just for a moment.

"And then the cops gave me that look too," Brian cut in. "Like the one you're giving me now."

"Sorry, I don't mean to." Amber looked out among the trees and the darkening sky. "I just don't know who would do such a thing. Emma had no enemies. Heidi didn't either. I mean..." Her eyes landed on a snapped branch that hung from a nearby tree. She squinted a moment and caught her breath.

"You okay?" Brian asked.

Her heart leaped into her throat and a rush of panic flushed her cheeks. "Yeah...yeah, I'm fine." She got to her feet. "You know what, Bri, I don't think we should be here. The cops don't want everyone wandering around and stuff. I should probably head back home."

He shot up. "Wait. Heidi, are you okay? You don't look it."

"Fine. I'm fine. I just want to go home, okay?" She kept her eyes on him, wondering if he saw the fear in her.

Brian shrugged. "Yeah, okay. Fine. Let's get out of here."

LIEUTENANT IRVING KNOCKED on the door of the Katz' home. "Mr. and Mrs. Katz? It's Lieutenant Irving. May we come in?" He glanced at the agents, who stood beside him. "I called to tell them we were on our way." When footsteps sounded on the other side, the handle turned, and the door opened. "Mrs. Katz, sorry it's getting so late. May we come in?"

Kate hadn't believed a more sorrowful look existed than that of a mother who'd lost her child. The utter despondency in their eyes. The frail tone of their voice, as though were they to speak any louder, they might shatter into a million pieces. It was a kind of pain Kate would never know. No loss could possibly compare. And then for those same parents to watch others rummage through their child's belongings, well, it must've felt like a violation.

Mrs. Katz stepped aside. "Come in."

"Thank you. As I mentioned, I brought the FBI folks, who are helping us to find whoever's responsible."

Kate walked inside with Surrey trailing. She offered her hand. "Mrs. Katz, I'm Agent Kate Reid. Thank you for allowing us to do this."

"Agent Jonathan Surrey." He extended a greeting. "Yes, thank you."

It appeared to Kate that this mother's suffering would worsen the longer they stayed. "We should get started so you can go on about your evening." She noticed Mr. Katz sitting in a recliner, peering at the television.

"What is it you think we have planned this evening, Agent Reid? Our daughter's been murdered. We won't be throwing any parties anytime soon," she replied.

"Of course, I don't mean to—"

"Emma's room is this way," Irving cut in. "Let's do what we came here to do."

Kate nodded her appreciation and waved for Surrey to follow.

As they reached the young woman's bedroom, Irving walked inside. "Like I said earlier, I've been in here before, so if y'all think I missed something, then please get on with it."

"I understand." Kate ambled inside. "Looks like they hadn't really touched her room since she went off to school." She peered up at the bookshelves. "A few ribbons and trophies."

"Emma was on the cross-country varsity team," Irving said. "Got a scholarship for college with that."

"Let's take a look at her books." She regarded Irving. "Do you have her laptop and phone in Evidence?"

"I do. Her folks didn't know Emma's passcode, so..."

"Do you mind if we give it to our people to take a crack at it?" Surrey asked. "And of course, you can pull phone records."

"Be my guest. I'll process the chain of evidence and you can hand it off to your people first thing in the morning," Irving replied.

"Thank you."

Kate opened the closet doors and shifted around the clothes. "Nothing appears out of the ordinary in here." She felt along the top of the shelf and then stood back for a better view. "I don't see anything there either."

A three-shelf bookcase lay against the side wall beneath a

window. Several books lined the shelves and Surrey sifted through them. He picked up each one and opened the covers, allowing the pages to come apart."

"What are you doing?" Irving asked him.

"Checking to see if she hid anything in the pages."

Irving folded his arms and pursed his lips. "I didn't think to do that."

"That's okay. I've had a lot of practice looking into people's lives. I know that they're often pretty good at hiding..." A photo slipped out from one of the books. He set the book down on the shelf and picked up the photo. "People are pretty good at hiding things, especially kids hiding things from their parents."

Kate made her way to them. "What is that?"

Surrey returned to his feet and examined the photo. "It's a Polaroid. Haven't seen one of them in a while."

"I hear they're making a comeback." Kate held out her hand. "May I?"

"Sure." Surrey handed her the photo. "Looks like a group of kids hanging out."

She examined it closely and returned a look at Irving. "Heidi and Emma were friends in high school."

"Yes, ma'am," he replied.

Kate pointed to the photo. "That's Heidi right there, isn't it, the dark-haired girl? And that's Emma, the redhead?"

Irving slipped on a pair of reading glasses. "Yes, ma'am. And that, right there, is Brian. Jason Gatwick, too."

Kate continued to study it. "There are a few other kids in this picture. And hang on, isn't that Sam Hardy over there off in the background?"

Irving looked at it again. "Good eye, Agent Reid. That is Sam, and it looks like Chris Pumphrey, too."

"Where was this taken?" she pressed on.

Irving turned down his lips. "Got no idea. In the woods some-where, by the look of it."

Kate raised a brow. "Two of the kids in this picture are dead. One of them is a person of interest."

Irving set his sights on her. "What are you getting at?"

She eyed the photo still between her index finger and thumb. "Lieutenant, I don't want to step on your toes, and I know we discussed meeting with these friends again. I'm convinced these kids share another connection that led to the murder of two of them. We should consider that the other kids in this picture might be in danger."

Amber adjusted her rearview mirror and locked her seatbelt before pressing the ignition. Brian waited until she entered her car before he left. And when his taillights disappeared into the dark-ness, she cut the engine and stepped out of her car. "They all think you did it." And what she'd seen while they were inside the clear-ing, a place he'd insisted they meet, could prove it.

Amber quickly twisted her long blond hair into a bun to keep it out of her face while she hiked up the hill again. She returned to the clearing with her phone's flashlight guiding the way.

This was the spot and Amber walked ahead to the tree with the broken branch. The wood inside looked fresh, as though the branch had only recently snapped. And then she saw red. Near the bottom of the tree trunk, Amber crouched low to see whether her mind had played a trick, or whether this was blood. To her knowledge, no one came up to the clearing anymore, and only a few people in town knew it was there. They'd all been her friends, but only one wanted to come back.

Amber shone the light from her phone onto the bark. She reached out her hand and touched it lightly with her middle finger. "It's dry. Maybe it was just an animal." Her head was playing a trick. It must've been. This was fear talking. Nothing more.

She got to her feet again and with her phone's light trained ahead, she walked a few more feet into the clearing. While the air had no chill to it, goosebumps rose on her bare arms and legs. Something about the look in Brian's eyes, like he hadn't wanted her to leave. "No, he couldn't..." Amber's right foot slipped just a little and her arms waved until she regained her balance. "What the?" She squinted at the ground and aimed her light at the spot, rocking back on her heels. "Oh my God! Oh my God!" She canvassed the grounds and hadn't seen anyone or anything around. Fear held her in its grip as she swiped open her phone and pressed on the camera feature. Shaking from head to toe, Amber aimed her phone at the pulpy, fleshy tongue that lay there as if it was a sacrifice—or a trap. The flash went off and the photo was taken.

She spun around and sprinted back to her car, hardly able to see through the tears that spilled down her cheeks under the blackened sky. Amber jumped behind the wheel and with a trembling hand, she pressed the ignition. Her tires spun on the blacktop as she slammed into Reverse and pulled out onto the single-lane road.

Speeding along the road into town, her mind raced. "The police. I have to tell them." Tears still clouded her vision and she struggled to catch her breath. Amber glanced into her rearview mirror and noticed a car drawing close. Its headlights shone brightly and forced her to squint.

With her attention diverted, Amber returned her gaze to the road and corrected the wheel as she'd begun to drift toward the shoulder. Her phone slid off the passenger seat. "Damn it!" She reached down, keeping eyes on the road, and felt around the floorboard. "Come on. Come on."

The sudden hit lurched her forward, and the phone slipped farther away. Amber pulled back up and glanced through the rearview mirror again. "What the hell?" The car behind her was so close now, that all she could see were its high beams in her eyes. "What are you doing?"

The car rammed her again and her tires skidded along the asphalt. Amber gripped the wheel tightly to stay in her lane. "Stop! Please, stop!" She slammed on the gas to gain distance, but it didn't work, and she was hit again. Her car veered off. Its front wheel tipped off the edge of the asphalt and onto the soft gravel shoulder.

The engine stuttered when she tried to speed up again to get all four tires back onto the road. The car's headlights shone too bright for her to see, and she pleaded, "Please don't hurt me. Please don't..."

The left front tire blew, and the steering wheel spun. Sparks flew from the rim as it scraped along the asphalt. The engine stalled. "No. No, no, no. Please, no." Amber pressed the gas, but nothing happened. Her steering wheel locked in place and the vehicle behind her pushed her onto the soft shoulder, tilting her car into the ditch along the side of the road. She rolled to a stop.

Amber spun around and peered through the back window, but the lights still shone in her eyes. "What are you doing?" She twisted around in every direction in search of the driver. "Where are you? Who are you?"

With her hand on the armrest, Amber reached for the button to unlock her door. The click of the lock sounded, and she gripped the handle to pull it open. The door flung wide, and she spilled out onto the gravel shoulder. Amber clawed at the ground to find the strength to stand. Gravel crunched underfoot from behind her.

Just as she started to pull up, the blow came. Blinding pain exploded from the back of her head. Warm blood streamed down her temple and onto her face. Nausea sent bile into her throat and vomit filled her mouth. She choked as it blocked her airway. Amber collapsed to the ground.

11

The evening brought with it a tepid breeze and Kate rolled down the passenger window of Irving's patrol unit. The air helped to clear her head. The photograph Surrey found added another layer to the case. While they'd discussed with Brian Keller their small group of friends, the photo contained another. Sam Hardy. And it remained unclear whether anyone else in that picture was in danger.

A call arrived on her phone and Kate answered. "Levi, hey, where are you?"

"I'm headed back to Quantico. I made a quick round at the Hardy's store."

She glanced through the sideview mirror at Surrey, who was in the backseat. "And did you come up with anything?"

"The man was in his office, so I kept to the front of the store and spoke to a cashier. She was the only one there. Place was pretty empty."

"I'll bet," Kate replied. "She was willing to talk to you?"

"When I said I was with the local news station, she perked up a bit. Long story short, she said that Heidi Sumner had come in on multiple occasions, apparently, and not to buy goods. She went straight back to the manager's office. Never stayed long, but how long does it take, you know?"

"Right. Do you know if Sam Hardy was there?"

"Not when I was there tonight, but if you're asking whether he was there when Sumner came in, it seems so. The cashier didn't say much more than that. Kept looking back like the owner might catch us talking."

"Sure sounds like an affair," Kate began. "And a motive. Emma worked there too, so we should consider that she discovered what was happening."

"That should give us some idea as to who you're dealing with," Walsh replied.

"It does. We found a picture in Emma Katz's bedroom of a bunch of kids in the woods that included our victims. Started thinking they could all be part of this thing and are being picked off one by one."

"If that's the case," Walsh pressed on. "It seems unlikely an affair with a girl in the group would be the motivator here."

"Yeah, that's what I'm starting to think." Kate eyed the road ahead. "Thanks for the intel, Levi. Drive safe and get back to me as soon as you have those labs."

"Will do."

Irving kept his hands on the wheel and eyes on the road ahead. "If you two are looking for a place to stay tonight, there's a budget motel near the east end of town. Cheap and cheery, if that's your style."

Kate returned her phone to her pocket. "Thank you. I'm sure that'll do just fine."

"That was Walsh?" Surrey pulled up from the backseat. "What'd he say?"

She peered over her shoulder at him. "At least one employee noticed Heidi Sumner inside the Hardy's store enough times that it drew her concern. Said the girl hung out in the back office with Randall Hardy. I'm not sure what that means for the kids in the picture we found." Kate set her gaze on the road again. "Maybe something happened in those woods that shouldn't have. Maybe Emma wanted to get it out into the open."

"It could be a situation of exclusion, too," Surrey added. "Someone who wanted to be part of the group but was denied. But what I don't understand is why wait till now to act? They'd all graduated. Moved on. What would be the point of acting out now if someone was rejected then?"

Irving's phone rang in the center console, and he pressed the speaker button. "Irving here."

"Lieutenant, we just got a call from Amber Hoffman's parents. They'd asked her to text them tonight to let them know she was okay. She was supposed to do that about an hour ago."

"All right," Irving replied.

"Lieutenant, with everything that's happened, they're terrified. They tried calling and texting her, but she hasn't responded. Can you do a welfare check at Amber Hoffman's apartment?"

"You got it. Text me the address. We'll head over there now."

"Thank you, sir."

He ended the call. "If someone else—"

"Lieutenant!" Kate gripped the handle above her door and braced against the seat.

Irving jerked the wheel and slammed on the brakes. The patrol car made a 45-degree spin and screeched to a halt. "Holy hell, Agent Reid. What in the—"

"Irving, look." Surrey pointed ahead. "There's something in the road."

"Shit!" Kate unbuckled her seatbelt and jumped out of the car.

This stretch of roadway was nearly pitch black and the patrol car's lights aimed toward the shoulder. Kate ran ahead and stopped on a dime in the middle of the road. "Oh my God."

Surrey joined her and quickly turned away. "Damn it."

When Irving reached them, it appeared he already knew what to expect. "Dear Lord." He closed his eyes. "Amber Hoffman."

Surrey caught sight of where the patrol car's lights shone. "Hey." He marched ahead. "Hey, that's a car. Reid, there's a car over here. Hurry!"

Kate jogged toward him with Irving keeping pace. "It must be hers."

Surrey stood before the car. "Looks like she was pushed off the road. Slid down this ditch." He walked around to the other side and aimed a light. "And she got out."

Standing beneath a starry sky on a dark road, Kate surveyed the area. "How did she end up in the street?"

Irving peered at the ground where Amber Hoffman got out of her car. "Agent Reid, you should come take a look here."

She walked over and stood next to them.

Irving aimed his light again onto the ground. "She was killed here. Blood's still pretty fresh. I'd say this happened within the last hour or so."

Kate drew in a deep breath. "What the hell was she doing out here alone?"

Surrey raised his brow. "She wasn't alone. She was with her killer."

Irving picked up his phone. "We need an ambo out here on northbound Route 340, near Homestead Road. Send me two units and I'm gonna need floodlights out here too." He nodded. "We got ourselves another murder. Amber Hoffman."

Kate squatted near the car to train her phone's light inside.

"What are you looking for?" Surrey asked.

"Her phone." She leaned into the driver's side. "I think I see it here. You got a pair of gloves handy?"

"I have a handkerchief." He pulled it from the pocket of his dress pants. "Here."

"Thanks." Kate reached over the seat. Inside the footwell on the passenger side, leaning up against the center console, lay her phone. "I think...yeah. I got it." She pulled out of the car and stood with the phone in her hand. "Screen's busted."

Surrey studied it a moment. "We need to see what's on that phone."

"We'll block off this area and do a search." Irving started back. "It's dark as hell, but we'll see if we can't spot the tire tracks. The back end of this car took a bad hit. Probably what knocked her off the road. There'll be skid marks everywhere. And we'll need to be on the lookout for a car with a damaged front end." He looked at Kate. "What's that in your hand?"

"Her phone. It still works."

KATE PULLED to a stop at the front of the motel room. She stared at the building while the engine ran.

Surrey set his sights on her. "Reid, Irving's taking care of it. The county's setting up patrols around the other kids' homes, and apartments."

She shot him a look. "Why isn't he going to tell them what's happening?"

"Because he doesn't know what's happening, and neither do we." He sighed. "If we start spouting off about the photograph and how we think everyone in it might be in danger? No, that can't happen. This town is already on edge. This will send them off a cliff."

"I'd rather that than more kids winding up dead," Kate replied.

"The media will come at this town hard. You know that. And any chance this killer's still here will evaporate. You know that too. So what would you prefer—Irving ensuring those kids are being watched by the county sheriff, or throwing a wrench in this case by suggesting to everyone in that picture that they're next?"

"I just don't want any more dead kids, okay?" she fired back.

"Hey, what's going on with you? This feels out of character."

"Oh?" She peered at him. "And you know me so well, do you?"

"I know you better than you think. I know that right now, you've completely lost your objectivity and that's a problem."

Kate opened the driver's side door and stepped into the warm night air. The door to her motel room was just ahead and when Surrey caught up to her, she turned to him. "A girl was just run off the road and murdered, her tongue cut out of her head. The third girl in, what, two weeks? I need to think this through. If I don't put myself in his shoes, I won't figure out who he is." She unlocked the door.

"And you can do that, can you? Get into the killer's head?"

Kate returned a hard stare. "You're damn right I can. I'll see you in the morning." She stepped inside and closed the door.

Surrey's door was adjacent to hers and she clearly heard his door slam. She was wrong to snap at him. It wasn't how a partner should be treated. He wasn't Quinn. Not even close. Kate slipped off her shoes and padded in socked feet to the bed. Maybe it was because she had no control over the investigation. It still wasn't under federal jurisdiction. Maybe that was the root cause of her helplessness. She couldn't tell Irving what to do even if it was completely obvious to her. Surrey was trying to say that, and she shut him down.

"Damn it." Kate buried her face in her hands. But there was no time for guilt or regret. Apologies would come, just not at this moment. Right now, Kate had to know more about this killer. Why this town? Why those kids? Had a connection existed relating to what the history teacher mentioned, and had she overlooked it because she wanted the answer to lay in that photograph or with Randall Hardy?

A knock sounded on the door that connected her room to Surrey's. Kate opened it and peered at him, doing her best to hide her regret. "Yeah?"

"Have you calmed down enough to think through this together, or should I leave you to sulk on your own?"

"I deserved that."

"Yes, you did." He stood with his hands in his pockets, still wearing the white button-down shirt and dress pants, but he'd removed his jacket and tie. "What's the plan, Reid?"

"How about we order some pizza and hash this out together? You know, like we were partners or something."

He proffered a crooked smile. "Okay, then. You want pepperoni on that pizza?"

"Anything but anchovies." She walked to the wood veneer table tucked under the window and retrieved the files and her laptop, but not before stopping a moment to pull back the curtain. "I saw Hardy's grocery store on the way over. Maybe I'll run out and grab some beer?"

"Sure. I wouldn't mind one. I can run out if you'd prefer."

"No, I'll go. And it'll give me a chance to see Randall Hardy. I need to look him in the eyes. This is a good excuse to make that happen." Kate slipped on her shoes again and snatched her keys. "Be back soon. You take care of the pizza."

Outside in the breeze, she inhaled a deep breath to refocus her energies. Kate climbed behind the wheel of her SUV and pressed the ignition. They'd passed by the store on the way over and she recalled it was only a minute or so away.

She headed back into town, and on its own, there it was. Hardy's. A big sign in red lights glared against the night sky. A sizable parking lot lay ahead, and she drove near the front, hoping the place was still open. And on checking the time, she figured she had a good shot since curfew wasn't for another hour. Kate had mixed feelings about Irving's decision to impose the curfew. People liked their freedom and when it was taken away, for whatever reason, it didn't always go over well.

She stepped out and made her way to the sliding glass doors that opened on her arrival. Inside, the air blew cold, and the harsh fluorescent lights shone brightly. But the place was empty. Soft rock music played on the speakers and echoed throughout, leaving an eerie, almost post-apocalyptic feeling. As Kate continued in, she spotted one person at a register and recognized him immediately from the convenience store video. "Mr. Hardy."

"You're that FBI agent, aren't you?" he asked. "My wife mentioned Howard was working with y'all."

"Yes, sir, I am." She surveyed the store. "Pretty slow tonight, huh?"

"Well, a killer roaming free and a curfew in place tends to keep folks in their homes. Summer's our busiest season. Guess all that's changed now. What are you looking for, if you don't mind my asking."

"Would love a beer right about now."

He chuckled. "Boy, don't I know it. Just over there, down aisle three. Pretty good selection, but if you're looking for them microbrews you find out where you're from, you're out of luck."

"I'm not really bothered by the brand." Kate headed toward the aisle. Plenty of cold six-packs were inside the refrigerated section and Kate grabbed the nearest one. She just needed something to get outside her own head for a minute. Give her an opportunity for some clarity.

For a moment, she wondered if that was how it started for Nick. His drinking problem. It seemed to stem from the job, which came as no surprise. But it wasn't in her personality. And having grown up with a father who drank was enough for her to know how not to be like that person. Regardless, it was hard not to make the comparison.

She carried on toward the register and set down the six-pack.

Hardy eyed her a moment. "Good choice. Nice, but not too nice." He rang it up. "Fifteen-thirty-seven, please."

Kate swiped her card. "Your son works here with you, right?"

"He does. But, uh, he's been struggling with the loss of Emma Katz. They were pretty close," Hardy replied. "Still can't believe she's gone. She was a bright kid. Good head on her shoulders."

"I have no doubt." She wanted to bring up Heidi Sumner just for a reaction but showing her cards now could put him on his guard, and her advantage would be lost. After all, while an affair seemed likely, murder was still miles away. "I'm surprised you're open tonight, especially considering what else happened."

"Sorry, what's that now?" he asked.

She hesitated. "Look, I'm probably not supposed to say anything, but unfortunately, another body was found."

"My Lord. Well, who was it?"

Kate focused on him with an eagle eye. Every twitch, every blink, every muscle that moved could reveal a man who had just killed or a man who merely feared for the lives of those in his community. "I'm afraid until I can be certain the family has been notified, I'll have to leave it to Lieutenant Irving." She watched him turn down his gaze and lick his lips as though he'd grown parched. His chest raised and lowered with mounting intensity. "I'm sorry, Mr. Hardy. We are doing everything in our power to put an end to this. I'm very sorry for your son. He's lost some friends and it won't be easy for him."

"It's not easy for any of us, Agent Reid." He handed her the receipt. "Maybe I'll just close up now. No one will be coming in here anytime soon."

"Good night, sir." Her eyes remained fixed on Hardy, who stood motionless behind the cashier's counter. He behaved like a bereft soul, not like a killer. Then again, it took a mastery of one's emotions to dish out violence against a son and hide that evil streak from the rest of society. As much as she thought she could enter the mind of a killer, if Hardy had been that killer, his mind proved impenetrable. Kate headed to the exit when he called out to her.

"Ma'am?"

She turned back. "Yes?"

"I don't know if you know this, but my son, well, he requires a bit of extra attention. And sometimes he says things that he doesn't really mean. You understand?"

Kate sized him up. "Not exactly."

"I suppose what I mean to say is that he's known for embellishing things on occasion. Only because he doesn't know any better. He has some measure of difficulty distinguishing truth from fiction."

"Why are you telling me this, Mr. Hardy?"

He shrugged. "I just figured because Sam's been so upset lately, and I know Lieutenant Irving's talked with him. I just want to be sure, you know, folks don't think he had anything to do with any of what's happening."

"I'll be sure to pass that along to the lieutenant." Kate carried on. "You have a good night."

THE BODY of Amber Hoffman had been loaded onto the ambulance. Irving and the county's CSI team remained on site to finish collecting evidence. Photographs of tire tracks had been taken. Her car had been hooked up to a tow truck to be moved to the impound lot.

A firetruck had also arrived as a matter of protocol. Jason Gatwick had been the one who aided the technicians with loading the body.

Irving approached him as he secured his gear back onto the truck. "Jason."

He turned around. "Yes, sir, Lieutenant?"

"Did you know her well?" he asked.

"Amber? I did."

"She was Emma's friend, and Heidi's. They went to high school together," Irving added.

"Yeah, I know." Jason pushed his hands into his pockets. "I don't think they're that close anymore, I mean—"

"I know what you mean," Irving cut in. "You've offered your statement and I do appreciate that, but I have another question for you. When Emma was taken from us, and I initially talked to Sam Hardy about the last day he worked with Emma, which was on the third..."

"Yes, sir?"

"He mentioned he'd seen you come into the store for a few things, and that he'd seen you talking to Emma," Irving continued. "So I went back and reviewed your statement, but you didn't mention that you'd seen her the day before she was killed."

"I didn't?" he asked.

"No, sir, you didn't." Irving zeroed in on him. "Care to explain why?"

"Well, I guess I probably didn't think about it. You know, it wasn't a conversation that stood out in my mind. Except to say that it was the last time I'd spoken to her. I did see her briefly the morning of the parade."

"Did you talk then?" Irving asked.

"No. We waved at each other, and I went about my business. I was pretty busy setting up everything." Jason paused a moment. "Lieutenant, why does it matter that I talked to Emma in the store the day before it all happened? It was Brian who was the last person to see her."

"And what about the others? Did you see either of the girls at the parade or at any time over the past month?"

Jason rubbed his arm. "Sir, I don't hang around them anymore, if that's what you're thinking. You know I went out with Heidi a couple times. Amber—she didn't care much for me anyway."

"Why is that?" Irving asked.

"I don't know, exactly. I hung out with them as a group a couple of times up in the woods."

Irving deadpanned. "In the woods?"

"Yes, sir. There's a clearing up there. The seniors used to go there, and smoke-I mean, you know, party and stuff. I'm a year older, but I hung out there, like I said, a time or two when I was seeing Emma."

Irving glimpsed the long dark road. "Don't suppose you can show me where that's at, can you?"

12

I t occurred to Kate how often she sat in a hotel room just like this one, late at night, with her partner, reviewing details of brutal murders. How, for hours on end, she examined the lives of the victims in hopes of learning why the unsub chose them. Uncovering some reason for the killings, as though a killer must've had one.

But in reviewing the lives of these young women, no reason had revealed itself. She sifted through Emma Katz's phone records that finally arrived and discovered Emma had spoken to the same people who'd already been interviewed. Without the phone itself, which would, of course, reveal text messages and other types of communication, this was all she had. And it did nothing to further the investigation. Nothing.

This was where Surrey proved himself invaluable to Kate. This was where he insisted she look at the situation through a different lens. A detached, unaffected lens, as he had. He called her out when she let her emotions take hold. He wasn't her protector. He didn't blow smoke. He was her partner. And as she glanced at him now, the true meaning of that word hit home.

"There's nothing here," Kate said. "Nothing in the phone records to suggest anything unusual had been going on in the days or weeks prior to Emma's murder."

Surrey pulled his attention from the laptop screen. "I've scoured her social media. No posts that would raise a flag. Nothing out of the ordinary."

"So where does that leave us?" she asked. "Three are dead now, and without Forensics breaking something loose..." Her phone lit up on the table. "It's Irving." Kate answered the call. "Lieutenant, what's going on?"

"I'm with Jason Gatwick right now. He showed me a place that, as dark as it is, might match the place shown in the photograph you found."

Kate's back stiffened. "You're there now?"

"Yes, ma'am. And I think it's best you both hustle down here. Folks have been here, and they have been here recently."

"Send me your location. We're on our way." She ended the call, bursting with renewed energy.

"What's going on?" Surrey asked.

Kate stood from the table. "Irving thinks he's found the place in the woods from the picture."

"How'd he manage that? I thought he was at the scene of the crash?"

"He's with Jason Gatwick. We'll ask questions when we get there." She checked her phone. "He just sent me his location."

Surrey gathered his things and shoved the last bite of pizza into his mouth. "It'll be dark as hell up there."

Kate snatched her car keys from the table and opened the door. "Then we'll use lights. Come on." She hurried outside and unlocked her Ford before stepping behind the wheel. When Surrey entered the passenger side, she started the engine.

"Where are we headed?" he asked.

Kate handed him her phone. "Take a look at the pin and tell me what direction to take."

He examined the location. "Oh wow. The place he's at isn't that far from where we found Amber Hoffman."

Kate reversed out of the parking lot and reached the single-lane road. "Irving said he'd already found evidence people had recently been there. Maybe Amber had too. But she wouldn't have been there alone."

She carried on along the roadway that was lit by the occasional streetlamp as they headed near the town's outer edges. "This could be where the murders are being committed. And if that's the case, then we'll have no choice but to assume all the kids in this circle of friends are in danger."

"There aren't that many left. "Surrey pointed ahead. "Make a right in about 500 feet. According to the map, there's a parking lot ahead."

"Got it." Kate made the turn. "Looks like a trailhead."

"I think so, but Irving doesn't look to be on a designated trail, according to the pin," he replied.

She pulled into a spot and cut the engine, peering through the windshield at the face of the mountain cast in darkness. "We'll have to hike up." Kate stepped outside. "It's dark as hell out here."

Surrey joined her and turned on his phone's flashlight. "Then we'll use lights."

She returned a knowing grin and gestured ahead. "Point us in the right direction. I'll follow your lead."

He started on at the trail's entrance and glanced at his phone for guidance. "It doesn't appear to be too far ahead." Surrey pushed away overhanging branches and traversed through the dense shrubbery. "Hope we don't run across any snakes."

"I might be more concerned about bears," Kate replied.

He glanced over his shoulder. "Thanks for that. I hadn't considered bears."

"That's what I'm here for." She followed him as they diverged from the marked trail, and lost her footing a moment, grabbing onto the back of his shirt.

"Whoa." Surrey turned around and took hold of her arm. "You okay?"

"Yeah. My foot caught the edge of a rock and slipped. I'm not exactly wearing hiking boots."

"Me either. We're getting there. I don't think it's much farther."

Several more yards and Kate heard voices. "Lieutenant?" she called out.

Surrey stopped in his tracks. "It's Agents Reid and Surrey. Where are you?"

"Over here," Irving replied.

Kate turned her head in the direction of the voice and saw a light. "That's him. He's shining a light. We see you, Lieutenant. We're coming your way now."

Within moments, they'd reached a place where the trees thinned, and the ground was free of brush.

"You made it." Irving approached them. "Listen, I know it's dark out here, but we're too close to where Amber was found to dismiss that as a coincidence. Especially given the picture you found."

"I agree." Kate held up her phone's light and aimed it at the area. "This is it. There's the makeshift fire pit. The downed logs lined up like they were used for seating." She caught sight of

Gatwick and knew he'd been in the photograph too. "Mr. Gatwick."

Surrey greeted the young man with a handshake. "What do you know about this place, exactly?"

Jason scoped the area. "I know that I came here a couple times with Brian, Chris, Amber Hoffman, and some of the other high school seniors at the time."

"Did that include Emma Katz?" Kate asked.

"Yes, ma'am. Emma, Heidi, Amber..." He looked away. "All of them."

Irving moved in. "Jason was at the scene of the crash and mentioned he knew about this place. Figured it was best not to waste any time and so we came over." He turned outward. "Then I started looking around and found this." He bent down to pick up a gum wrapper from the ground. "It's not much, but it looks to have been recently discarded, then I started looking around some more." He moved through the fire pit area and looked back. "This is where you folks might want to follow me." Irving walked on.

They caught up to him when Irving stopped and aimed the light at the ground.

Surrey reeled back. "Oh, shit. Have you touched this?"

"No, sir. I saw it after I called you. I had a look around for more evidence folks had been here recently. Came up to this. Damn near fell over backward when I saw it."

Kate approached the bloodied tissue. "This isn't human. Looks like it could be a cow's tongue. Whoever left this wanted it to be found."

WALSH ENDED the call and stood from behind his desk. "It's about time." He made his way to the corridor and caught sight of Fisher from the corner of his eye.

"You look like you're in a hurry," Fisher called out.

Walsh stopped and waited for him. "Been expecting the lab to get back with me on the sample I brought in last night. Finally got the call for the results." He started on again with a hurried pace while Fisher kept up.

"I just got off the phone with Reid." He reached out to Walsh. "Hold up a second. She said another victim was discovered last night. In fact, they almost ran her over. The body was left in the road. After the lieutenant had the county's CSI team on site, one of the town's firefighters mentioned something about a clearing in the woods. Evidently, it was a hangout. Long story short, an animal's tongue was found."

"An animal's tongue?" Walsh asked.

"I imagine she'll be calling on you soon, but given where that sample was collected." Fisher shrugged. "It could be from a dead cow. Reid believes it was a warning aimed at the kids who frequent that clearing."

Walsh set his hands on his square hips. "That's not going to move the needle, is it?"

"Not likely. Listen, they're heading back out to the woods this morning for a better look. With the light of day, they stand a chance at finding more evidence."

Walsh started on again and the two soon arrived at the elevators. "This ups the ante in terms of the killer setting the stage. I'll see what the lab came up with and contact Kate afterward." He stepped onto the elevator. "I'll keep you in the loop." As the doors shut, he eyed the numbers while his thoughts reeled as to who sent this message, this warning that the supposed cow's tongue represented. It was a pivotal moment in the investigation, and they needed answers quickly.

Walsh reached the Quantico labs and headed inside the state-of-the-art facility to retrieve the results. "Morning, I got a call that my results were in. Levi Walsh, Unit 4."

"Good morning, Agent Walsh." The technician typed on his keyboard. "Here they are. DNA from a blood sample."

"Yes, sir."

"I'll print that off for you as well as email a copy." He retreated to the back and quickly returned. "There you go."

"What's the good word?" Walsh flipped through the report.

"Inconclusive." He wore regret. "Sorry, I wish I had better news. The sample was fine, but the DNA that was pulled couldn't be identified."

"Tell me this, was it human?" Walsh asked.

"What's that now? Human?" The tech eyed his computer screen. "Uh, yes, sir, it was. Had you expected different results?"

"Given what I've just been told, possibly. This, however, is a better result—I think. But you don't have a match, meaning the DNA isn't in the database."

"No, sir. I'm afraid not."

Walsh rubbed his forehead. "Okay, I'll keep at it."

"The profile is in the system now, so if you do find your suspect, and get a sample, we'll have something to compare it to."

THE RISING sun drove rays of light through the treetops high on the mountain, while the clearing below was still cast in shadow. The agents returned to the scene of the disturbing find to see yellow police tape that cordoned off the grounds.

Kate bent low to slip beneath the tape and found officers documenting the scene, including the man in charge. "Lieutenant

Irving?" She glanced back and noticed Surrey, who was much taller, raise the tape to get under it.

Irving took notice of their arrival and started back. "Morning. Did you manage any sleep last night?"

"Not much, no," she replied. "Now that it's light, we'll be able to have a better look around."

"Agreed," Irving said. "I do have my people checking the parking lot for tire tracks and whatnot."

Surrey joined them. "We saw a couple of officers down there."

"I'd like to say we'll find a match to the tire tracks found at the scene of the crash, but time will tell," he replied. "I also touched base with the Roanoke coroner's office to get a status update on the autopsies."

"And?" Kate asked.

"He'll be sending over Emma Katz's results this morning. Cause of death was brain bleed, secondary to blood loss."

"From the blow to her head." Kate skimmed the area. "What still eats away at me is that none of the three victims were killed in exactly the same manner. I've studied and investigated serial murderers long enough to know that these people take time to perfect their techniques. It rarely changes."

"What are you getting at, Agent Reid?" Irving asked.

"Katz was our only victim who survived the initial attack," Surrey cut in.

"True," Kate began. "It would be easy to write that off as a mistake or an interruption, but I'm not so sure. Then you have Heidi Sumner, who was dragged out to the river."

Surrey tucked his hands into his pockets. "And now we have Amber Hoffman, who was rammed off the road, we assume, then struck in the head. The differences could be attributed simply to opportunity. The unsub attacked when he had the chance. At this point, I think it's safe to rule out any sort of ritualistic fantasy this killer has."

Kate regarded him. "I agree with you. I see no undertones that point to religion or ritual killings. But let's go back to Emma Katz for a second. We found no evidence of defensive wounds. This could be because the killer struck her in the head from behind. She hadn't expected it."

"He wanted to talk with her," Surrey added. "Things didn't go as he'd planned. She went to leave, and things turned ugly."

Irving raised his finger. "Let's not forget this person carried a hunting knife. If he hadn't intended on murdering Emma, why bring the knife?"

Kate considered his question. "Is this hunting season?"

"About the only thing to hunt around here in the summer is the coyote," Irving replied. "Don't know too many folks who do that. Most everyone hunts in the fall."

She nodded. "Then the only reason to bring a knife was to threaten; to scare her into doing what he wanted. But I don't think he believed it would go that far, and when it did, he cut out her tongue in retaliation. Maybe she said something to him he didn't like, and his anger drove him to the act. But I won't rule out the possibility she knew something or was about to say something, and the killer did what he did as a message, not unlike the tongue left here last night."

"That starts to make some sense, if any sense is to be made of this," Irving said. "But your point regarding the differences in these murders?"

Kate had mulled over this idea for a while. The three deaths seemed different in a way she struggled to articulate. Besides the obvious, which Surrey pointed out as an opportunity. But this was more than opportunity. This was... "Revenge. But not for the same reason."

"You know what you're saying?" Surrey asked. "You think we're either dealing with two unsubs, or the killer thought Emma had spoken to her friends and he feared what they knew."

"The latter is the more logical conclusion, unless or until I can find evidence the former rings true." Kate walked toward the tree where the bloodied tongue had stained the ground. She squatted low to examine the area again. "For now, someone's cow is dead. This threat cannot be ignored. I imagine a call will be coming into you this morning about that, Lieutenant. When it does, we'll want to note the location of where the cow was killed and its proximity to this place. If the owner saw something, or someone, then so much the better for us."

Surrey drew closer to Kate. "And you know what's really interesting is that the animal's tongue didn't get carried off by a bear or wolf or whatever else lives in these woods."

"Animals would've gotten to it quickly." Kate returned to her feet and eyed the lieutenant. "And Jason Gatwick brought you here, what, about an hour after we found Amber?"

Irving nodded. "Which would've been a couple hours after she died."

"Let's be sure we know where that kid was when he got the call to assist at the scene." Kate noticed her phone ring and looked at the caller ID. "It's Levi. He must have the DNA results." She answered the call. "Levi, good morning. Tell me you have something for us."

"Inconclusive," he replied. "I'm sorry, Kate. The DNA profile is in the database now, so if you find something to compare it to, then you might get somewhere. Fisher mentioned you found the tongue of an animal. I did question the lab to ensure the sample was human. It was."

Kate rubbed her forehead. "I suppose it makes sense there

wouldn't be a match in the system. And yeah, we're pretty sure what we found was from a cow."

"Then this isn't the silver bullet you'd hoped for," he replied.

"Not yet, but thanks for the help, Levi. We're expecting the Katz autopsy later this morning. If I get the DNA profile with the autopsy, I'll let you know. We'll check for a match there." Kate ended the call. "We're running out of options until our victims' labs break free. So, here's what I would like to suggest, Lieutenant. We gather DNA swabs from the people who know about this clearing. Everyone in that photograph that was found in Emma's room. Our team can cross-reference those with the sample you found that currently has no match, according to Agent Walsh."

Irving appeared resigned. "You want me to ask those kids for a DNA sample?"

Kate raised her palms. "We have no choice. We collect samples from the Voss' to rule them out since this is their property, and then we get the rest to submit. And when you receive labs back on the victims, we'll also compare. Process of elimination is where we're at right now, Lieutenant. You have three dead kids here. None of us wants anymore."

IRVING'S TEAM remained at the clearing as they continued the hunt for evidence, particularly as it related to the parking lot and matching tire tracks to what was found on the scene of Amber Hoffman's murder on the highway.

A consensus had been reached to home in on the young men in the photo, asking if they would voluntarily submit a DNA swab. Jason Gatwick was the first one to approach. His shift continued at the fire station and the agents headed that way.

Kate sat behind the wheel of her Explorer and glanced at Surrey. "Do you think I overstepped?"

"You mean with insisting on swabs?" He raised a shoulder. "Maybe. But I think your point came across well enough. I get why he wasn't keen to move forward—"

"He doesn't want to believe one of those kids could be a killer," Kate cut in.

"That, and we run the risk of setting off a chain of events that could backfire on us."

She drew in her brow. "How so?"

"This is a small town. The parents of these kids all know each other or are acquainted in some way. We start suggesting one of these young men is the killer, the town will turn on itself. And I don't know how we prevent that, but we'll have to find a way to spin it such that it appears as a way to rule out rather than confirm a suspect."

"That, we can do," Kate replied.

"Then you have to think that whoever the unsub is, he'll understand that we know about the clearing, about the group of friends. That could invite him to finish the job he started quickly, or he could take flight. We lose either way," he added.

"What choice is there? How can we move forward without ruling out the three remaining people in this circle of friends?"

"Four." Surrey glanced at her. "You're forgetting Sam Hardy. Listen to your gut on this one, Reid. You're not wrong to want to go at him."

"And his father," Kate added. "Although, it's appearing less likely that Randall Hardy would murder these kids for suspecting they knew about his affair. Why would that matter to them? It would've only mattered to Heidi Sumner." Kate made a left turn and the firehouse came into view. "I want to proceed with the swabs. I see no other way to give this case forward momentum."

Surrey nodded. "It's your show, Reid. If this is what your gut's telling you, then you have to push on."

Kate drove onto the parking lot toward the side of the fire station. "My gut tells me this kid, Gatwick, who was there when two of these girls were killed, should be who we hit up first."

Lieutenant Irving knocked on the door of the Hardy home once again and when Carol Hardy answered, he regarded her. "Good morning, Mrs. Hardy. I believe Randall's at the store with Sam right now."

"That's right."

"Then may I come in and talk to you?" he asked.

"Of course." Carol stepped aside.

"Thank you." Irving removed his hat and followed her to the kitchen table. "I wanted to talk to you about Sam's relationship with his father."

Carol walked to the coffee pot and poured a mug. "Can I get you a coffee, Howard?"

"Sure. Thank you." He awaited her return and took a sip. "That's nice. Appreciate it."

Carol sat down and laced her fingers on top of the table.

"You don't have to be nervous. As you know, this entire situation is, well, it's just unthinkable, really. I know how afraid everyone is."

"They're all leaving town, Howard. Everyone," she replied. "You know what that's going to do business at the store? We only just recovered after all this COVID business. Everyone shopping online. It nearly destroyed us."

"I have no doubt, but right now, Mrs. Hardy, three young women have been murdered right here in our town."

"What's it got to do with Sam and Randall?" she pressed on.

He took another sip of coffee. "Most folks know your husband has some difficulty controlling his emotions." Irving raised his hands. "Now, I'm not laying blame, here, you understand? I'm just trying to wrap my head around all this."

"All what, exactly, Howard? I don't think I understand what you mean."

"Sam's been pretty bent out of shape over what happened to Emma Katz."

"Well, of course, he has. They were close friends," she replied.

"I understand. But the other night, I found Sam wandering around Market Street alone. Now, I know that's not particularly usual for him, except that it is under these circumstances, you see. But worse than that, I saw the young man's face. The bruises. He said nothing about it, and I didn't ask. Suppose that's on me. Point being, he knew all three girls. I'm going to need him to make an official statement as to his whereabouts on each occasion those girls were killed."

Carol drew in her brow. "I'm sorry, are you telling me you think Sam killed them?"

"I'm saying, I need to let these FBI people know that Sam had nothing to do with any of it. Now, you can help me prove that to them, or you fight me on it."

She raised her chin in defiance. "What do I need to do?"

"Let's figure a way to get Sam to the station and offer an official statement," Irving began. "I don't want to draw the ire of your husband because I know he prefers to keep your family life, well, in the family. So we do this under the right circumstances, okay?" He looked away a moment. "Mrs. Hardy, I don't like what goes on between Sam and your husband and I damn well know you don't either. So maybe you should think about making some changes. Maybe Sam could go live with a relative or the both of you can...I don't know, I just figure something has to change and this God-awful situation is the best catalyst. Do you understand what I'm telling you?"

Carol drew back her shoulders and her face masked with indignation. "I'll have Sam go and make a statement down at the station. Frankly, I don't see Randall having a problem with that. Despite what you think you know, Lieutenant, my husband will protect his family. He wants to find whoever's terrorizing this town just as much as anyone."

Irving realized her objectivity was skewed to the point that it could not be overcome. "Okay, Mrs. Hardy. Okay."

13

The garage doors at the front of the firehouse were open and the mid-morning sun warmed the inside. Loud music played while two firefighters wiped down the truck that had just been cleaned. Kate recognized one of them as Jason Gatwick, and she eyed Surrey. "We should separate them first. I don't know the other guy, but I don't want Gatwick feeling anxious."

"You mean, more so than he probably already is?" Surrey asked. "No, I get it. We can do that." He stepped into the garage and cupped a hand around his mouth to amplify his voice. "Morning."

Jason looked in his direction and stepped down from the ladder on the side of the truck. He grabbed his phone and pressed a button. The music stopped.

Another young man on the other side stepped into view. "What'd you do that for?"

Jason turned to him. "Feds are here."

"Feds?" the man peered over at them. "Oh. What can we do for you?"

Kate displayed her badge. "FBI. We'd like to have a brief word with Mr. Gatwick."

Jason tossed down his towel and eyed his colleague. "I'll be right back." He made his way toward them as they stood just inside the entrance. "What can I do for you, Agent Reid, Agent Surrey? Is this about last night at the clearing?"

Kate eyed the other firefighter as he appeared to linger. He seemed to catch on and soon disappeared into the back. "Mr. Gatwick, first of all, I'm very sorry for the loss of your friends. I can't imagine what must be going through your mind right now."

He cast down his gaze. "It doesn't feel real, ma'am. I come here, do my job, and I just feel numb."

"I have no doubt," Kate continued. "And we appreciate you showing the lieutenant the clearing last night."

"Did it help you guys at all?" he asked.

"I think so, yes. And it's part of the reason we're here." Kate retrieved the photo. "This was found in Emma's bedroom, inside one of her books."

Jason took hold of the picture. "Looks like all of us at the clearing last year."

"So you recall when this was taken?" Surrey asked.

"Kind of. I mean, I didn't go there a lot. I'm a year older than those guys, but I went when Emma and I dated. My roommate tagged along once or twice. Hung out with all of them. We were all friends—up until recently."

"Three of the people in that photo are dead," Kate continued. "Four remain. And you're one of them."

He returned the picture to her. "What are you trying to say, Agent Reid?"

Surrey stepped in. "We'd like you to submit a DNA swab so

that we can rule out your involvement in the murders of your friends."

Jason placed his hand on his chest. "You want my DNA?"

"Yes, sir," Kate replied. "In order to rule you out as a suspect. It seems to me that would work in your favor." She kept close watch of his reaction. His lips parted slightly as he breathed through his mouth. His eyes blinked with greater frequency. His throat appeared dry as he swallowed with some effort. He fit the profile. Shorter in stature, making an attack on women of about the same height easier from behind, or by surprise. Strong enough to wield a blunt object against a skull. Strong enough to put them in a choke-hold. "What do you think, Mr. Gatwick? Can you help us find the person who killed your friends?"

"What about Brian?" Jason asked. "He's in this picture too. Chris and Sam."

"We'll be asking them for their help as well," Surrey replied.

"Your roommate," Kate began. "I think you mentioned to Irving that you don't see him much because you work alternating shifts."

"That's right," Jason replied.

"So he was home last night?" she continued.

"Probably. I was on shift, which was why I was there at the accident. Chris was with me and Hughie at the fireworks stage when we found Emma that night." He turned away as if his emotions rose to the surface.

"I'm sure that must've been devastating for him, too. Was he as close to the group as you were?" she continued.

"No. He was at home a few times when Emma was at our place, and we'd start talking about getting together with everyone. I sort of invited him a couple of times because I felt bad. Honestly, he and I aren't that close. He's a little older and I think it was awkward for him."

Jason used the back of his hand to wipe sweat from his brow. "So does this DNA test hurt?"

Kate grinned. "No. It's just a cotton swab in your mouth. We can be finished in less than two minutes, and you can go on about your day."

Dust from the dirt road kicked up as Kate's Ford rolled on toward the Voss Farm.

Surrey kept his eyes ahead. "We'll have to track down Brian Keller since he didn't answer his phone. Irving insisted he'd handle Sam Hardy."

"That leaves us with Chris Pumphrey. According to Gatwick, he's at the apartment. We'll hit there next."

Surrey raised a brow. "Not the result you expected?"

She turned to him. "Huh?"

"The Gatwick kid. You seem disappointed he agreed to the swab. This is a good thing, Reid. We'll have something to cross-reference with Irving's sample from the gate."

"Yeah, I get that," she replied. "He cooperated and that speaks volumes. I still can't shake the idea he was there when Emma died and was one of the first on the scene of the crash, even before some of Irving's people. I understand he was on duty, but something about it doesn't feel right."

"Then having his DNA on file is a good thing, no matter how this shakes out," Surrey added. "For now, we shift our focus to the Voss farm. The blood was found on their gate. Their son believed he'd seen someone on the other side of their fence. And we'll learn pretty quickly whether they have a dead cow on their hands."

Kate pulled to a stop at the bottom of the long driveway. She glanced toward the newer model Chevy pickup. "Looks like someone's home."

Surrey opened his passenger door and stepped out into the midday sun.

Kate climbed out of the driver's side and walked atop the pea gravel driveway toward the large farmhouse with a wraparound porch. Cicadas buzzed in the tall trees that provided a lush green backdrop. She climbed the steps that led to the front door and when Surrey caught up to her, she knocked.

The door opened almost instantly, and Kate retrieved her credentials. "Good afternoon, Mr. Voss?"

"Yes."

"I'm FBI Agent Kate Reid and Agent Jonathan Surrey."

The thickset man with a heavy beard stood at the door. "FBI?"

"Yes, sir. We're working with Lieutenant Irving, and we'd like to talk to you for a moment," Kate replied.

"I didn't know the FBI was involved. Howard didn't say anything like that." With a narrowed gaze, he appeared menacing, but the tone in his voice expressed grief.

"We're here to help him, but the case still rests with the Jansville Police. May we talk to you, Mr. Voss?" Kate pressed on.

"Sure. Come inside. It's already getting too hot out here."

The kitchen was on the right, and Kate noticed a few breakfast dishes on the counter. An empty box of cereal. Inside the living room, the television was on with no sound. The oversized sofa and loveseat looked well-worn. "I understand this farm has been in your family for generations."

"Yes, ma'am." Mr. Voss closed the door. "My great-grandfather bought the place."

"Is that so?" The nearly 200-year-old murders sprang to mind as Kate realized no one had yet pulled the archived files. With the death of Amber Hoffman, resources were severely stretched, and maybe she was putting too much stock into that idea. DNA samples would tell them everything they needed to know.

"Anyway, I figured one day my boy would live here with his family." He choked back his emotions. "Please excuse the state of our home. Mrs. Voss is packing up. After all that's happened, it's time she and my boy get the hell out of town."

"I understand," Kate replied. "We've come here to ask you a few things, Mr. Voss."

"All right." He stepped into the kitchen. "Can I offer you a cup of coffee?"

"No, thank you, sir." She followed him while Surrey walked beside her.

Bruce turned away from the sink and eyed the agents. "Then ask away, Agent Reid."

She peered through the kitchen window. "Have you been out to check on your livestock recently?"

He raised a brow. "My livestock?"

"Yes, sir," Surrey cut in.

"Not since yesterday afternoon. Normally, I'm working the farm from six in the morning to six at night, but things have been so God-awful, well, I'm struggling to keep up. Why are you asking me this?"

Kate's attention was drawn to the entry, where a young man appeared. "Hello."

Anson Voss looked with hesitation at his father.

"It's okay, son. They're with the FBI. They're trying to help figure out all this mess."

Anson stepped closer to his father. "Did you tell them we think someone was out on our land the other night when I went to check on the chickens?"

"I think the lieutenant may have mentioned something like that," Kate replied.

Bruce swatted at the idea. "He went out to check on the chickens and swore up and down he caught a glimpse of someone on our land. Never did see anyone, myself, and nothing since. We made mention of it to Lieutenant Irving."

Surrey looked at the kid. "Can you describe this person?"

"Well, no, sir." Anson turned down his gaze. "I just sort of heard footsteps. Looked over and saw the trees moving like someone just passed by. I didn't see a person."

"So, you see, I'm afraid there really isn't much to say on that matter," Bruce replied.

Kate regarded him. "Would you mind showing us where your son thinks he saw this person? We can check out the cows too, if that's all right."

"Can I ask what's got your interest in my cows?" Bruce asked.

She glanced at the boy, and it seemed the father understood.

"Anson, go on and get yourself packed up now. You and your momma will be leaving soon."

"Yes, sir." The lanky kid walked away.

Bruce turned back to the agents. "All right then. I'll show you around."

PATIENCE WAS key when dealing with Sam Hardy. Irving waited while Carol called him back home and the young man just arrived. "I appreciate Mr. Hardy letting him take an hour so that he could speak to me." That wasn't entirely true. He'd prefer to have done this at the station and without the knowledge of the senior Mr. Hardy. Almost defeated the purpose.

"Like I said, you misunderstand Randall. He had no problem whatsoever when I said you were here and wanted to ask Sam a few questions. But I figure it's best to do it here, you understand.

No need to agitate Sam any further." Carol's attention was drawn to the door as Sam walked inside. "Son, come into the kitchen, would you?"

Sam arrived with his sights aimed at the ground and shuffled to the kitchen table.

Irving smiled. "Hi, Sam. You feeling a little better than when last we talked?"

"Yes, sir," he mumbled.

"Good. I'm glad to hear it. Now, I just have a few questions I need to ask, all right?"

Sam pulled out a chair. "Yes, sir."

"Okay, Sam. I'd like you to take a look here." He handed him the photo. "You remember this picture and where it was taken?"

"I think so. I haven't been there since Emma took me last summer. I was only there once, I think. Mostly, it was for the high schoolers to hang out," he replied.

"You recall who all came out there? Anyone besides the ones in this picture?"

Sam reluctantly peered at the photo again. "They're all dead."

"Yeah, Sam, they are, which is why I need your help. You might be the only one who can help me, do you understand what I'm telling you?"

"Uh-huh." Sam took the picture and studied it closer. "Emma took me out there. I didn't drive there myself. Why don't you ask Brian? He was the one who talked to Emma last. He's in that picture too."

"We have, Sam, we have. And maybe that's why I'm coming to you now. You see, I don't know who did these awful things. But if it's someone else in that picture, maybe I don't want them to know, you understand?"

Sam nodded. "Uh-huh. If Brian did all that, he might go back there and hide the evidence."

Irving needed to tread lightly here. Better to get to the point. "When I saw you on Market Street the other night, can I ask what you were doing?"

"Just walking home, like I told you," he replied.

"Sam." Irving tried to make eye contact with him. "I need you to be more specific. I need to know exactly what you were doing and where you were doing it. Because here's the thing. Now, I'm not trying to scare you, but someone bad is walking around freely in this town. And you shouldn't be."

"Yes, sir," Sam replied.

"So, you see why it's important I know where you'd gone? Now, take your time. Think about it. And tell me where you were going on that night and when Heidi and Amber were taken from us."

Sam glanced at his mother.

"Go on, now, Sam. Tell Lieutenant Irving where you were. It's important you be truthful, all right?"

"Okay." He picked at his fingernails in his lap. "Last night, when Amber was in that car accident—"

"Yes, son?" Irving pressed on.

"I was out back, in the shed."

Irving glanced at Carol and set his eyes on Sam again. "What were you doing out there?"

"I was upset about Emma. I miss her, sir. I miss her a lot."

Carol folded her arms. "You see? He was home."

Irving set his eyes on her. "Did you know he was back there?"

"Lieutenant, I'm not sure I get your meaning, but I do the best I can with my son. He's still a grown man and no, I don't keep him on a leash, if that's what you're asking."

Irving raised his hands. "That's not what I meant, Mrs. Hardy."

"Isn't it?" she asked.

"Stop it," Sam called out. "Stop yelling."

"No one's yelling, Sam," Irving said. "You were out back. All right. And what about Heidi? You remember where you were three nights ago when she didn't come home from the convenience store?"

Sam raised his eyes as if thinking about the question.

Irving tilted his head after he'd remained quiet for too long. "Sam?"

He set his gaze on the lieutenant once again. "I was home. I was in my room, like most nights since this happened. I came home from work early 'cause Dad didn't need me. Not many people are coming to the store anymore, so I went home. I was in my room, listening to my music. That's all."

Carol waved her hand. "There you go."

Irving drew in a deep breath and leaned back. "Mrs. Hardy, I'm going to need you to vouch for Sam, you understand? You or Mr. Hardy, either one."

"Of course. I don't see a problem with that at all."

He turned back to Sam. "Did you drive home from the store just now?"

"Yes, sir."

Irving considered the damage that would be visible on the vehicle that drove Amber Hoffman off the road. "So your car's just outside?"

"Yes, sir."

In a way, Irving felt relieved. Yes, the killer was still out there, but it hadn't appeared to be Sam Hardy. "I appreciate you talking with me, Sam. There is one other thing I'm going to need from you."

"Okay."

"In order to completely ensure you had no part in any of

what's happened, I'm going to need you to allow us to take a DNA test."

"What?" Carol asked. "You just heard the boy, didn't you? He told you where he was, now you want more?"

"Mrs. Hardy, this is all standard procedure. I believe Sam is telling me the truth, so this won't be a problem." He turned to Sam. "Isn't that right? You're a grown man, who can make his own decisions. You don't need permission from anyone, do you understand me?"

"I understand."

"So, will you agree to me putting a little cotton swab against the inside of your cheek and collecting your DNA? Do you understand what that means?"

"It's like what they do on those crime shows, right?"

"That's right, son. Just like on the crime shows," Irving replied.

Sam glanced at his mother and nodded. "Okay. If it'll help you find out who took Emma away from me, then I'll do it."

Bruce Voss threw the column shifter into Park. We can get out here and have a look." The driver's side door of his old Chevy truck squeaked as it opened.

Surrey stepped out of the passenger side and lent a hand to Kate as she slid out of the bench seat.

"Thanks," Kate said.

Bruce stood in front of his truck and peered out over his pasture. "I only got ten head of cattle, so it'll be fairly easy to spot whether one was missing. So, let's go see." He started toward the fence and opened the gate. "You still haven't told me what it is you think we're about to find, Agent Reid."

"Well, Mr. Voss, we believe we found what appeared to be a cow's tongue in the woods late last night."

Bruce raised his brows. "I'm sorry, what's that now?"

"A cow's tongue," Kate repeated. "I'm no expert, but it was large, and I knew it wasn't human. So, given that Lieutenant Irving discovered blood on your perimeter gate..."

"Again, what's that? What did he find?"

"Sorry, I—I thought he would've mentioned it to you." Kate grew uncomfortable. "He followed a trail that led from the road heading out of town to your gate. It was an a-frame style gate."

"So the one on the west side of the property," Bruce replied.

"Must be, yes," she continued. "Anyway, he found dried blood on the gate and was able to get a sample and we had it analyzed. Unfortunately, we don't know who that blood belonged to, but we'd like to get a sample from you to make sure we aren't spinning our wheels."

"It's starting to make sense now that my boy might actually have seen someone out on our property," Bruce replied.

"It's possible," Surrey added. "But before we get too far down that road, if what we found was the tongue from a cow, it would make sense it came from your farm."

"You're telling me I got a dead cow in my pasture?" Bruce asked.

Kate eyed him. "I hope not, Mr. Voss."

They continued into the pasture and Bruce pointed to the right. "They're over there, by the pond. They like to hang out near the water in the summer. They'll cool themselves down by walking in it sometimes." He started ahead.

Kate trailed him and Surrey wasn't far behind. If what she suspected was true, then the Voss farm had just become much more important to this investigation than she would've expected. The blood on the gate, the son believing he saw someone on the property, and now this. She slowed down and waited for Surrey before leaning in to whisper, "Do we have a statement from him?"

"I don't think so," Surrey replied. "But right now, I've got some questions."

"And if we find a dead cow," Kate began. "We're going to have a whole lot more."

Bruce arrived first at the pond and began a head count. When it was clear he was one short, he walked the perimeter.

Kate and Surrey soon caught up and looked on as he appeared to search for the missing cow. "He doesn't look like a guy who expected this."

"No," Surrey began. "He's upset. What do we think? What if he doesn't find the cow?"

And just as Kate was about to speak, they both turned when Bruce called out. "I think he just did."

The agents jogged several hundred feet ahead and caught up to the farmer. Kate looked down and saw the dead animal. "I'm so sorry, Mr. Voss."

Surrey squatted to peer at the animal's mouth. "Tongue's been cut out."

Bruce dropped his head into his hands. "Oh, my Lord. How could someone do this? Why?"

She placed her hand on his back in a feeble attempt to offer comfort. "Mr. Voss, whoever did this was someone who knew your farm. Knew the layout, where your cattle would be. Do you have anyone working here right now? A farm hand or someone like that?"

"No, ma'am. Not right now. I do get some local boys to do odd jobs, but mostly, it's me and my family who run the place."

Surrey stepped up. "Did your son know any of the girls who've died?"

Bruce regarded him. "I'm sure he did. He's a slight bit younger than they were, but he probably would've been a sophomore when they were seniors. And most of the kids know each other around here."

"We should have Irving talk to him," Kate added.

"Whoa, now, hold on." Bruce raised his hands. "You think my boy is somehow involved in all this?"

"That's not what I'm saying at all, Mr. Voss," Kate began. "I'm saying it would be a good idea to understand how your son might know these kids. Possibly interacted with them recently. We want to get to the bottom of this just as you do."

He closed his eyes a moment. "I'm sorry, Agent Reid. Of course you're right."

Kate's gaze was drawn out to the horizon. "How far does this property extend?"

Bruce shielded his eyes as he peered out. "There's a fence along the boundary. We can ride it if you want."

"With your permission, we'd prefer to check things out ourselves, so that if we do find any evidence someone was out there, we don't risk contaminating it," Kate replied. "In the meantime, it'd be a good idea for you and your son to sit down with Lieutenant Irving. Just in case you have information you don't realize could be valuable. And of course, to obtain a swab. That'll put you and your family in the clear."

"Yes, ma'am. Uh, of course. You can check things out. I don't know how I'm going to explain any of this to my family." He looked at the carcass again.

"I'll let the lieutenant know what's going on. He'll head your way soon, I imagine. Thank you for your time, Mr. Voss. And I am sorry about this." Kate returned to her SUV and when Surrey stepped in, she pulled out toward the fenced boundary of the property. "It's pretty out here. Reminds me a little of home."

"Oh yeah? Where's home?" Surrey asked.

"Originally, Rio Dell, California. It's north. That was where I grew up."

"And where it happened?"

"Yeah. Where *it* happened. I lived pretty close to the Redwoods. These trees are nothing like that, but the greenery reminds me of it, I guess. Being surrounded by mountains and hills. I will say that the weather isn't the same. It's a lot hotter here."

"And you moved to San Diego for school, right?" he continued.

"I did." She pulled up along the fence line. "Where did you go to school?"

"Actually, I grew up in New Mexico. Lived in Albuquerque and went to school at New Mexico State. I joined the Bureau shortly after and then, of course, you know the rest when I worked out in Denver."

"Look at you, actually talking about your life for once." Kate smiled.

"Well, you asked. I'll answer just about any questions you have," he added.

"Oh, really?"

He held up his hands. "Within reason, Reid. Within reason." Surrey glanced through the passenger door. "Hold up. Pull over."

Kate rolled to a stop. "What is it?"

"Come on." Surrey jumped out and headed toward the fence.

Kate joined him and looked out into the forested hillside. She shot him a look. "How did you spot that?"

"The trail? I don't know. Maybe I had a hunch."

"Might be better than mine," she quipped. "I would like to know where it leads. You feel like taking a hike?"

"In the middle of the day, in the middle of summer, with no water?" he asked. "Sure. What could possibly go wrong?"

"We'll see where this goes and then head back toward the gate. Mr. Voss didn't mention a trail from this land," she added.

"Maybe he didn't know."

Kate squeezed between the barbed-wire fence and stood on the other side. "Think you can get through? I can use my shirt to raise it."

"I got it." Surrey bent over and pushed one leg through, lowering his back between the barbs. "Damn it."

Kate heard the tear. "You all right?"

He made it to the other side and took off his jacket, examining it. "Nice." The back had a large tear in the fabric. "I loved this jacket."

Kate appeared sheepish. "Sorry about that. It's too hot for it anyway."

Surrey dropped the jacket to the ground and carried on next to her. "Let me see if I can get my bearings straight."

"I believe over there," Kate pointed northwest, "heads back out of town."

"So over there would be toward the clearing we saw?" he asked.

"I think so. That has to be a solid two miles, maybe three."

"If the trail leads out that way, that could be our connection to this farm," Surrey added.

"Doesn't explain why Emma was in the park before she was attacked." Kate turned around. "Unless this trail heads in that other direction too."

"I'd say that's possible. What do you think?" Surrey asked. "Which direction do you want to take?"

Kate examined the dirt path. "You think we could borrow ATVs? I don't know if the trail stays this wide all the way, so we could get stuck somewhere."

"If that happens, we get off and walk. But this is going to take some time." Surrey looked up at the bright clear sky. "I think we're going to need to prepare for this, Reid. Let's head back and ask Voss if we can borrow a couple of vehicles and get some water."

14

The wreckage that was Amber Hoffman's silver 2013 Toyota Corolla, had been towed to the impound lot at the Jansville police station. The back end had folded like an accordion. The front passenger tire flattened and hung off its rim. Blood had splattered on the driver's side door.

"Go ahead and unhook it," Officer Erin Calvert called out to the tow truck driver. She stood back as the man disconnected the electrics and then unlashed the tires from the truck bed. He and his colleague led it down the ramp.

"There you go. If you'll just sign the papers for me," the driver said.

"Sure." Calvert signed the receipt and returned the man's pen. "Thanks."

He looked back at the vehicle. "This from another murder? I live in nearby Woodstone. Shame what's been happening here."

"Yes, sir. A shame indeed," Calvert replied.

"Well, I'll leave you to do your job."

When he and his partner returned to the truck and drove

away, Calvert examined the vehicle and stopped and the back end, where most of the damage had occurred. She squatted and was eye-level with what remained of the back end. Blue paint marred the bumper.

Calvert retrieved her phone and photographed the paint. "If I can figure out what color this is, I can get a make and model."

"What's that, Calvert?" Abrams meandered over and eyed the car.

"I was just saying that if we can identify this paint, we'll find out what kind of car it was that ran Amber off the road."

Abrams raised his chin and nodded. "It would take some time, but it's possible. You want some help with that?"

CAMERON FISHER HAD GOTTEN the call from Unit Chief Cole, the man in charge of the entire BAU, regarding an update on his team in Jansville, Virginia. Word had reached the chief that the case had ballooned, and the media had suddenly become very interested in the small town, given the gruesome nature of the crimes.

When word reached the chief, it was rarely a good thing, so Fisher headed to Walsh's office for an update. "Hey, you have a minute?"

Walsh looked up from his desk. "Of course. Come in." He appeared to notice Fisher's expression. "What happened?"

"Chief Cole happened." He pulled out a chair to sit. "I tried Reid and Surrey, but their phones went straight to voicemail. Tell me you know what's going on."

"I reached out to them this morning. The results of their sample came back inconclusive, which wasn't exactly what they'd wanted to hear."

"I'll bet not. What's their plan? Are you heading out there today?"

"Not today. They're due to touch base in a few hours for an update," he replied.

Fisher sucked on his toothpick as he appeared to consider his options.

"I do think, and Kate agrees," Walsh continued. "That it's worth talking to Emma Katz's college roommate, ruling out any involvement from someone at the young woman's university. I'm working on getting Katz's class schedule and finding out who was in her circle at school."

Fisher nodded. "Okay and what about Duncan?"

"I've only spoken to her in passing today. She should be in her office."

"I'll talk to her next." Fisher cocked his head. "Cole's getting heat from above since this isn't a federal investigation, so whatever we can do to help those guys in Jansville is what we need to do. I imagine the Roanoke Field Office is getting antsy as well. They're going to want to put in their two cents. I should make a call to my buddy and ask him to smooth things over since he was the one who brought this to us. In the meantime, get Reid what she needs. I'll try her again here shortly."

"All right. I'll let you know what I dig up," Walsh replied.

Fisher made his way back into the corridor and grabbed his phone. "Scarborough, it's Fisher. Is this a bad time?"

"No, what's wrong? Is Kate okay?"

"Walsh spoke to her this morning, but I've been trying to get hold of her or Surrey and neither is answering."

"All right. What can I do to help?" Nick asked.

"I know you two talk about cases."

"Not so much anymore, but go on," he replied.

"Has she mentioned anything to you about this Jansville investigation?"

"A little. Why do you ask?" Nick replied.

"It's been over a week and now three kids are dead," Fisher said. "Cole's riding my ass to get our team out of there, but you know your wife. She won't go until she's finished."

"Oh, I know."

"I guess what I'm asking is whether you have any insight about her progress. Is she making any because all I'm hearing is that they're coming up against a bunch of brick walls?"

"Come on, Cam, you know as well as I do, that's how this works," Nick said. "I've talked to Kate about it, but I think the real problem is with the local investigator. She feels hamstrung and there's nothing any of us can do about that."

"No, I suppose you're right," Fisher replied.

"And as far as Cole goes, look, get the Roanoke field office involved if you have to. Let this be their case to prosecute. BAU doesn't do that anyway. That way, you get Cole off your back and Kate can work with those guys without the heartburn."

Fisher reached his office and walked inside. "You think Reid's going to be okay with me bringing in more feds?"

"I didn't say it would be easy. Otherwise, you do what I used to do."

Fisher sat at his desk. "Which was?"

"Be the whipping boy," Nick replied. "You protect the work your team has already done by being that layer in between them and Cole. It'll hurt, but you'll heal. Trust me."

"Yeah, okay. Hey, thanks, man. I appreciate the advice. You know, I never gave you the credit you deserved running this team. I'm sorry about that."

"No apologies necessary, friend. Things turned out just as

they were supposed to. Hey, I gotta run. I'll try Kate later and let her know to touch base. See ya, Cam. Bye."

NICK RETURNED his phone to his pocket and noticed Georgia at his office door. "Hey, come in."

"Am I interrupting anything?"

"No, just finishing a call with an old colleague," he replied.

She continued inside and sat down. "Anyone I know?"

"Don't think so. He's BAU, in my old job."

Georgia returned a crooked grin. "Oh really? Looking for a handout or a hand-up?"

"He's a good guy and since he works with my wife, he thought I had intel, but I didn't, so, I couldn't help him anyway."

Georgia lowered her gaze and kept her smile. "Agent Reid has turned out to be quite the profiler, hasn't she?"

"That she has. She did learn from some of the best," Nick replied. "You included."

"I appreciate that, but considering she's the head profiler at BAU, I'd say she's done pretty well on her own, and you know, she deserves it. She went through a lot to get to that spot." Georgia folded her hands in her lap. "I'm glad things worked out for you two. I always knew she was the one for you."

"Even before I did," he replied.

"What can I say?" She pushed away the strands of red hair from her cheek. "When the man you're in love with loves someone else? A girl knows." She chuckled. "Although, I suppose I learned that a little too late about my own husband."

There it was again. Being around Georgia didn't feel as easy or as comfortable as it once had. She'd made it clear on multiple occasions that her marriage wasn't all sunshine and roses. What was Nick supposed to say to that? While he didn't hold a grudge over her infidelity, and probably should have thanked her for sending him straight into Kate's arms, a part of him felt like she was getting what she deserved. The problem was, that he was her boss now, for the most part. He needed to find a way to shut down what he perceived as her attempts to perhaps win over what was once lost. That was never going to happen.

Sure, he and Kate had their share of problems, mostly stemming from his alcoholism recovery. But he would never jeopardize what he had with his wife. They'd been through far too much and were as strong as steel because of it.

"Listen, Georgia, I'm sorry that you don't seem happy in your life. Truly, I am. However, I need to know that you have the focus necessary to do this job. Personal problems, as you are well aware, can create distraction. On this team, there's no room for it. I can't afford it. This job means too much to me."

"What are you saying, Nick?" Georgia pinched her lips and narrowed her gaze.

"I'm saying, the past has to stay in the past. And I need to know you can see to that."

THE AFTERNOON SUN WANED, but the heat and humidity persisted. The trail had, so far, produced nothing, but a long way was yet to be traveled.

Kate wiped the sweat from her brow as she rattled atop the ATV along the rugged trail. She glanced back at Surrey and waved at him to slow down. They stopped and Kate climbed down from the vehicle. "Okay, I may have underestimated the effect of this heat."

"You think?" Surrey squinted up at the sun. "Look, we can do this before the sun goes down. We've already gone a mile."

"With nothing to show for it," Kate replied.

"If we reach the end of this trail and it leads us to the clearing, then we'll have plenty to show."

Kate looked down along the trail. "I know you're right. I was hoping we'd find evidence that the killer has been using this trail to move around."

Surrey opened his phone. "It's still possible. Let's see how far we are from the river where Heidi Sumner was found."

Kate moved in and peered at the map on Surrey's phone. "Irving would be the one to call on this." She grabbed her phone. "Lieutenant, yeah, we found a trail from the Voss farm, and we think it could lead us to the clearing, which would give us a pretty good idea of how our unsub is moving around. That said, can you text me the location of where exactly Sumner was found? There's a chance that river could be easily reached from this trail as well."

"You're on a hike in this heat?" he asked.

"I know it seems a little drastic, but this could be the connection we've been looking for. Mr. Voss confirmed a dead cow on his property, too, so that reinforces the idea. We borrowed ATVs from him to check out the trail. We're not out here on foot."

"All right. Let me shoot that over to you now. Hang on."

Kate waited for the ping on her phone. "Got it." She opened the map. "Jonathan, take a look. Irving says this is where Heidi Sumner was found."

Surrey looked at the pin and set his index finger on her screen. "And we're over here." He traced back the location.

She eyed him again. "We're not that far."

"No, we're not."

Kate returned to the call. "Lieutenant, it doesn't appear we're that far from the river. If there's a way to get there from here, and this leads to the clearing..." She wore excitement in her eyes for the first time on this case.

"Then, by all means, keep at it, Agent Reid. Call me when you know more. I'll head over to have a word with Voss' here shortly, given the situation with the cow. I'm still at the Hardy home but will be wrapping up soon. Oh, and just so you know, young Sam Hardy agreed to a DNA swab. I also confirmed his whereabouts on the days Heidi and Amber were killed."

"Did you take a sample from him?" Kate asked.

"I did have a kit, so yes. Now we have two of the four."

"What about Sam's alibi? You on board with it?" When the line went quiet, Kate pressed on. "Lieutenant?"

"I'm still working on that, Agent Reid. You'd better get back at it if you hope to be done before day's end."

"Thank you, Lieutenant." She returned her phone to her pocket.

Surrey looked at the map again. "Your hunch strikes again, Reid. We need to keep going. If our unsub travels this trail, then we'll find signs of him." He returned to his ATV. "Let's keep moving."

Kate mounted her vehicle, turning the key to start it up again. She rolled ahead at a slow speed so as not to miss any clues along the way. Any signs of life would help, but right now, there were none.

A trail this deep into the woods appeared to have been made for one purpose. It wasn't a designated trail, meaning the general public wouldn't have used it. No, this was created in a matter of days probably by nothing more than a scraper on the back of an ATV to clear the path.

Several minutes went by when Kate stopped again. When Surrey stopped beside her, she pointed ahead. "What's that, up there?"

He raised his hand to shield his eyes. "More woods."

"No, look...there's a..." She expressed an audible gasp and looked at him. "It's the clearing. You see it? We were right."

"I see it." He eyed her. " And *you* were right."

IRVING PREPARED to leave but stopped and eyed Sam once again. "I thank you for helping us out today, I really do. But could I ask you one more thing, son?"

Sam glanced at his mother, and she nodded her approval. "Sure."

"Would you like to press charges for those marks on your face?" Irving continued.

Carol launched from her chair. "That's enough, Howard. You are way out of line now."

Irving wouldn't look at her and kept his sights on Sam. "You're an adult. You have the right to make your own decisions, son." He watched the young man reel with confusion and realized he may have pushed too far.

"He liked her," Sam whispered.

Irving leaned in. "I'm sorry? Who liked who, now?"

Sam glanced at his mom and looked back at Irving. "I saw him talking to Emma about how she was pretty, and she could come to him with anything she needed—"

"What?" Carol asked.

Irving drew back in surprise. "Your dad? Was this your dad who said these things to Emma?"

"Yes, sir. On the day she died. She came in to get her paycheck. I was sweeping the floor and I heard them talking."

Irving regarded Carol. "Do you know what he's talking about?"

No, of course not. I'm sure Sam must've misunderstood what transpired. That doesn't sound like Randall. I'm sorry, Howard, but that doesn't sound like him at all."

"You know what, Sam?" Irving began. "I want you to think about all this real hard, okay? Think about what you saw. Then tomorrow morning, I'll come pick you up and we'll grab some breakfast. Would that work for you, son?" Irving nodded to Carol. "Thank you for your time, Mrs. Hardy."

Anger heated her round face. "You don't believe he's right about this, do you, Howard?"

"I got three dead girls in my town. I don't want any more blood on my hands." Irving was walking outside when his phone rang. "Impeccable timing, Agent Reid. I'm just leaving the Hardy's home now."

"Did you get what you wanted?" Kate asked.

"Well, out of the blue, Sam mentioned something about how his father essentially hit on Emma and that he had been witness to it. Mrs. Hardy jumped to his defense, for obvious reasons. After that, I figured it was best to get Sam alone. I'm going to see him first thing in the morning. I'll know more then, but as I said before, I got your sample."

"I know I've been focused on the kids in the photo, but all things considered," Kate continued. "Randall Hardy is not an innocent man. He still has a connection to Heidi Sumner. I'm not sure it leads us to murder, but I do believe he has played a part. Agent Walsh mentioned the store's employees believed something was happening between those too as well."

"Yes, ma'am, that is a fact. One I have not forgotten. How are you two faring out there on the trail?"

"We found it, Lieutenant. That was the reason for the call. The trail that passes by the Voss farm leads to the clearing."

"Well, hell." He opened his patrol car door and slipped inside. "You there now?"

"We are," she replied.

"I'm on my way."

RANDALL HARDY NOTICED his son's return and approached him near the cashier's counter. "Decided to come back, did you? You were with Lieutenant Irving all this time?"

"Yes, sir. He had a lot of questions."

"And what did you say to him, son?"

Sam raised a shoulder. "I don't know."

"You don't know." Randall nodded. "Did he ask you about Emma and the others again?"

"Yes, sir, and I told him the truth. I said I didn't know anything and that's the truth," Sam replied. "I really don't think I helped him very much. He asked me to let him put a cotton swab in my mouth, so I did. He promised it would help him find whoever killed Emma."

Randall tilted his head. "You gave him a DNA sample?"

"That's what he called it."

15

The stately architecture of the university lent itself to the notion of serious learning. However, Levi Walsh recalled his days back at college, and at the University of Alabama, he rarely took his studies seriously.

Today, though, he was here to speak to Emma Katz's roommate, who, as luck would have it, was taking a summer class and had remained on campus. Good thing because the girl lived in Washington State.

He was scheduled to meet with her in the common area of her dormitory. Walsh parked in front of the tall building and headed inside where a front desk remained empty. "Hello?" He craned his neck to see behind it but found no one. "Hello? Is anyone here?"

"It's summer session. They only have a part-timer working the desk."

Walsh spun around and saw a young woman. Shoulder-length wavy blond hair. Brown eyes and freckles across her nose and cheeks. "Oh, okay. Maybe you can help me. I'm looking for Lauren

Marsden." He retrieved his credentials. "I'm FBI Agent Levi Walsh."

"Hello, Agent Walsh." The girl offered her hand. "I'm Lauren. I saw you park outside and you kind of looked like FBI, so I came downstairs."

He smoothed down his Oxford shirt. "I'll have to work on my appearance. It's nice to meet you and I'm sorry to have to come under these circumstances."

"Me, too," Lauren replied. "Emma was my friend. I can't believe what happened to her." She turned around. "Follow me. We can talk in the common room. No one's in there right now."

Walsh trailed her to a large open area with plush sofas, a couple of foosball tables, and a flat-screen television on the wall. "This is nicer than anything I remember having at my school."

She turned back to him. "Where did you go?"

"Bama."

Lauren smiled. "Nice. And now you're an FBI agent. Did you study Criminal Justice?"

"No, actually, I didn't. I was in ROTC and then went straight to into the Army after that. Intelligence, mostly."

She sat down on one of the sofas. "Makes sense. So, I did speak to Emma's parents. They told me the funeral service wasn't scheduled yet. How come?"

Walsh sat down across from her. "Unfortunately, because of the nature of her death, the investigation takes precedence, and burial can't happen until all the forensics testing is completed."

"Oh, I see. How can I help you then, Agent Walsh? If all this happened to Emma back home, how does it involve the school?"

Walsh leaned over with his elbows on his thighs. "Do you know if Emma was seeing anyone?"

"Well, a lot of boys liked her. Emma was pretty and smart. Everyone loved her." Lauren looked away and wiped her eyes.

"She'd dated this one guy, but it didn't last long. I think it was over by Spring Break."

"Do you know who broke it off?" Walsh continued.

"Emma did. But it seemed like the guy was cool about it. I mean, I saw them talking a few times weeks later. You know, like it was no big deal. I'm pretty sure she was single when she went back home at the start of summer." Lauren wore a pained expression. "That doesn't help you at all, does it?"

Walsh looked up as if considering the question. "Do you recall hearing Emma speak to anyone on the phone? Like this ex-boyfriend, or other friends."

"You mean did she talk on the phone? Of course she did."

"What I'm asking is do you recall overhearing any unusual conversations with friends, family, anything like that."

"No, I don't. Emma and I had different class schedules. We were hardly in the dorm together. I mean, don't you have the ability to like, check her phone records or something?"

"We have and she had spoken to her friends at home as well as family. But unfortunately, the contents of those conversations with the friends, we don't know because they're dead too."

Her lips parted as shock masked her face. "Oh, my God. I had no idea. What is happening there?"

"If I knew, Lauren, I wouldn't be here," he replied. "What else can you tell me about Emma?"

Lauren turned down her gaze. "She didn't have a mean bone in her body. She got along with everyone. I don't know what else I can say about her." She peered at Walsh again with reddened eyes. "Emma smoked weed, like most everyone on campus, drank a little bit, but you know, she kept up on her studies. She was a lot like me, I guess."

He cocked his head. "I don't suppose Emma ever mention someone named Brian?"

Lauren shrugged. "Sure. He was her boyfriend back in high school. Why?"

"Did you ever meet him? I mean, did he visit her here?" Walsh continued.

"Not that I'm aware of. Emma and I talked sometimes. She mentioned Brian. Mentioned Jason."

"Jason Gatwick?"

She nodded. "That's the one. I think they traded messages and stuff, but it wasn't like, you know, any big deal, or whatever. It was just a sort of mentioned in passing."

"And Emma never said anything about a creep hanging around or getting weird text messages?" he asked.

"Not that she ever mentioned," Lauren replied. "Do you think someone was stalking her?"

"Honestly, it's not likely, given what we currently know about the case, but I have to ask." Walsh got to his feet. "Thank you for your time, Lauren."

"Of course, yeah." She choked back her emotions as she joined him. "I'm sorry she's gone. Everyone around here will be too."

"I'm sure they will. I appreciate your time, Lauren."

THE HIKE along the rugged trail combined with the rising heat of the day made the wait for Irving near the clearing barely tolerable. But when Kate's attention was drawn ahead, it seemed their wait was about to end.

"Looks like Irving's finally here," she said.

Surrey glanced in the same direction. "Good. We're burning daylight."

Irving climbed the slope toward them. "How goes it?"

"Could be better, but thanks for meeting us here. I noticed your team was gone," Surrey replied.

"They finished up a while ago. They'll have their hands full cross-referencing tire tracks, but fingers crossed, we'll get a hit. And I have people taking a look at Amber's car. There's blue paint on the rear bumper. Could help us establish a make and model."

"If we get that far, we'll be almost over the finish line," Kate replied.

"What happened at the Hardy home?" Surrey asked. "Any idea how the father ties into this, besides knowing he was hanging around Heidi before she was killed?"

"We now know, according to Sam, that Randall Hardy hit on Emma the day she was killed. And we know he was probably the last person to have seen Heidi alive."

"Two out of the three," Kate replied. "Is there a reason the man isn't already in cuffs?"

"Agent Reid, you asked me to gather DNA samples. I've done that. You asked me to speak to the Hardy family. I've done that too. Now, I appreciate all you've done for me here, but this is still my investigation, as you've reminded me. So, when I feel I have what I need to make an arrest, be assured, I'll do so."

Surrey thrust his hands into the pockets of his dress pants and rocked back on his heels.

Kate noticed his reaction and knew she'd crossed the line—again. "I apologize, Lieutenant. I don't mean to overstep."

Irving swatted at the air. "Never mind that now. Are we ready to head down to see if that trail meets the river?"

"Yes, sir," Kate replied.

"Then I'll make my way back with y'all and have a talk with Bruce on his own. Then his boy," Irving said.

Kate's phone rang in her pocket, and she retrieved it. "Levi, hey. How'd it go at the college?" She stepped away a moment.

"Not as well as I'd hoped. Except that I did learn something," he replied.

"I'm listening."

"Emma Katz had been messaging her ex-boyfriend in Jansville."

"Brian," she replied.

"No, Jason Gatwick. She'd had a boyfriend here at school, but they'd broken up in the spring. And her roommate says Emma mentioned Brian a few times, but it hadn't seemed like they stayed in touch."

"But no mention of anything else?" she asked.

"Afraid not, so it wasn't a very fruitful trip, except to say it's safe to rule out someone at school followed her home and went on a killing spree on her friends," Walsh replied. "And let's not forget the intimate knowledge our unsub has about the town."

"Which reinforces the idea the killer isn't someone from school," Kate said. "In my opinion, Keller's alibi is on shaky grounds. The kid says he lost his phone, so the police here have had no way to confirm his whereabouts, although his parents saw him later in the day. The exact timing isn't clear."

"Convenient," Walsh replied.

"Isn't it?" Kate sighed. "I'd hoped to gain some clarity here, but it just puts us right back in this circle of her friends that we're struggling to break free from."

Walsh grunted. "If that's where you keep landing, then you might ought to take a closer look."

16

The sound of running water captured Kate's attention. She stopped the ATV and looked back at Surrey, who'd taken Irving along for the ride. "I hear water nearby."

Surrey pulled up beside her and checked his phone before turning back to Irving. "Are we in the right place?"

Irving climbed down off the vehicle. "Yes, sir. This is it." He surveyed the area. "It's over there, to the right. Come on. I'll show you where she was found."

Kate hopped off the ATV and joined them. "It's looking more and more like this trail is the key. It leads to the clearing and now here, to the river."

"We didn't see any evidence along the way," Surrey added.

"No, but we can't ignore how easy it would be for the unsub to travel along this route," Kate replied. "We could get drones to assist in the search for evidence." She turned out toward the sound of the water. "Something is happening in these woods."

"I have to agree with Agent Reid. Follow me." Irving walked

on. "The fisherman who found Heidi was standing just over here. And downstream, the body was heading his way."

"The body came from farther downstream?" Kate asked. "This trail leads upstream. The unsub would've had to continue down that way for what, a quarter mile, and then dump the body so it would travel here. We initially thought the body was moved from the park, thinking the murders were in the same location. Given the size of the tributary near the park, there was only a small chance that could've happened. But to go beyond this spot here, and make it appear the body headed in the opposite direction, what's the point in that?"

"You have to hand it to the killer. He's not making it easy to track," Surrey replied.

"I guess the point is," Kate continued. "It appears the killer is using the trail as a way to move around town unseen." She turned in the opposite direction. "And I'll guarantee that if we went back to the Voss farm and headed along the trail in the opposite direction, we'd come across Town Park, where Emma Katz died."

"If we're to assume this trail is key, what's our next move to home in on our unsub?" Surrey asked. "Drones could work, provided the unsub doesn't see or hear them. What other approach do we have?"

Kate considered Surrey's question. He always prodded her. Forced her to look deeper for answers. And he wouldn't back down. The option to lean on him, at least in these terms, wasn't an option at all. He made her rely on her gut instincts, even when she didn't always believe her gut was right.

"We're dealing with an unsub who knows the town well, as we've discussed," she began. "Who may be using what had been barely a path and turned it into a trail."

Surrey folded his arms. "I can see the wheels turning. You have a theory?"

"One we have considered, but in light of the speed our unsub has set to accomplish his goals, it has fallen by the wayside. And it's time to revisit it." Kate's gaze shifted between Surrey and Irving. "We haven't put much thought into what the history teacher talked about. The 1835 murders. I'm wondering if that's what's missing here."

"Care to elaborate, Agent Reid?" Irving asked.

"At the very least, it could have provided inspiration. Because here's the thing, I've been looking for a reason the killer would've severed his victims' tongues. What if there isn't one? He wanted them dead for a reason, certainly, but maybe this unsub is someone who admired the man who committed those murders and chose to emulate him. It wouldn't be the first time a copycat killer surfaced."

Surrey regarded her. "It's a valid point. But what about the cow's tongue? Why go through the trouble? And are you now suggesting there is no secret the unsub wanted to keep? No message to deliver to the other friends in this group?"

"Let's consider this," she continued. "What if the so-called message was to point us to Hardy's likely affair with Heidi Sumner? Set our sights on Randall Hardy and away from anyone else?"

"It's not enough," Surrey replied. "There must be a reason this killer has chosen these kids."

Irving peered out over the river. "Look, here, we can debate this later because right now, I don't give two shits about a motive, Agent Reid. You point me to the person who's doing these things. That's all I care about."

Kate's chest tightened with growing frustration. "Lieutenant, in this instance, motive is the only thing that matters. And the only thing that will lead us to the killer."

IRVING STOOD outside the Voss farmhouse with Bruce while the federal agents drove down the gravel driveway and disappeared beyond the corner. He turned his attention to the man. "I appreciate your willingness to talk, Mr. Voss."

"Didn't think I had a choice. Come on in. I don't know if the agents mentioned this, but my wife and son are heading out soon. I don't want them here. Not until this is over."

"I understand." Irving followed him inside. "I'll try not to keep you from your family."

Bruce continued into the kitchen. "Might as well take a seat. Can I get you a glass of water? Must've been damn hot out there today."

"Appreciate it, sir. Thank you." Irving sat down at the table. When Bruce returned, he accepted the glass and took a long drink. "Much better, thank you."

"So what is it you want to ask me, Howard?" Bruce sat down across from him. "I already lost a cow today. My boy thinks he saw someone just outside our property. Could have lost him then, come to think of it. Just like poor Dave and Sharon, and all the other parents in this town mourning the loss of their child."

Irving removed his hat and set it on the table. "I know a thing or two about that, Mr. Voss."

"You do?"

He looked at Bruce. "It's a long story that I don't feel much like talking about right now, but know that my only purpose on this planet is to find the son of a bitch who's killing our young people. It starts with you telling me where you were when those girls were killed."

Bruce inhaled a deep breath and heard Anson walk into the

kitchen. He turned to him. "Not right now, son. I'm busy with Lieutenant Irving."

"Yes, sir." Anson set his gaze on Irving. "One thing I forgot to tell those FBI people was that our dog went missing that same day I thought I saw someone on the other side of the fence."

"He did? Well, I'm sorry to hear that," Irving replied.

"Oh, we found him again. Poor boy was covered in muck and blood."

Bruce turned to Irving. "He'd been gone a day or two. Figured he got into a tussle with a squirrel or raccoon or something. We washed him up and he seemed fine. Wasn't injured at all."

Irving nodded. "Where you end up finding your dog, son?"

"In the woods, along one of the trails. Came out of nowhere. Me and my dad, we looked everywhere for him. And then there he was."

After discussing with the agents how the killer may be traveling unchecked through town by way of a makeshift trail, it occurred to Irving this dog could have come upon something far more sinister than a squirrel or raccoon. He eyed the boy. "He had blood on him, huh? You think you could show me where you found him?"

Anson looked at his father, who nodded his approval. "Yes, sir. Course I can."

Brian Keller had, so far, been difficult to track down. They needed him to offer a sample, so while Irving talked to the Voss family, Kate and Surrey arrived at the Keller home.

"No one's talked to this kid since Amber Hoffman was found." Kate knocked on the door. "He already thinks the town's after him, so I don't know how willing he'll be to submit a swab."

"If he wants to prove his innocence and offer an alibi for last night when Hoffman was killed, he'll talk," Surrey replied.

A moment later, Mrs. Keller opened her door.

Kate displayed her credentials. "Afternoon, Mrs. Keller. I'm FBI Agent Kate Reid. This is my partner, Agent Jonathan Surrey. We're here to speak with your son, Brian."

She eyed them for several moments before opening the door. "Fine. Go see what he has to say for himself."

Kate walked inside and returned a surprised look at Surrey. It seemed an odd response for a mother about her son. She turned to the woman. "Mrs. Keller, was your son here with you last night?"

"I don't know," she replied.

Kate furrowed her brow. "You don't know?"

"He comes and goes as he pleases."

"With everything happening around here, Lieutenant Irving has implemented a curfew of eleven o'clock," Kate added. "Can you at least tell me if he was home by that time last night?"

"You'll have to ask him yourself, ma'am," Mrs. Keller continued. "Like I said, we don't pay much mind as to what he does."

"Would you call him out here to speak with us?" Surrey asked.

She sighed and turned on her heel, disappearing into the corridor.

"Okay, that was strange," Kate whispered.

"When Brian came in to make a statement about Emma," Surrey began. "He told Irving his parents didn't believe him. Seems to me, they still don't." He glanced into the hall. "Here he comes now. Given this situation, we should probably speak to the kid outside."

"Good call," Kate replied.

Brian approached them. "What's going on? Who are you guys?"

Kate glanced into the living room and noticed the mother standing nearby. "Why don't we speak outside?"

"Okay." Brian walked outside and stood with his back against the porch railing. When the agents joined him, he continued, "So, what's this about?"

"Brian, we're with the FBI," Kate replied. "We're here to help Lieutenant Irving. I'd like to ask, when was the last time you spoke to Amber Hoffman?"

Brian shoved his hands in his pockets and shrugged. "Last night."

Kate drew back her shoulders. "You spoke to her last night? In person?"

"Yeah."

"So you saw her before she was murdered?" Surrey asked.

Brian's face heated and his eyes reddened. "Yeah, I did, okay? I was the last person to see her alive, just like Emma, all right? So, clearly, I must've killed her, too." His eyes filled with tears.

Surrey held up his hands. "That's not what's being said right now, Mr. Keller."

"Really? Sure sounds like it."

"Okay, I think we're getting off on the wrong foot, here," Kate began. "How about you start by telling us where and when you saw Amber."

Brian wiped away the tears with the back of his hand. "Look, all of us are freaking out, okay? My friends are being picked off, one by one. You see that, right? So I asked Amber to meet me. To talk about all this craziness."

"And where was that? What time?" Surrey pressed on.

"I don't know. It was just getting dark, so maybe eight o'clock or so. I wasn't interested in the time."

"Where?" Surrey asked again.

"We met in the parking lot of a trailhead."

"Near the clearing?" Kate asked.

Brian narrowed his gaze. "How do you know about that place?"

Kate looked toward the driveway. "Where's your car, Brian?"

"Uh, it's in the garage. Why?"

"Show us." Kate stepped off the front porch. "Now."

"Okay, I just need to get my keys." Brian returned inside.

Kate hurried along the path to the driveway and stood with Surrey at her side as the garage door raised.

Brian was behind the door and came into view as it rolled up, and so had the car. "Here. It's right here. You can look if you want. I'm telling you, I didn't do what you think I did. Amber was my friend. One of the only ones I had left."

Kate's shoulders sank. 'It's not blue."

Surrey walked into the garage and walked toward the front of the vehicle. "It's not blue and there's no damage."

Brian meandered toward her. "Am I in trouble for driving my car, ma'am?"

She returned her attention to Brian. "Why didn't you come forward after you'd heard about the crash that you'd seen Amber shortly before it happened?"

"I was scared." He cast down his gaze. "Everyone already thinks I killed Emma. When I left the parking lot, I made sure Amber was inside her car and had turned on the engine. I thought she was safe after that, ma'am. I swear it."

"Mr. Keller, I'd like nothing more than to be certain you had nothing to do with any of this, so I'm going to ask you to let us take a DNA swab. Do you know what that is?" Kate asked.

Brian's chin quivered. "It's so you could see if I killed my friends. If my DNA was on them or whatever."

"That's right. Will you agree to it?" Kate waited for his answer.

"If you want everyone in this town to know you're innocent, as you say, this is how you do that."

"Well, do I, like, need a lawyer or something?" Brian asked.

"If you feel you need one," Surrey cut in.

Kate fixed her eyes on him. He was scared. The young man's hands trembled. "Brian, I'm very sorry all of this has happened. I honestly don't know what you're going through right now. If it makes you feel any better, you're not the only one we've asked to do this, okay? Others knew and were around Emma and the other girls, same as you. So, will you agree to a swab so we can work to clear your name?"

Tears streamed down his cheeks now as he looked away. "Fine. Whatever I got to do to make people understand that I loved Emma. That the other girls were my friends too. And I would never do anything to hurt anyone."

"Thank you." She nodded to Surrey, who stepped back to the SUV to retrieve a kit. "Was it just you and Amber at the clearing last night?"

"Yes, ma'am. Like I said. I talked to her because I was scared. I know she was too."

"Did anyone else know you were there? Anyone at all?" Kate pressed on.

Brian turned away as if thinking about the question. "No. I-I didn't tell anyone. I don't know if Amber did."

"Excuse me a moment." She walked toward Surrey while he retrieved the kit. "All these kids are willingly submitting a sample."

He eyed her a moment. "Just about. We're not quite finished yet, but yeah, kind of makes it hard to think they'd do that unless they were innocent."

BRUCE VOSS PULLED alongside the shoulder of the road and parked. Behind him, Lieutenant Irving arrived in his patrol car and stepped out to meet Bruce and his son on the slight embankment that led to the trees.

"This is the spot?" Irving asked as he set his sights on the woods.

"Yes, sir," Anson replied. "Me and Dad had started down that way—"

"Where there's parking off that gravel turnaround," Bruce added.

"Okay," Irving turned back to Anson. "And you reached here, then what happened?"

"We'd been looking for him for a couple of hours and Dad kept telling me we'd find him, but I started thinking we wouldn't." Anson walked ahead into the trees. "Then we got near here, where that trail is right there."

"I see it," Irving said.

"And we just kept walking till I heard footsteps. Next thing you know, there he was. Only he looked awful. I thought he was hurt, but his tail was wagging—"

"The dog was fine," Bruce cut in. "Like I said, I thought he'd just gotten into a fight with a raccoon or something. But he wasn't hurt. Just dirty and had some red on him. He was plenty scared and hungry too."

"So I called him and he came running like it was nothing," Anson continued.

Irving set his hands on his hips. "He got out of your property the evening you went to the coops, and you hadn't seen him since?"

"No, sir. Me and Dad searched our property everywhere the first day, then on the second day I begged him to come search down through here."

"What made you think he'd come here?" Irving asked.

"Nothing, really, except he's real smart. He knows where to find water and I know that stream comes through here, so we sorta walked in the direction of that stream," Anson replied.

Irving entered the woods. "You say there's a stream around here?"

Bruce pointed toward his right. "Just down that way. I don't know if that's where the dog came from, but it's possible."

"I'll tell you what," Irving began. "You two go on back home. I'm going to check things out here and just see what's what."

"What are you expecting to find, Howard?" Bruce asked.

"I'm not really sure, but something tells me this is worth my time."

"All right. Me and the boy will head on out."

"I thank you for your time, Mr. Voss. And again, I'm sorry about what happened to your cattle. Is there anywhere you can keep the rest till all this is over?"

"I think I got a place. Guess I have to send everyone and everything I love away from this town." He eyed Irving again. "I hope you find the son of a bitch soon, Howard."

"You and me both." Irving pushed on deeper into the woods, toward where the Voss' believed lay the stream. He didn't know what he might find, except Agent Reid made a connection he hadn't considered. So if the killer was traveling through here, maybe he was camping out in here too. With few options, and a dog who returned to its owner covered in blood, this seemed the best strategy.

He traversed through the dense woods, climbing over fallen limbs, avoiding boulders, and taking care not to slip on the thick cover of dead leaves that lay on the forest floor. He wasn't much of an outdoorsman and preferred a weekend filled with football, or baseball, depending on the season. But now he faced a situation the likes he'd never seen. To say he felt underqualified would be putting it mildly. Even back in Asheville, what homicides he worked on were nothing like this. This town deserved better, and he would have to do better.

Irving walked into what became a valley, of sorts. The somewhat steep hillside led down to a flatter bottom that had probably once been a river thousands of years ago. Now, it was covered in greenery and wildflowers.

He kept on toward the sound of a stream when the stench hit him. His face screwed up as he covered his nose and mouth with his hand. "Dear Lord." Ahead, several more yards, was where he came upon the source of the rancid odor. A stony expression masked his face. Half-eaten animals lay on the ground and hung in the trees. Blood stained the earth. Crows pecked at carcasses, pulling at whatever meat and skin remained.

Irving reached for his phone. "Agent Reid, I think you and Agent Surrey need to get down here."

"Where are you?" Kate asked.

"I'm in the woods." He looked around. "Not exactly sure where, but I'll send you a pin. Best get down here just as quick as you can."

"What did you find, Lieutenant?"

He peered out over the scene. "A horror show, Agent Reid. A damn horror show."

THE FORD's high beams shone along the dusky stretch of road that wove in and out of the trees. "How close are we?" Kate asked.

Surrey checked the map on his phone. "A little less than a quarter mile. It'll be on the left. Hang on. I see a car...yeah. Over there. Pull in over there. That's Irving's unit."

Kate checked her sideview mirror before crossing the lane. As she reached the shoulder, she stopped behind the lieutenant's car and grabbed her phone. "Lieutenant, we just arrived. You want to meet us at your car?"

"Be there in a minute."

She ended the call. "I don't see any other units. I'm not sure what he's waiting for."

"It's his case and his call." Surrey stepped out of the car and lost his footing for a moment on the embankment. He looked back at Kate as she walked toward the ridgeline. "Careful. It's slippery."

"Got it." She made her way to the bottom, and both waited for Irving. Kate focused her sights ahead. "I think that's him heading our way." Irving soon reached them and the look on his face was one Kate had seen too many times before. "How bad is it?"

He shook his head. "Ma'am, I don't know the kind of things you must see every day in your job, but this? I never seen anything like this in my entire life."

"Better show us, then." The rundown shack in Texas jumped to mind as Kate recalled the photos of the women on the walls. The room that came to be known as the "kill room." Yeah, she'd seen plenty.

As Irving started ahead, he continued, "I got to talking to the Voss' and the boy, Anson, he's about 16, he mentioned their dog got loose on the day he thought he saw someone near their property. Anyway, father and son came out looking, found the dog right around here. Poor thing was covered in mud and blood."

"Blood?" Kate asked.

"Yes, ma'am. Father chalked it up to a fight with a squirrel or some such thing. But I had an itch and figured I'd scratch it, so I came out to see for myself."

Kate recoiled as she slowed her steps. "What is that smell?"

"You're about to find out." Irving soon reached the area in the valley. "What the hell you two make of this?"

She used the crook of her arm to cover her nose. "It's him. It's our killer. How close are we to the locations where the murders happened?"

Irving appeared to gather his bearings. "About a mile from where Heidi was found. The clearing's up that way, I'd say about two miles." He turned around. "And down there is the Voss farm. So, it puts us smack dab in the middle of this monster's territory."

Kate took in the grisly scene while the stench seemed to soak into her skin, hair, and clothes in the same way campfire smoke clung to everything. "This isn't where Heidi was killed."

"How can you be so sure?" Surrey asked.

"She was leaving the convenience store through the rear exit, where she parked her car," Kate continued. "No obvious trail of blood or spatters was found in the vicinity, which suggests he took her somewhere else, leaving behind her car."

"Which is what we've been operating off of," Surrey replied.

"Yes, but he didn't bring her here. I had believed there was some sort of killing grounds where the murders took place. The idea Heidi had been killed where Emma was attacked seemed viable, given the proximity of the tributary. But after what happened with Amber, that theory no longer stands."

"All right." Irving regarded her. "If this place isn't where he takes his victims, which I reckon I understand your thought process on that, then what is it?"

She crinkled her nose as the putrid odor of carrion penetrated her senses again. "This is his refuge. A place to act out his aggression, where he expected no one to ever find." Kate took measured steps until she reached several dead cats tied to a rope by their legs and hung from a branch. "He kept most of the carcasses off the ground, but not before any number of animals caught the scent and came here for a few meals. These cats," she continued. "Their tongues have been severed." She aimed her index finger at the remains. "You see here?"

"I see it," Irving said. "So he comes here because of a growing appetite for killing?"

Kate looked to her partner for consensus. But he refused to display agreement, disagreement, or anything in between. Instead, his eyes revealed a trust in her ability to read this killer. And so, she turned back to Irving. "He comes here—for practice."

17

The lieutenant's plan was to bring in spotlights, teams of CSI, and officers to search the grounds for evidence that could reveal the killer's identity. However, Kate pushed back on the idea.

They returned to their vehicles to breathe air that wasn't laced with death and decay. And under a clear moonlit sky, Irving made his displeasure known by pacing the gravel shoulder and shaking his head.

Kate leaned against her Ford and looked on. "He's not happy about this."

"Oh, he's making that abundantly clear," Surrey replied.

She heard Irving grumbling under his breath. "He must see that this is an opportunity."

"He does see that, just not in the same way you do." Surrey ambled toward her. "He sees that the unsub left behind evidence and that if it was identified, it could put an end to this nightmare."

"While I agree that's possible, the better scenario is to stake out the area until he returns, which he will do. I promise you, he will," Kate said. "If we set up spotlights and have the side of the road teeming with cars and the entire forest lit up, what do you think the odds are he'll return?"

"Not good. I don't disagree with you, Reid. But again, we're here to help him, not order him to do what we want." Surrey peered down the darkened road. "And the possibility exists that the unsub has already seen us. So, it's a toss-up as far as I'm concerned."

"Lieutenant?" Kate called out as she approached him.

Irving stopped and turned to face her. "Yes?"

"I see your point, and my partner has reminded me that this is your case. I have no right to insist on anything. I'm here to help you identify the killer. We've come a long way toward that goal. Maybe this is the final leg." She focused on the woods. "To get back in there and uncover whatever he might've left behind. I can't say you won't find anything. That place was his secret, and to the best of our knowledge, he believes it remains a secret."

Irving set his hands on his hips. "Thank you, Agent Reid. Please don't think I'm not grateful to you and your team. If you hadn't uncovered the likelihood this killer was traveling back and forth through these woods, I wouldn't have considered asking the Voss boy where they'd found their lost dog. You've done an awful lot for me here, but I do believe we've reached the end of the road. I prefer to finish this with my own people and the help of the county's CSI." He fixed his gaze on her. "You've done all you could do, ma'am."

"Okay. Well, good luck to you, Lieutenant. I have no doubt you'll see this to its rightful end." Kate headed back to her SUV and unlocked the door.

Surrey caught up to her. "Where are we going?"

She raised her brow and smiled. "Home. Our services are no longer required."

His lips parted as surprise masked his face. "Are you serious?"

"Oh yeah." Kate stepped inside and buckled her belt while waiting for Surrey to get in and close his door. She turned the engine. "Irving says he prefers to use his own people to finish this out. And that we'd done everything we could do."

Surrey appeared stunned as he buckled his seatbelt. "We've been kicked off the case?"

Kate checked her sideview mirror and pulled off the shoulder onto the road ahead. They drove by Irving as she stood at his patrol car. "First time that's ever happened. I've worked with local detectives who hadn't wanted me there, but to be dismissed, well, I guess there's a first time for everything."

"Give him some time to come around," Surrey began. "We both know he's in way over his head."

"I don't think he'll change his mind," Kate replied.

"It's late anyway. We have the hotel. Let's stay there tonight. Irving can set up his search in the woods. If he finds something, great. But if he doesn't, he'll come knocking, I promise you. And we still need to process the DNA swabs."

"Irving sent two of them to the county," Kate added. "He'll be lucky to get them back inside of three days."

"Well, there you go."

She glanced at him. "What do you mean?"

"Right there proves the man is in too deep. We volunteered our lab to expedite things. He went another route."

"Just like how he hasn't brought in Randall Hardy for questioning." Kate felt her gut tighten. "That man was the last person to see Heidi Sumner, and he refuses to get a statement from him."

"Another example," Surrey continued. "There's the hotel. Do me a favor? You and I will keep working the case. We stay here tonight and see if anything breaks free tomorrow. Can we do that? I think you'll regret it if we don't."

Kate sighed. "I'm not trying to be stubborn—"

"I know that. You were right about that place he found. You've been right about everything so far, so, don't let down the people here."

Kate parked at the hotel and stepped out of her SUV, waiting for Surrey to close the passenger door before she locked it.

They walked along the sidewalk and reached the breezeway. Their rooms were next to each other, and Kate grabbed her key as they arrived.

Surrey stopped at his room and eyed Kate. "Get some sleep, Reid. You'll see this more clearly in the morning."

"I hope you're right. Goodnight." She walked into her room and slipped off her shoes. The hem of her dress pants looked like they'd been dipped in grime and her shoes wore a layer of dirt an inch thick. The day's hike had exhausted her. The practice grounds that had been discovered left her sickened. And the abrupt ending to her part in the investigation had been the proverbial icing on the cake.

Kate picked up her phone. "Hey, it's me. Are you busy?"

"Hi, uh, no. I just got home," Nick replied. "Where are you?"

"Still in Jansville. Jonathan and I are staying at a motel. We just wrapped up for the day." Kate dropped onto the bed and fell backward.

"You doing okay? I thought you'd be coming home tonight."

"I might be home tomorrow, if things go the way they did today."

"That's a good thing then, right?" he asked.

She rubbed her forehead and cracked a smile. "Depends on whether it would bother you if you got fired from a case."

"What? Kate, what happened?"

"It's been a struggle since I got here. The lieutenant didn't ask for help. It was a friend of Cam's who has some relative who lives here in town. So, from Day One, I've gotten relative pushback. Tonight, it came to a head. What we found, Nick...let's just say it was a warning of just how dangerous this unsub is."

"And the lieutenant thinks he has a handle on it. I've seen that before. So why didn't you just drive home?" Nick pressed on.

"Jonathan convinced me to wait until morning. He insists the lieutenant will see the error of his ways, I guess. We'll see."

"What about the rest of the team?"

"Levi's been a huge help. I haven't had much for Eva or Cam to run with. What we need are the DNA results on the rest of the victims and our persons of interest," Kate replied. "Then we can at least cross-reference them with what we already have."

"It does appear to be a big pill to swallow for this lieutenant," Nick added. "Sounds like he is in over his head."

"That's exactly what I said." A siren blared outside, and Kate shot up from the bed. "What the hell?"

"What's going on?" Nick asked. "Are you okay?"

She walked to the front window and pulled back the curtains. "I'm fine. It sounds like a fire alarm." A fist pounded on the adjacent door. "That's Surrey. He's next door. Hey, let me see what's going on here. I'll call you when I can." Kate ended the call and opened the adjoining door.

Surrey stood on the other side. "You hear that too, huh?"

"Kind of hard to miss. It's coming from Market Street, I think. I'll meet you out front." Kate closed the door again and pulled on her shoes. As she stepped outside, the sound grew louder. Surrey joined her. "I don't think it's coming from Market Street. It's really loud." She retrieved her keys and unlocked the car. "Let's check it out."

Kate reached the main road and drove back toward town. "I can still hear it. We must be getting closer."

"If that alarm is tied to the police department, we should see a unit heading that way soon," Surrey added. "With the town being practically deserted, it could be a break-in."

Kate peered through the windshield and noticed shadowy black smoke rising in the night air. "Oh no. Isn't that the library?"

"I think so." Surrey picked up his phone. "Irving must already know, but I'm going to call him anyway."

Kate pulled into the parking lot as flames pierced the roofline. Black smoke drifted into the night sky. "Oh my God. What if someone's inside?" She unbuckled her seatbelt and threw open the door.

"Reid, wait! No one's going to be..." He returned his attention to his phone. "Irving, it's Surrey. Reid and I are at the public library. Damn thing's on fire. The alarm..." He nodded. "Yeah. Okay good. Is there anything we can do? Do you think anyone could be inside?" Surrey stared into the parking lot. "No. I don't see any cars... Okay. Okay, we'll sit tight."

Kate aimed her sights at the approaching fire engine. "They're coming."

"We can hear the fire truck now," Surrey continued on the call. "Okay. See you in a minute." He dropped his phone into his pocket. "He's on his way."

Kate looked on. "I hope no one's inside."

"Not at this time of night and inside a library?" He looked on at the growing flames when he craned his neck to the left.

"What is it?" She gazed out in the same direction. "Do you see something?"

"Son of a bitch. Someone's running." He opened the car door and jumped out, taking to a sprint.

"Damn it." Kate hurried out of the driver's side and rushed to catch up to him. "I see him. Hey!" she called out. "FBI!" With her hand on the butt of her gun, Kate pumped her legs, but Surrey was taller and had a wider stride. He pulled out in front. "Hurry! Stop him!"

In the dark, it was impossible to see more than just the shadow of a figure running off in the distance. "Where the hell did he come from?" She fell back and slowed to a stop while Surrey pressed on.

The fire truck arrived and raced toward the building where Kate quickly returned. She rushed toward firefighter, Chris Pumphrey, who jumped out of the truck. Out of breath, she pointed ahead. "Someone just ran away from the building. My partner went after him. I have no idea if anyone is inside."

"Who are you?" he asked.

"FBI. You have to get in there."

Pumphrey gestured to Gatwick and another firefighter. "Gear up! We might have people inside. Let's go!"

Kate looked on while they hurried to douse the flames. Through the glass doors at the entrance, she saw the sprinklers raining down, but it seemed to have the effect of spit on a campfire. She jogged back toward the side of the building where Surrey chased after the runner, but he was nowhere in sight. "Where the hell are you?" Kate reached for her phone.

"Reid?"

Her attention was drawn ahead. "Oh, thank God. Are you okay?" She examined Surrey for injuries.

"I lost him. Whoever it was knew this area and knew exactly where to go." His breath was labored and sweat dripped from his forehead.

"Do you have any idea who that was?" Kate asked. "Did you get a look at him?"

With his hands on his hips, and catching his breath, Surrey lowered his gaze. "I couldn't see shit out there."

Kate set her sights on the burning building. "They're trying to get inside to see if anyone is trapped."

Surrey eyed the increasing flames. "If there is anyone, I doubt they're getting out of there alive."

THE LIGHTS from patrol cars and fire trucks lit up the sky almost as much as the flames that danced on the roof of the library. Kate was helpless to do anything.

Jason Gatwick stood near the truck and wrenched the hose. She watched him work. This was the same kid who'd found Emma Katz clinging to life. The same kid who offered aid at the scene of the Amber Hoffman crash.

She stood with Surrey, witnessing the ongoing efforts to contain the blaze when Lieutenant Irving made his way over.

He peered at her with awkward resignation.

The tension between them lingered a moment until Kate began, "What are the odds this was an accident?"

"The library?" He set his sights on the building. "Considering we requested those archived files on the past murders, they aren't great."

"When we arrived," Surrey interrupted, "We caught a glimpse of someone who seemed to be coming from the building. I chased after him through those woods there, but it was too dark. I lost him."

"Back through that way?" Irving thumbed behind him.

"Yes. I couldn't give you a description if I tried. He wore black, and that's all I know."

"Then it makes all the more sense this was arson, and the timing is suspect." Irving turned to Kate. "I owe you an apology, both of you.

This fire here could've been the result of getting that perimeter set up in the woods. A way to divert our resources so he could get back in there and clean house. We'd only just begun, but like you said, Agent Reid, he was likely to come back, and maybe he did." He watched the firemen. "Now this. Seems to me this was done to destroy any link we might find between the killer and the past murders, as well."

"We can't rule it out. And no apology necessary, Lieutenant. What can we do to help?" From the corner of her eye, Kate noticed a vehicle turning into the parking lot. "Who's that?"

Irving looked out. "It's Randall Hardy's truck. What the hell's he doing here?"

"We passed his store on the way," Surrey began. "And it was curfew. He must've closed up, headed out, and saw the flames."

Kate felt an opportunity had just presented itself in the form of Randall Hardy's arrival. But would Irving see it that way? "Lieutenant, there are things about that man that don't sit right with me. And I don't think they sit right with you. He was the last person, we believe, to have seen Heidi Sumner alive. He hit on Emma Katz. Please, may I speak to him? He's the one who came here. I'm not going after him."

Irving appeared resigned. "You know what, Agent Reid, I can admit when I'm outmatched. Evidently, not very quickly, but I do come around. I can also admit when I'm outmanned. I will say that I'm not convinced an affair would lead to multiple murders, but then again, I'd be a fool to disregard the possibility. You want to talk to him, be my guest."

"Thank you, Lieutenant." Kate carried on toward the truck before she stopped and turned back to Surrey. "Do you want to join me?"

Surrey jogged ahead. "Yeah."

Randall Hardy stepped out of his truck while his eyes fixed on the blaze. "What the hell happened here?"

The agents drew near when Kate continued, "That's what Lieutenant Irving is trying to find out. What are you doing here, Mr. Hardy?"

"I closed up and started home. I heard the alarm, of course. Had no idea it was this place." He focused on her. "Is everyone okay?"

"They're trying to get inside. I don't know the status." She studied him as he looked on. The bright flames reflected in his eyes while beads of sweat arose on his forehead. And as she let her eyes rake over this man, something else came into focus.

Kate nudged Surrey to capture his attention. When he looked at her, she eyed Hardy's right arm and pointed at her wrist. It seemed he noticed it too. A tan line from where a watch was worn. "Excuse us a moment, Mr. Hardy." She nodded for Surrey to follow her as they stepped several feet away. In a low tone, Kate continued, "He wears a watch."

"But he's not wearing one now," Surrey replied. "The watch found in Heidi's bedside table?"

"Could be." Kate fixed her gaze on the man, who continued to view the flames. "We're all but certain he was having an affair with Heidi, which serves as a pretty good motive for murder. And if Heidi told anyone?"

"That could be the secret."

They returned to Hardy, and Kate regarded him. "Mr. Hardy, would you be willing to come down to the station to talk to us and the lieutenant?"

"About what?"

"We've been wanting to speak to you about Heidi Sumner. You showed up on security footage from the convenience store. It was on the night she was killed."

He shot her a look. "I'm sorry, what's that now?"

Surrey stepped in. "We saw you on the store's security footage that night. You went inside and talked to Heidi for a while before eventually leaving without having bought a thing. Can you tell us why you were there?"

Randall returned an incredulous gaze. "Are you serious right now? This building is on fire and you're asking me about Heidi?"

"Yes, sir," Kate replied. "If you think this fire is unrelated to what's been going on in this town, then you're not as smart as I thought you were."

"I don't have to stand here and take this." Randall marched back to his truck.

"So we'll see you in the morning at the station?" Kate called out.

He stepped into his truck and slammed the door before rolling down the window. "If the lieutenant wants to see me, he can ask for me."

Kate turned on her heel and started back toward Irving. When she and Surrey reached him, she drew his attention. "Lieutenant?"

He turned away from Fire Chief Burrows. "Yes, ma'am?"

"You remember the watch we found in Heidi's apartment?"

"I do," Irving replied.

She fixed her gaze on him. "Randall Hardy appears to be missing his."

18

Walsh removed his reading glasses and rubbed his eyes as he sat in his office. It approached midnight, and he'd offered to scour the phone records for Heidi Sumner after a call from Kate to step in. And when a pattern developed, he knew he was onto something. "Almost every day. Either a text or a call over the past two months. Son of a bitch." Walsh picked up his phone. "Hey, are you still at the fire?"

"It's out. I'm just staring at a burned-out building now," Kate replied.

"I've been going through those calls, like you asked, and found something interesting. You have a minute to walk through it?"

"Absolutely."

"Randall Hardy's phone number shows up several times on Heidi's phone records. Calls, texts. Of course, I don't know the content of the messages, but the point is, he was in contact with your victim on a regular basis."

"Then it's starting to come into focus," Kate replied. "Thing is, Lieutenant Irving reached out to the Hardys just minutes ago and

Randall Hardy's wife gave him an alibi. She claimed he went straight home after he stopped at her store. But given we found a man's watch in Heidi's bedroom and then Hardy getting defensive, now this? It's not looking good for him."

"There's something else, isn't there?" Walsh asked. "I can tell you're holding back." He heard her sigh on the other end of the line. "What is it?"

"We've been running in several directions with this investigation," Kate began. "With these murders happening within days of each other, it's been beyond difficult to home in on a single theory as to the killer's motivation, and where he might go next. The fact we're only just now delving into Sumner's phone records shows you where we're at. But I suppose what gets me about one particular theory is that unless Sumner had threatened to expose the affair, why would he have killed her? And on top of that, we have the other two victims. Supposing she had made that threat and she had told her friends, could this really be motive enough?"

Walsh leaned back in his chair. "All right. Let's play this out. Sumner and the other young women were friends. Emma Katz had recently returned home from college. What's to say Heidi didn't confide in her friends about the affair? Randall Hardy appears to have standing in the community—"

"Is that really enough motive to murder all of them?" she pressed on. "This man has complete control over his family. He's an abuser. His wife, I'm guessing, wouldn't have left him had she learned about it. And his son, Sam, well, he's already scared to death of his dad."

Walsh rubbed his lined cheek. "It sounds to me like you don't believe your theory. This man was obviously having an affair with one of your victims, but I think you've answered your question."

"Maybe. We'll know more when our samples are processed. According to the lieutenant, Emma Katz's report was due today. I don't know if he's received it. But as far as Randall Hardy is concerned, I can't dismiss him yet. Thank you for scouring the call records. It confirms the affair and I'll let the lieutenant know. It's his call," Kate replied.

"Listen, you know I'm here for you," Walsh said. "You need anything else—"

"Be on the lookout for our DNA swabs. I only have two right now, but the last one I need is from a man who's here now. Irving sent a couple to the county and that could take days, so can you or Fisher try to pull some strings and rush the ones we have?"

"You got it."

"Thanks, Levi. Go home and get some sleep. I'll touch base in the morning."

"Goodnight, Kate. Stay safe."

THE SMOKE DISPERSED in the moonlight skies. While blue and red lights still swirled atop the emergency vehicles, the firefighters packed their gear. Water pooled on the dimpled asphalt parking lot. The glass doors of the building had been forced open. Black soot clung to every surface.

Kate leaned against her SUV and watched Chris Pumphrey with a close eye. As Gatwick's roommate, he'd had some interaction with Emma Katz and was also in the photo, though he'd been far off in the background. Regardless, he was the last to cross off the list. She caught sight of Surrey as he approached. "We should get with Pumphrey now, while we have the chance." She led the way to the fire truck and caught up with Gatwick. "Mr. Gatwick?"

He turned around. "Agent Reid. I hear you and Agent Surrey were the first on the scene."

"Not that we could've made a difference. Listen, would you

mind introducing us to your roommate? He might be more willing to talk if he knows we've spoken to you."

"Uh, yeah, sure. Follow me." Jason carried on toward Pumphrey. "Hey, man."

Pumphrey set down his helmet on the bumper of the fire truck. "What's up?"

"These guys are with the FBI. Agents Reid and Surrey. They've been going around talking to all of us who knew Emma and them."

"Oh, okay." Pumphrey set his sights on Kate. "What can I do for you? I've already spoken to Lieutenant Irving. I thought I'd answered all his questions."

"Recently?" She quickly sized him up. He appeared about five-feet-nine, maybe five-ten. Broad shoulders. Sturdy build. The soot in his hair made it appear almost black. He was slightly larger than what she'd profiled.

"Well, I talked to him after what happened to Emma. I was there when, you know..." he replied.

"But you haven't spoken to him since?" Surrey asked.

"No, sir. Should I have?"

"Mr. Pumphrey, my partner and I have been doing what we can to assist Lieutenant Irving," Kate said. "We've been speaking to Mr. Gatwick and others, who were friends with the young women. Those of you who are still alive." She gauged his reaction, but he appeared indifferent.

"Look, Agent Reid, I'm really sorry about the awful things that have happened here, but I have to tell you, I'm not really friends with those guys. I mean, I live with Jason, sure, but we don't hang out that much." He looked at his roommate. "Didn't you tell them?"

Jason nodded.

"I don't see how I can help you," Pumphrey added.

"Hold that thought a moment, would you?" Kate walked to her car and grabbed the photo. On her return, she held it out. "Are you in this picture, Mr. Pumphrey?"

He examined it. "Yes, ma'am. I'm the guy in the back."

"So you did hang out with them?" Surrey cut in.

"Well, yeah, I guess, but like I said, not often. That picture was probably only the second time I'd seen all them together."

"Dude, they're just trying to rule all of us out. They want a DNA swab from you. That's it," Jason said. "I did it. Brian did it. We're all trying to help, you know?"

He raised a shoulder. "I mean, I guess that's okay. I kind of feel like I should ask a lawyer or something first, though. Like, aren't my rights being violated here?"

"We aren't forcing you to do anything, Mr. Pumphrey," Kate replied. "We're just trying to find whoever killed three young women, who you were acquainted with."

He glanced back at Jason, who nodded. "Well, okay."

A DNA DRAGNET. That was what this investigation had amounted to, and it was a technique Kate never needed to employ before. Police everywhere conducted such sweeps to "rule out" possible suspects. But with so little information back from the coroner's office and the rapid pace at which the unsub had operated, what choice was there?

Nonetheless, Pumphrey cooperated, as had everyone else. So where did that leave them in the interim? Looking into the dubious connection between the killer today and the murders committed almost 200 years earlier in hopes that they might find a copycat.

Irving waved over the agents. "You folks wanted to get inside the library. Now's the time. We got the all-clear from the fire chief."

As Kate and Surrey reached the lieutenant, Kate began, "Did the town librarian suggest a place for us to look? I don't want to wander through the building when it may not be safe to do so."

"He said records would be located on the computers, but also paper versions would be in the fire-proof safes in storage. He's on his way now to let us in." Irving looked ahead. "In fact, I'll bet that's him now."

An older man stepped out of a small white pickup with the town's logo on the door. Tears streamed down his cheeks as he set his sights on the destruction.

Irving quickly approached him. "George?" He offered his hand. "Thanks for coming down."

The man absentmindedly returned a greeting, never taking his eyes off the scene. "Lieutenant, thank you for calling me. I just can't believe this. It's gone. Everything's gone."

"It will be rebuilt, sir, I promise you that," Irving replied. "Right now, we sure could use your help. You know all that's been going on, so I won't bother rehashing it for you. The point is, we need to find the records. Electronic, paper, I don't care how, but we need to find them. We're certain the library was targeted."

George cleared his throat and wiped the tears from his eyes. "Then follow me. I'll show you." He started onward to the entrance.

"George." Irving waited a moment for Surrey and Kate to catch up. "These folks are with the FBI."

He nodded. "Well, I guess it's good y'all are here. I'll show you what you're looking for."

Inside the library, soot covered the walls and ceiling. Books, papers, and files floated in the two inches of water on the carpeted floor. Chairs and tables were blackened, some overturned. The scent of burnt paper lingered.

George looked on in disbelief. "Dear Lord. How could this have happened?"

Without absolute certainty the fire was intentionally set, Kate held her tongue. But she knew—the rest of them knew—this was arson.

"Watch your step, now, George." Irving trailed him. "Just take us to the archives. We'll get through this."

"Yes, sir."

Surrey rubbed his nose with the back of his hand and coughed while he fell back a moment.

"You okay?" Kate stopped for him.

"Yeah. It's just the smoke."

She studied him. His demeanor. His composure. Even in the face of the destruction, the precipice of learning who might be behind all this, he remained entirely unmoved. "How do you do it?"

"Sorry?" he asked.

"Stay so damned detached from all of it. Like before, with what happened between Irving and me. Now, in here—"

"Because if I wasn't detached, I'd start questioning my job, just like you've been doing lately." He cocked his head. "Didn't think I picked up on that? I can see it all over your face, Reid. You know how many times I've seen it on other agents' faces? Plenty." He squared up to her. "You're wondering how much more you can handle. How many more monsters you have to slay. When the questions you should be pondering are, 'What can I do to create a system whereby these serial killers are more easily identified? What can I learn from each of these monsters that will enable me to predict their actions?' Do you see what I'm talking about? That's detachment. That's a way to keep going without losing sight of the objective, which is to prevent these monsters from ever taking lives to begin with."

Kate had never heard it put that way. She had been looking at things from the standpoint of slaying monsters after the fact, rather than learning to identify them before they slay their victims. Everything she'd learned up to now was almost in direct contrast.

Surrey focused in on her. "Part of the reason you are so damn good at your job is because you can see into their minds. You do know who they are because you've been up close and personal with them. You've been one of their victims. So I understand why you feel the way you do, but it's time to change your perspective, Reid. Otherwise, you won't survive in this field for much longer."

"You two coming?" Irving called out.

"Right behind you." Surrey placed his hand on Kate's back. "Lead the way."

Kate caught up to Irving and the librarian. Soon, they reached the storage facility at the back of the building, behind a fire door. And when George keyed the lock and opened the door, she stepped inside. "Everything's intact."

"Yes, ma'am. That's sort of the whole purpose of the fire door." George walked inside. "The file cabinets are fireproof as well. Everything that's ever happened in this town is in these files." He set his sights on her. "We may be a small town, but we cherish our history. This is Virginia, ma'am. Where it all began."

"Yes, sir." She grinned. "You have no idea how appreciative I am about that right now. So, can you take us to the date in question?"

"Of course." He started on toward the shelves. "We do have much of this on the cloud, too, but not going back as far as what y'all are looking for. That, we'll find right over here." George reached the back corner where several dusty metal cabinets lined the wall. "These are separated by month and year. Right here, this is what you want." He reached for his keys and unlocked the cabinet. "Lieutenant Irving, you might want to come take a look for yourself."

"Yes, sir." Irving approached him and aimed a flashlight at the drawer. "Right in here, you say?"

"This is one of the files, but I know the month and so, yes, this is what you're looking for."

Irving searched through the files. "Looks like quite a few."

"Oh yes. There are records of most things. But if you want to narrow it down, I suggest you look under the Great Fire."

"Is that what they called it?" Kate asked. "When the fields were burned."

George turned to her. "Yes, ma'am. The fires lit up the sky. Burned hundreds of acres. I'm no historian, but I am well-versed in the history of this town." He looked away. "I can only imagine what they'll call what's happening now."

Irving continued to search. "Here we go. This is what we're looking for." He reached for a thick file and carefully pulled it from the large drawer. "Will this also have a census so we can look at the names of people who lived here at the time?"

"Yes, sir. Now, if you're wanting lineage, that will mean logging onto the servers."

"I have my laptop in my car," Kate interrupted. "I can bring it in while the lieutenant goes through the documents."

Surrey extended his hand. "I'll grab it. Hand me your keys."

"Thanks." She dropped the keys into his palm. "Back seat."

"I know." He started out.

Irving set down the large file on a nearby folding table. "We just need names, George. You think you can help me locate that?"

"Yes, sir." He walked to Irving as the two reviewed the documents.

It seemed only moments passed when Surrey returned with

Kate's laptop. She took it from him. "Thank you. How's it looking out there? Anyone left?"

"No. The fire department's gone. Patrol cars are gone." He raised his sights to the ceiling. "You know what? We should have a look around. Irving can handle this. Whoever darted away from this place could've left something behind."

"You're right. No point in wasting resources." Kate approached the table and opened her laptop. "We're going to walk the perimeter. This is ready for you to access your servers, George."

As they returned outside, a hint of sunrise peeked just above the mountains. Dawn was near and the feeling that closure was, too, propelled Kate to push through the exhaustion. As she carried on toward the front of the building, Surrey stopped cold, almost tripping her up. "What is it?"

"Whoever started this fire knew how to do so without injuring himself."

"You mean like a firefighter," she replied.

"Exactly." He turned to her. "Someone who knew the library or had scoped it out...say...after figuring out we'd be looking into the history of the murders."

Kate considered his theory. "A lot of people from town were at the station that day and heard what the history teacher said."

Surrey continued ahead toward the side of the building. "I saw the man come from right about here, where we're standing, and then he sprinted out this way." Surrey aimed his flashlight into the trees. "Through here. Come on."

"What are you looking for?" Kate asked as she was just steps behind him.

"I'm looking for where he would've ended up. I need to know what's on the other side of this. If my hunch is right, then that'll put one more nail in the coffin."

"Whose coffin?" she asked.

He continued through the woods, walking faster now as grey light spread through the trees. "We're close. Keep going."

She waited for the great revelation he seemed prepared to make. And after about a hundred more yards or so, that revelation came into view. "Oh, my God."

Surrey pushed away a few more branches and stepped out into the open. He turned back to her when she joined him. "There you go."

Kate looked on. "Hardy's grocery store. You're telling me, it was Randall Hardy who ran?"

With certainty in his gaze, Surrey continued, "Back to his store, jumped in his truck, drove to the library as if he'd just happened to see the fire."

"He's no firefighter, but I can't argue your timeline of events." She returned a knowing smile. "Hitting on Emma Katz. The affair with Heidi Sumner. And this makes Strike Three."

19

S
am tossed and turned for much of the night, never really settling on any sleep. His mother told him about the library, and he'd been up since then, finally hearing his father return home a few hours ago.

Now, in the early light of day, Sam heard his mom walk out of her room and head into the kitchen. Mumbled voices reached him, and he knew his parents were both awake. Moments later, he pulled out of bed and walked into the hall, stopping just behind the wall of the staircase. He listened to their conversation.

"What's going to happen now?" Carol asked. "What are we going to do for money, Randy? No one's visiting the store. Now with the library..."

Sam heard the fear in his mother's voice. There were things she didn't know. Things that Sam had seen. Things that he knew. People thought he was stupid; that they needed to explain everything to him as though he was a child. But he understood some things quite clearly. Like how his father behaved around Emma. Sam hated seeing her face when he said things to make her uncomfortable. And how Heidi sometimes showed up at the store and went to the office to talk to his dad. She wasn't there for work either.

"We have no choice but to stay open, Carol," Randall said. "I can't just close the place. People still need food. And until the cops pull their heads out of their assess and find out who killed those kids…"

Sam emerged from behind the wall and walked into the kitchen.

Carol caught sight of him. "What on earth are you doing up so early?"

"I couldn't sleep." He swiped his keys from a bowl on the kitchen counter. "I think I need some fresh air."

"Where do you think you're going?" Randall asked. "You have any idea how dangerous it is out there right now?"

Sam lowered his gaze. "I'm going out, Dad, and you can't stop me." He started toward the living room.

Randall jumped to his feet, nearly knocking over his chair. "What did you just say to me, boy?"

Carol grabbed Randall by the arm. "Leave him! Just leave him for once."

He stopped and fixed his sights on her. "You too, huh?"

Sam walked through the front door and jumped in his car. He'd grown tired of the fights. The screaming and yelling. He'd grown tired of being his father's punching bag. After slipping behind the wheel, he turned the engine and made it onto the road ahead.

Soon, he reached the Keller home. Three cars were parked in the driveway, and he recognized one of them as Brian's. He opened his door and stepped out into the gray morning, where heavy clouds formed along the horizon.

When Sam reached the front door, he knocked on the screen

and stepped away but remained under the awning of the narrow porch. Footfalls sounded inside and then he noticed the handle turn. He smoothed his shirt and when the door opened, Brian stood on the other side.

"Sam, what are you doing here? It's really early." He pushed open the screen door and stepped over the threshold. "Your folks know you're here?"

"Can we talk for a minute, if that's okay?"

Brian's eyes raked over Sam. "About what?"

"Um, well, you heard about the library?"

"Course I did. Everyone knows. Were you there when it happened?" Brian asked.

"No, my dad was, though." He shoved his hands in his pants pockets and shook away the hair in his eyes. "Um, I was wondering if you talked to Heidi, you know, um, before..."

Brian glanced over his shoulder and stepped outside, letting the screen door close behind him. He crossed his arms and regarded Sam a moment. "Last time I talked to Heidi was on the day she was killed. I mean, well, she was killed after her shift..."

"I saw her that night too," Sam replied.

Brian furrowed his brow. "You did?"

"She was driving to work, and I was walking in town. She asked if I wanted a ride. Anyway, um, can I tell you something?"

Brian placed his hand on Sam's shoulder. "Of course, bud. What is it?"

Sam's mouth dried and he shifted his feet. "Um, I think maybe my dad and Heidi were together."

"What's that now? Together...what do you mean?" he asked.

"I mean, like I think they were like boyfriend and girlfriend."

Brian's face deadpanned. "You sure about this, man?"

Sam nodded. "Pretty sure. I saw Heidi's phone on her passenger seat, and it rang. I recognized the phone number."

Brian stepped out onto his porch until he reached the railing, leaning over it on his elbows. "Damn. Okay. Okay, so what does that mean? Like, did your old man..."

Sam joined him. "I don't know. I thought maybe she said something to you."

"Nah, nah, we didn't talk about anything like that. Just mostly about the old gang and how, well, most of them are dead now."

"Yeah, sure," Sam replied. "I was wondering if you wanted to come with me."

"Where to?" Brian asked.

"Maybe I should say something to the police about my dad."

Brian pulled up again. "You sure about that, Sam? I mean, like, it could be bad news for him."

He shrugged. "Could you come with me?"

"Yeah, okay." Brian nodded. "I'll tag along."

20

While inconclusive, Surrey's discovery of the Hardy's store on the other side of the trees left little doubt the man, at the very least, needed to account for his whereabouts, without a wife who would say whatever he demanded. But for now, they returned inside the fire-damaged library, to Irving and the man who ran the place.

Kate set her sights on Irving. "Do you have a name?"

He unleashed a heavy sigh and turned her laptop screen toward them. "We found the census in the file, and of course, already knew the name of the man who'd committed the murders. The history teacher was right. They had no children, but the man had a brother."

"We also checked the names of the other citizens registered at the time," George said. "There are a few familiar names, but were otherwise, not directly connected to the killer."

"What were the other names?" Kate asked.

"The Bunns, for one. The Andersons," Irving replied. "But take a look here. This is who you're going to want to see."

Kate leaned closer while Surrey peered over her shoulder. It took a few moments to find the names, but as she began to read, she glanced back at him. "Are you seeing this?"

"I see it."

She pulled upright again and set her sights on Irving. "He's one of the firefighters, isn't he?"

Irving nodded. "And Jason Gatwick's roommate. Chris Pumphrey's great-great-great grandfather on his mother's side was the brother of the man who murdered all those people."

Kate felt almost disappointed by the news. "Are you sure? I was certain It was Randall Hardy. Almost certain it could've been Jason Gatwick, who seemed to turn up every time someone was killed."

Surrey firmed his stance. "After what we found on Randall Hardy, no way are we ruling him out. Relative or not, he's got a part in this. And if this other guy does too, then we bring them both in."

IRVING KNOCKED on the Hardy's door once again as mid-morning arrived. Only this time, he was left with no choice but to insist Randall come down with him to the station. After what the FBI figured happened, the time had come to confront the man.

The door opened and Carol stood on the other side. Irving removed his hat. "Mrs. Hardy, good afternoon."

"Afternoon, Howard. Come in." She pushed open the door.

"Actually, Mrs. Hardy, I'd like to talk to Mr. Hardy, if he's around." Irving noticed her expression turn dour.

"I see, well, I'll go get him for you." She let the screen door close and disappeared inside the home.

Irving gazed out over the front yard before eyeing the driveway. "Sam's not here?" He walked toward the side of the house where a long driveway led to the garage set far back from the main home. The garage door was raised about a foot off the ground. The sound of the front door opening again captured his attention.

Irving hurried back to the porch. "Mr. Hardy, hello."

He narrowed his gaze while his eyes shifted between Irving and the side of his house. "Carol said you wanted to see me, and said you didn't want to come in. What's this about, Howard? Did you find out who burned down the library?"

"Interesting you should ask about that." Irving glanced at the hat in his hands and slid his fingers along its brim. "Uh, Randall, I'm gonna need you to come down to the station with me."

"What for?" Agitation mounted in his tone.

Irving peered beyond the large man's shoulders into the home and spied Mrs. Hardy listening to their conversation. "Probably best we talk about it in my office."

Randall sucked his teeth a moment and looked at Irving with mild derision. "Fine. I'll go with you." He turned back inside. "Carol, I'll be back soon. Mind that boy isn't gone too long, you hear me?"

"All right," she called out.

Irving cleared his throat for attention. "Where is Sam, if I might ask?"

"Not sure. Got smart with me and decided to leave. Probably under stress like everyone else around here." Randall snatched his wallet and keys that lay on the entry table just inside. "Well, let's get this over with."

Irving returned to his patrol car and slipped behind the wheel, waiting for Hardy before he turned the engine. "I appreciate you working with me on this, Mr. Hardy. Just want to clarify a few things."

The short drive and uncomfortable silence soon ended when

Irving pulled into the station. He stepped out and helped Randall from the passenger side. "All right, I'm gonna have you speak with the federal agents helping out with this investigation in a little while, too." He continued toward the entrance and opened the door. "Go on in, sir."

Randall stepped inside. "Well, lead the way."

THE APARTMENT COMPLEX was about a quarter mile down the road. Kate clenched the wheel, her knuckles turning white, and kept her eyes fixed ahead. "He cooperated with us only hours ago. Are we sure this is who we should be after?"

Surrey peered at her from the passenger seat. "We have more on Randall Hardy than we do on this guy. Sure, his relatives go back to the murders, but we both know that's not enough. He was clearly on duty when the call came in at the library. I don't know. We check it out and see where it takes us."

"Process of elimination," Kate replied. "His only connection to this case is that he lives with Jason Gatwick. He was with Gatwick when Emma died. I'm having trouble coming up with a possible motive, too." She pulled into the complex. "What was the building number?"

Surrey checked his notes. "C. Building C, Unit 2087."

Kate arrived at the building and cut the engine. She stepped out of the car and gave Surrey a moment to catch up. "As far as I'm concerned, Randall Hardy seems the most likely, but something about Gatwick keeps gnawing at me. So, maybe since both Gatwick and Pumphrey were there when Emma was found, we should consider they're in this together."

"Two killers?" Surrey asked.

"We've noted the differences in the M.O.s, or one does the dirty work, and the other gets rid of the bodies."

They approached the second-floor apartment and Kate knocked on the door. "Gatwick and Pumphrey were on duty last night at the library fire. They may both still be at the firehouse." After a few moments, she knocked again.

Impatience grew as she eyed Surrey. "No answer." Kate pounded on the door and shouted, "Chris Pumphrey, FBI. Open the door."

Surrey eyed her. "He's not here."

"Then we need to get to the fire station. Now."

IRVING STARTED into the hallway and reached his office. On opening the door, he motioned for Randall to step inside. "Take a seat, Mr. Hardy. Can I get you a cup of coffee? I think we have some fresh donuts in the breakroom."

"No, thank you. I'm fine." He sat down.

"Fair enough." Irving closed the door and returned to his desk. "I'd like to ask you about Heidi Sumner, Mr. Hardy."

"Okay."

Irving opened his desk drawer and retrieved a file, laying it on his desk. "During the course of our investigation, Mr. Hardy, we pulled the phone records from Heidi Sumner." He pulled out the documents and set them in front of Randall. "The highlighted number is yours, sir. In addition to that." Irving opened another desk drawer and retrieved an evidence bag. "Inside Ms. Sumner's home, we found a man's watch in her nightstand." He noticed Randall's eyes flicker and set down the bag on the table. "Is this your watch, Mr. Hardy?"

Randall glanced at it and returned to Irving. "What are you

getting at, Howard? You think I killed that girl? You think I killed all of them?"

"I'm just trying to get the full story, here, Mr. Hardy. Were you involved with Heidi Sumner, romantically? Bear in mind, we also have video evidence that puts you at her place of business only hours before we believe she was murdered."

Randall fixed his gaze on Irving. "You caught me, all right? I was having an affair with the woman."

"She was nineteen, sir."

Randall looked away. "I didn't kill her. I didn't kill Emma or Amber, either. I know what you think of me, Howard. What the entire town thinks of me. But I'm no killer."

"You've been in this town a long time," Irving continued. "You know most everyone here. And I know your boy has done some work over at the Voss farm on occasion."

"So, what?"

"You must be pretty familiar with the place, too."

"I guess," Randall replied.

"Did you know someone killed one of their cows the night before last? Cut out the poor creature's tongue and left it in the woods at a place where all the young kids hang out. Looked like some kind of message. Same message whoever killed those girls left."

"I got no idea what in the hell you're talking about right now," he said.

"You were there last night at the library, too, why?" Irving pressed on.

Randall shrugged. "I told you last night. I closed up and started to leave. Heard the alarm and drove over." He narrowed his gaze. "And why the hell would I have reason to burn down the library, if that's what you're thinking."

"Mr. Hardy, I'm going to need to place you under arrest."

"What the hell?" He pulled back his shoulders. "What for? I didn't kill anybody. Are you messing with me?"

"You're welcome to contact a lawyer, but until we get a few other answers we're looking for at the moment, you're the only one who had a reason to kill Heidi Sumner."

"And what reason is that, Howard? Cause I was screwing her? Really? You're going to arrest me for that?"

"You deserve a whole lot worse, you ask me," Irving replied.

Randall nodded. "Ah, I get it now. This is really about Sam, isn't it? You have no idea what goes on in my family—"

"I have some idea. Now, come on. We'll get you booked into custody. You can call your lawyer after that."

Kate's Ford Explorer raced onto the driveway of the firehouse. She shoved the gearshift into Park and cut the engine. "If Pumphrey isn't here, we get Irving to issue a BOLO." She opened her door.

"Got it." Surrey stepped outside and headed toward the firehouse. "I don't see anyone in there."

"Won't know for sure till we get inside." She marched on. "Hello? Anyone in here?" Kate walked on. "Hello? FBI. Chris Pumphrey, are you here?"

A moment later, she heard footfalls and from behind the firetruck, Jason Gatwick emerged. "Agent Reid? What are you doing here?"

"We're looking for your roommate," she replied. "Is he on duty?"

"No. He's not scheduled for work until six o'clock tonight. Why? Is everything okay?"

"When was the last time you saw him, Mr. Gatwick?" Kate pressed on.

"The three-alarm at the library. You know that. You were there too." Jason regarded the agents. "What's going on?"

"He's not at home," Surrey cut in. "Do you know where else he might be?"

Kate raised her hand. "Are you aware whether Chris was interested in any of the girls? Did he ask them out? Had he asked out Emma?"

"No." Gatwick shook his head. "He wouldn't ask Emma out. She was my girlfriend."

"But she hadn't been in a year," Surrey replied.

"I know that, but—no, he didn't have a thing for any of them. Not that he ever told me about."

Kate noticed his eyes shift. He appeared hesitant. "What are you not telling us right now, Mr. Gatwick?"

Jason shrugged. "Nothing. I mean, I don't know. Look, Emma didn't care too much for Chris. It wasn't like anything ever happened; it was just a personality thing."

"You're sure nothing happened between them?" Kate asked. "Did Emma tell you she didn't like him? When was that?"

Jason raised his hands. "Okay, just give me a minute." He took a breath. "Chris was with me when we found Emma, so he didn't do this."

"Was he with you the entire day?" Surrey asked.

"Well, no—"

Kate rubbed the back of her neck. "Listen, Jason, we need to talk to Chris and clear all this up, you understand? He volunteered the sample, and that speaks to his cooperation. Regardless, we have to find him. If you know where he might be, or how to get in touch with him, please tell us."

THE CALL RANG in on Irving's cell phone as he waited inside Booking. "Lieutenant Irving."

"Lieutenant, it's Dr. Rozier."

He stepped away from the desk. "Dr. Rozier, I hope you're calling to tell me you have the results back from the autopsies."

"I do, sir. I also have the results of the DNA profile from Emma Katz, and Heidi Sumner. I've just emailed all the reports to you, but I thought we could take a look together so that I might answer any questions. I know what's at stake, so I wanted to waste no time."

"Yes, sir, absolutely. Give me one moment." Irving hurried back to his office and got in front of his computer. "Sorry about that, Doctor. Yes, I see them. Okay, I've opened the Katz file and I'm reading the summary now." Irving squinted to view the screen as he hurried through the passage. "You found foreign DNA."

"Yes, sir. I thought you might like to know that. No match yet—"

"Any foreign DNA found on Heidi Sumner?" Irving opened the file for her report and quickly read through the summary. "Semen."

"Yes, while I found no indication of sexual assault, I did find semen and I ran the DNA, but of course, no match."

"What about the samples I sent you? The one from Jason Gatwick and the one from Sam Hardy."

"Let me check on that. Hang on." He placed the call on hold.

Irving tapped his fingers on his desk. "Come on. Come on, Doc."

Rozier returned to the call. "Yes, sir. The cross-referencing was just completed, and I do have those results for you."

Irving closed his eyes. "What'd you find, Doc?"

"The sample from Jason Gatwick was negative. No match to your victims' profiles. Bearing in mind, I don't have Amber Hoffman's profile back yet."

"Okay, and Sam Hardy?"

"Uh, yes, the foreign DNA found on Emma Katz was a match to Sam Hardy."

Irving returned a stony gaze. "It was? Where was the foreign DNA found on her body, Doc?"

"Her right cheek."

"I'm sorry, her cheek?" Irving asked.

"Yes, sir. Touch DNA or trace DNA, requires very small samples and can be picked up using essentially strips of tape. So anyone who touched her with any part of their body could easily leave behind skin cells that can be picked up."

"None of this trace DNA was found on Heidi Sumner?" Irving continued.

"No, sir. She was found in the water and over time, the foreign cells would've washed away. Only the semen was found, and as I said—"

"You don't have a match. Well, I have a pretty good idea who it belonged to," Irving replied. "Thank you, Doc. I know we're still awaiting Amber Hoffman's results, so as soon as you have them—"

"Of course, Lieutenant. I have my team working on this day and night."

"Thank you, Doctor." Irving drew in a deep breath and placed the phone to his ear once again. "Agent Reid, we have some results back."

"Go on," Kate replied.

"Heidi's body was void of foreign DNA except semen. We can all guess whose, but that's something I'll have to handle. But here's the real problem. Sam Hardy's DNA was found on Emma Katz."

21

F rom the passenger seat of Sam's older model gray Chevy Trailblazer, Brian noticed the police station ahead. "You're sure you want to do this?"

"I'm sure," Sam replied.

Brian turned to him. "Listen, man, I can't imagine what things are like for you at home, but I'm sure it's not great. And I know how much Emma meant to you. She used to talk about you a lot, you know."

Sam appeared to swallow his emotions as he kept his gaze fixed on the two-lane road.

"But I gotta ask...what did your dad do that makes you think he's responsible for all this? I mean, I don't get it. He's an asshole, if you don't mind my saying, but to kill our friends? Why?" He soon noticed that Sam hadn't slowed to make the turn into the station. "Hey, you're gonna miss the turn..." And when they drove past it, he shot him a look. "Sam, what are you doing? You drove right by it, dude."

"I want to show you something first. It'll prove what I'm telling you." Sam glanced at him. "Is that okay?"

Brian raised his shoulder. "Yeah, I guess so. Where is it? Where are we going?"

"Just up the road a little more," Sam replied. "Don't worry. It won't take long, and then we'll turn back and go see Lieutenant Irving."

Brian's gut knotted. "When did you know that your dad was cheating on your mom with Heidi?"

"She told me when I saw her phone that night." Sam pulled off onto the side of the road. "This is it. This is what I want to show you."

Brian checked his surroundings. "Why not park up ahead near the trail? What's over here?"

Sam removed his keys from the ignition and opened his door. "I told you. This is what I want to show you before we go to the police station." He stepped out of the small SUV.

That knot in Brian's gut tightened and he felt it rise into his chest. But this was Sam. Sam had put up with a lot of crap in his life and still found the time to smile at everyone who walked by, to ask everyone how their day had been when he saw them at the store. And this was Sam, who Brian was certain had loved Emma in a way she either hadn't known or chose to ignore. If he wanted to show Brian something, then it must've been important.

He stepped outside as the sun shone above in a cloudless sky. With the trees before him and no one else on the road, Brian made his way over. "Okay, Sam. What do you want to show me?"

Sam started into the woods, stepping over broken branches, navigating around jutting boulders, and walking atop the years' worth of decaying leaves. "It's just over here."

After several yards, the smell came. Brian crinkled his nose. "What the hell is that stench?" And as he continued to trail Sam, he noticed the yellow tape. Inside that yellow tape were bloodied garbage bags, dead animals, skinned and half-eaten, and police markers everywhere. "Oh my God."

Sam stopped on a dime. "They found it. I guess the police know about it now."

Brian stepped back and kept his gaze fixed on Sam. "What is this place, Sam, and what do the police know?"

It was the look on Agent Reid's face that sent Jason's mind to worry. He stood before the federal agents, who'd accused him of hiding the details of his roommate's whereabouts, and waited for her to speak. "Who was that on the phone, ma'am? You look like you got some bad news."

She turned to Agent Surrey. "We need to talk to Sam Hardy. That was the lieutenant. He received information from the ME."

Jason eyed the other agent. Something bad had just happened and neither was going to say anything in front of him. "Listen, I don't know what's going on right now, but I have no idea where Chris is. I'm telling you the truth."

Agent Reid reached for a business card and offered it to him. "If you see or hear from Mr. Pumphrey, please call me imme-diately."

He took the card. "Yes, ma'am. I will. But I don't understand what's going on here. Is he...did he—"

"We have to go," Agent Reid cut in. "We'll be in touch."

Jason watched them return to their car and pull away. "What in the hell was that?"

"Hey."

He spun around. "Oh, Chief, I didn't know you were here."

Fire Chief Barrows glanced out as the vehicle pulled away. "Was that them FBI agents? I heard Irving was getting help."

"It was. They're looking for Chris." He regarded his boss. "Do you know where he is?"

"Not a clue, son," Barrows replied. "Why are they looking for him?"

Jason shrugged. "Have no idea, but they got a call and just took off."

"Maybe something finally broke loose on this thing, huh?" the chief asked. "Have you finished your reports for the library fire?"

"Uh, no sir. Not yet. I'll get on it now." Jason retreated to the rear of the firehouse and walked inside the common room. A kitchenette lay at the back. A sofa, a couple of chairs, and a television were near the front. And off to the right was a dining table and a couple of workstations.

He headed toward the workstation and stopped for a moment while he considered the odd event. Jason reached for his phone and pressed the contact button. When the call was picked up, he continued, "Where are you, man?"

"Dude, I'm in the woods with Sam. Something's not right. I need to leave. There's like dead animals and shit."

"What?" Jason asked. "You're with Sam?"

"Listen, I can't talk. I have to get the hell out of here. Something's not right."

The call ended and Jason stared at his phone as he'd been cut off from the call. "Dead animals?"

KATE MADE the turn into the police station and parked near the front. She cut the engine and eyed Surrey. "Levi might have the results back from the samples we sent. It's worth a call before we go in there."

"Irving's booking Randall Hardy on suspicion of murdering Heidi Sumner because he was the last one to see her and semen was found during her autopsy," Surrey began. "But he doesn't have a match because Hardy never submitted a sample. But then Sam Hardy's DNA was found on Emma Katz." He regarded Kate. "Are we considering the idea both these men are the killers? And if so, what was the point of the library fire and learning of the Pumphrey connection?"

"None of this is making a lot of sense right now," Kate peered through the windshield at the station's entrance. "It is possible the father and son are responsible for the murders. I don't know how Pumphrey fits, except to say he has a connection to the past murders, which doesn't hold a lot of weight. But let's not forget what Gatwick said."

"About how Pumphrey didn't seem to get along with Emma. Yeah, I hear that." Surrey picked up his phone. "I'll call Walsh and see what he has." He waited for the line to answer.

"Walsh here."

"Hey, it's Surrey. I'm here with Reid and I have you on speaker."

"Got it. What's happening?" Walsh asked.

"We were kind of hoping you might know," Kate replied. "We're looking for results on the swabs we couriered late last night. Brian Keller and Chris Pumphrey. Any chance they've come back this morning?"

"Hang on. Let me see if I've received anything recent."

They listened while Walsh typed on his keyboard.

"Okay, I do have something here," Walsh replied.

"Thank God," Surrey replied. "We're ready when you are."

The silence continued for a moment before Walsh returned to

the line, "Keller's sample is negative against the Katz results and... hang on. Yeah, we just got the sample entered for Amber Hoffman."

"Hoffman? I didn't think we had those yet," Kate said.

"Looks like the ME just entered them into the database," Walsh replied. "Your lieutenant may not have been notified yet. But it does appear... uh, it's negative, too against Keller. And Pumphrey's results are still pending. I see you have Heidi Sumner in here too, but nothing's hit there either."

Kate slammed her palm against the steering wheel. "Damn it. So what we have is Sam Hardy's DNA on Emma and that's it. Negative for Keller. Negative for Gatwick. Sam's DNA wasn't on Heidi, we know that. And we don't have a sample from Randall Hardy to confirm against Heidi Sumner."

Surrey cast his gaze on her. "This is what we've been waiting for. But if all we have is Sam Hardy, then it's best we find him."

"Thanks, Levi. I appreciate the help. We'll be in touch," Kate added.

"Thanks, man." Surrey ended the call. "The father's inside. You think he knows where his son is?"

SAM PEERED over his shoulder at Brian. "Who are you talking to?"

He slipped his phone into his back pocket. "No one. Listen, man, we should get going. Obviously, the police don't want people here or they wouldn't have taped it off. I don't know what any of this is, Sam, but—"

"I tried to control it," he cut in.

"Control what?"

"When they took Emma, I was mad. I was so mad I came here

and did these things. My dad kept telling me it was all my fault. I thought it would make me feel better, but instead—"

"Wait. You did this?" Brian's pulse quickened. He felt the tingle of adrenaline as it surged in him. He took a step back and it seemed Sam took notice.

Sam raised his hand. "Don't go."

"This isn't right, man. You know this isn't right." He stepped back again. Sam took a step forward. "You're fucking crazy." Brian spun around and darted through the trees. The uneven terrain forced him to stumble, but he quickly regained his balance and pushed on.

He heard Sam's steps behind him. While the two were evenly matched from a physical standpoint, it was clear Sam knew this area well and he closed in on Brian. "Jesus." His heart raced and his breath echoed in his ears, but he knew the road was nearby. If Sam reached his vehicle, it would be all too easy to catch up to him while he ran on foot. But the hope was that other cars might come. That someone might see him.

A tear fell down his cheek, realizing this must've been what his friends felt just as they were about to die. It was impossible to believe Sam had done it. Then again, after what he just saw in the woods...

As the road became visible through the trees, Brian's chest swelled with relief. Still, Sam was close.

"Brian, wait!" Sam called out.

"Fuck you, man. I'm not waiting," he yelled back. He cleared the trees and stepped onto the soft gravel shoulder of the roadway. The embankment was only feet in front of him, and so was Sam's car. "Just go, man! Go!" He leaped over the narrow ditch and landed on the other side, just off the road.

The police station was at least a mile back. He could get close, but Sam would get closer, faster, in his car. As Brian turned back, he crossed the road and hustled as fast as his legs could carry him.

His phone bounced in his pocket, and he thought, *maybe.* Brian reached for it and pressed the emergency button. The call rang through to 911. "Yeah, it's Brian Keller. I'm being chased by..." Brian looked over his shoulder and veered off into the road. When the tires screeched, he whipped back and saw the car quickly approach. He dropped his phone and dove off toward the side.

The car skidded to a stop and the driver jumped out. "Oh my God. Are you okay?"

Brian's left shoulder felt like it had popped out of its socket. He rolled over to see who it was, but he had recognized the car. "Jason, dude. Get me out of here."

RANDALL HARDY SAT in an interview room while Kate huddled with Surrey and the lieutenant. She shifted her gaze to the door before her. "What the hell do we do about Sam Hardy?"

"I asked Mr. Hardy if he knew where his son was, and he said he didn't," Irving replied. "So we have the fire, which you, Agent Surrey, believed that it could've been the elder Mr. Hardy who ran from it. And now we know the results of Heidi Sumner's autopsy. So, the question is, how do we get Randall to submit a sample?"

"It's a waste of time to wait for that," Kate cut in. "It'll be important, but it's not important in light of what we suspect regarding Sam."

"Which is?" Irving asked.

Kate's attention was drawn to the officer who quickly approached, and she turned back to Irving. "I think he's looking for you."

Irving eyed the officer. "What is it?"

"Lieutenant, a 911 call came in only minutes ago. The caller identified himself as Brian Keller. He said he was being chased when the call cut out."

Irving's expression blanked. "Did he say where he was?"

"No, sir, but under the current circumstances, it doesn't sound good."

"It does not. Thank you." He turned to the agents. "Keller's the only one we don't have the results for—"

"Actually, we do now," Kate replied. "Agent Walsh from my office said he'd just received the cross-match." She shook her head. "Nothing. All we have on this case is Hardy DNA. It's safe to say, Sam's going after Keller. He's working off the photo and crossing everyone off down the line."

Irving nodded. "We need to get a location on Brian's phone."

"Didn't he say he lost his phone a few days ago?" Kate asked.

"As a matter of fact, he did, but I suppose he could've gotten a replacement." Irving checked his weapon. "We'll be sure and ask him just as soon as we find him—alive, I hope." He turned around and headed back toward the bullpen. "The 911 operator should have received a dispatchable location within about 30 seconds from the time the call was placed. That will tell us where he was when the call was dropped." Irving hurried through to Dispatch and called out to the two operators on shift. "Give me the location of the 911 call that came in from Brian Keller."

One of the dispatchers set his sights on his computer. "Yes, sir. Just give me one second." As he fixed his gaze on the screen and typed with speed, the answer, it seemed, had arrived. He looked up at Irving. "Lieutenant, the call came from about half a mile east."

"Son of a bitch." Irving rushed toward the lobby and glanced behind him. "Agent Reid, if we are to believe Sam Hardy is the man we're after, I suggest you two follow me to where Brian Keller made that call, and pray to God he's not dead."

BRIAN PEERED over his shoulder at the rear window of Jason's two-door pickup. "We have to tell the police."

"Tell them what, man? That Sam showed you that place? They already know about it," Jason replied.

"Yeah, they know, but I'll bet they don't know it was Sam who did it." He returned his attention ahead. "He said he was mad about what happened to Emma, and that he went there and like, I don't know, started killing all these animals. You didn't see it, dude. They were skinned, cut up. Some looked like they had their tongues cut out."

Jason winced. "Seriously? So, do you think he killed everyone?"

"I don't know, man. I'm freaking out. As soon as you almost ran me over, he kept on going. He had to know I'd tell you all this."

"Then we need to tell the cops what just happened," Jason replied. "These FBI people came around and took my DNA, and they didn't even look at Sam."

Brian shook his head. "None of us did. He said his dad was sleeping with Heidi."

"What?" Jason shot him a look. "No way. No friggin' way."

"I think it's true, man." Brian glanced through the passenger window. "Something's going on with that family and it's not good."

"And you think the cops will listen to us?" Jason asked. "You don't have anything except Sam went psycho on some animals. Did he come after you? Was he trying to hurt you?"

"I didn't want to stick around to find out." He narrowed his gaze. "Hey, that's Hardy's store. I bet Sam went there, probably to tell his dad what happened."

"What do you want me to do?" Jason asked.

"Turn in. We'll see his Chevy and call the cops. He won't get away this time."

Jason parked at the front of the store. "Dude, this is a mistake. Man, what are we doing? Sam's car isn't her."

Brian opened the door. "Maybe his dad is. The dude was sleeping with Heidi, man. Come on. He's not innocent in all this. You know what Sam's like. Maybe it's his dad who's pulling the strings, you know?" He stepped outside.

"Where are you going?" Jason called out. When Brian didn't answer, he opened his door. "Damn it. Dude, wait up."

Brian waited for him to catch up. "No one's even in this place. The entire town is practically deserted."

"What are you going to do if you find Sam's dad, huh?" Jason asked. "Look, we're not cops. I don't have a gun. This is friggin' stupid, bro. I know you're hurting cause of Emma and all them. I am too, but this isn't the answer."

Brian stopped at the store's entrance and turned around. "I just want to see him, okay? If Randall Hardy is here, we call the cops. That's it. Sam won't be far behind after that." He walked inside the empty store. "Jeez, is anyone even working right now?"

"Friggin' crazy is what this is," Jason muttered under his breath as he trailed Brian. "You know, those federal agents are looking for my roommate."

"Chris?" Brian glanced back. "Why?"

"They didn't say. He wasn't home. I don't know where the hell he is or why they want him."

"What are you getting at?" Brian continued.

"Just saying, you know, maybe we don't have the whole story, here," Jason replied. "I don't like being here, man. I don't think anyone's even friggin' working. Like, why was the place unlocked?" He followed Brian to the back storage area. "It's hotter than hell back here." He stopped at a noise. "What in the...? You hear that, man?"

"Hear what?" Brian pushed through the doors and into the storage area where pallets lay stacked with dried and canned goods. "It doesn't look like Sam or his dad are here."

Jason stepped quietly toward what he thought may have been items that had fallen from a pallet. He took a few more steps and heard footfalls behind him. "Brian, dude, we gotta go."

With his back still turned, a hand clamped down on his face. Jason's eyes widened and panic spread through him. He tried to speak, but the hand pressed on his lips so hard, he felt his teeth cut through them.

"Shhh..." the man said.

Jason had to see the face. He had to know who this was, so he used his legs for leverage and with all his strength, began to turn his shoulders. But the headlock tightened, and he grew dizzy. His legs wobbled. If his shoulders could just pivot a little more, he could get a glimpse...

A heavy blow struck the back of his skull. Jason went limp.

BRIAN RETURNED to the front of the storage area. "Jason, where are you? You're right. Neither Hardy is here. Let's just go straight to the cops." He walked back to the doors. "Jason, come on, man. Quit screwing around." Brian looked toward the forklifts and saw blood run like a river from behind a pallet. His stomach turned. "Oh, no, man, no. What the..." He hurried to find the body. Blood pooled on the concrete floor. "Oh my God." Brian kneeled to check Jason's pulse. "Dude. Dude, don't be dead, man, please."

Tears fell down his face and stung his eyes. He took hold of Jason's head and saw his gaping mouth. Bile climbed in his throat, and he cried out. "No!" With shaking hands, he lowered Jason's head to the ground and returned to his feet. "Where are you, Sam? Where the fuck are you?" he screamed. "Coward!"

Through his sobs, Brian reached for his phone.

"Reid, here."

"He's dead," Brian pleaded.

"Brian? Who's dead? Where are you?" Kate asked.

"I'm at the store. Oh God, you have to come here quick. It's Sam Hardy. I know it. He killed Jason. He cut out his tongue."

KATE DROPPED her phone into her pocket as she stood roadside where skid marks blackened the street. "It was Keller. He was with Jason Gatwick. Someone got to him."

"Where are they?" Surrey asked.

"Hardy's store." Kate rushed back to her car. "Lieutenant, we'll meet you down there. You'll need an ambulance. We have another body." She stepped into her Ford and waited for Surrey to climb in. "Damn it. The kid took off with Jason and now Jason is dead."

"Why the hell wouldn't he just come down to the station?" Surrey buckled his seatbelt. What were they trying to do?"

"I don't know. Keller's got a lot to answer for right now." She turned the engine.

Several moments went by when all Kate could do was stare at the taillights on Irving's patrol car ahead of them. She thought they had been so close and now another kid was gone. One she initially suspected. Turned out, her gut was wrong. It seemed to have been wrong a lot during this investigation. She still hadn't known what

Pumphrey had to do with any of this. Maybe it was just a coincidence that he was related to a murderer.

Kate pulled to a stop near the front of the store and caught sight of Brian running outside. "Oh my God. He's got blood all over him." She threw open her driver's side door and jumped out. "Stop!"

Brian halted immediately and held up his hands. "He's dead. He's dead."

Surrey quickly got into position and had his weapon trained on the trembling kid with tears streaming down his face.

Irving jumped out of his car. "Hold up! Relax. Put down your guns."

Kate maintained a firm grip on her sidearm. "Jason Gatwick is dead?"

"Yes," Brian replied.

"Did you kill him?" Surrey shouted.

"No! No, I swear it." Brian peered over his shoulder. "I made him come with me. It was Sam. He took Jason's tongue, just like the others. Please, you have to help." He fell to his knees.

"Calm down, son. You said it was Sam?" Irving pressed on. "Are you sure about that?"

"He came after me. He took me to that place in the woods with all the dead animals—"

"What?" Kate called out. "You were there?" She looked at Surrey. "Jesus, I thought he had officers on that site."

"Yeah, and he freaked me out, so I took off. Started running. That was when I called 911, but then Jason found me. Sam kept on driving after that. We came here because...because I thought Sam was here, or maybe his dad. I was only going to call the cops when I found them."

Kate kept her eyes fixed on the young man, who was covered

in blood. "Is that Jason's blood on you? And I'm supposed to believe you didn't kill him?"

Irving set his sights on Brian. "Are you armed, son?"

"No. No, Lieutenant, you have to believe me. I was in the back when it happened."

"So you didn't see anyone?" Surrey cut in.

"No." He lowered his hands and wept.

"For Christ's sake." Irving holstered his weapon and hurried toward the kid, grabbing him by the arms to raise him. "Come on, now. Get up." He quickly patted down Brian and turned back to the others. "He's unarmed."

The agents secured their weapons and Kate marched toward the entrance. "Is he inside?"

"Yes. In the back where they keep the pallets," Brian whispered.

"If the killer was just here, we'd better hope he left something for us." Kate pushed through the doors.

Surrey was only steps behind her. "In the back."

"Got it."

Kate was the first to reach him. "Over here. I see him." She stepped around the pool of blood to get a better look. When Surrey caught up to her, she continued, "It's Jason Gatwick. Jesus, how did this happen?"

22

Given the town was already on edge, this latest news spread like wildfire. People arrived at the grocery store to learn what had happened to one of the town's firefighters.

The lieutenant opened the back door of the other patrol car and helped Brian inside. "I wish it didn't have to be this way, son, but I'm going to need you to make a statement at the station and go from there."

"What do you mean, 'go from there'?" Brian asked.

"It means what it means, son. Now, go on. Get in and buckle up. I'll have Officer Toomey take you back and get your statement. I'll be there later to sit down with you." He closed the door and turned to Kate. "Ambulance is on the way. Should be here any minute."

Kate waited for the officer to return to his vehicle and drive away with Brian inside. She kept her eyes on the kid, trying to figure out if he was in on this with Sam Hardy. He fit the profile to a T. But there was a lot more to it than that. "If we're looking at a situation where Keller did this, and he was unarmed when you patted him down, that means the knife used to cut out Jason's tongue could be here somewhere. Probably hidden."

"So you do think he did it? After everything that points to the Hardys?" Irving asked.

Kate noticed the look in his eyes. Sadness, disappointment. "Look, Lieutenant, I don't really know what to think at this point, but Sam's clearly involved in this, and we'll have to find out whether Keller was too. And where the hell is Chris Pumphrey?" She raised her hands. "Hell, I don't know, given how Sam has grown up with violence all around him, it's feasible he's responsible, like Brian said. Regardless, we need to search the building. There's a chance the knife is here." She peered over her shoulder at the growing crowd. "You have people out there who demand answers, so let's try to find them."

"Yes, ma'am."

She returned inside and led Irving to Jason Gatwick's body, where Surrey continued his search for the knife. "Have we found whatever was used to knock him out?"

Surrey eyed them. "I haven't touched the body, but just by looking at the source of the blood, it's likely he was caught by surprise from behind. Just like the others. Bruises are turning up around his neck. He was strangled, probably to subdue him. He's a strong young man. But if he was grabbed from behind, he could've been put in a headlock and passed out long enough to do the deed."

"Lieutenant, you seem to know the Hardys well," Kate began. "Sam, in particular. What are your thoughts? Is he capable of this? And if so, is it possible Randall Hardy is either helping him or pulling his strings?"

"I would've never believed that in a million years," Irving replied. "That said, we know Brian's sample came back negative against the victims. Makes his claim seem legit. And Sam's DNA was found on Emma."

"But not the others," Kate added.

"No, ma'am. Not the others. So to suggest Randall Hardy could be behind it? I'd say it's possible."

Kate placed her hands on her hips. "Then we have to find Sam."

"I'll get out the word, then I'll head over to the Hardy home myself," Irving replied. "The young man relies heavily on his mother. There's a chance he's gone back home, not knowing what to do. That's where I'll start."

"Okay. We'll do a search of the perimeter in the event the knife was left behind. Then we'll head back to the station and pull together a plan to find Sam and get his father to talk."

"And Chris Pumphrey?" Irving pressed on.

"Can you put a unit at his apartment and call Chief Burrows to keep eyes out for him?" she asked.

"I can and I will." He turned to leave.

SWEAT DRIPPED down Brian's forehead while he sat inside the room hardly bigger than a prison cell. Not that he'd ever seen a prison cell except for on television. He'd called his folks and when he said he was there to make a statement, for the first time, it seemed like they believed him. Like maybe they hadn't believed the worst thing in the world about him. They were on their way. But he wasn't a kid anymore, they couldn't help him with this.

"Oh, man. Jason. I'm so sorry." Brian wiped away the sweat with his hand and eyed the door that remained closed. And as if he'd forgotten his shirt was covered in Jason's blood, he looked down in shock. "Oh my God. Get this off me."

At that moment, the door opened, and Lieutenant Irving walked inside. "I'm very sorry to have kept you waiting, son. As you know, we've got several things happening at once around here." He pulled out a chair and sat across from Brian. His eyes raked over him. "I'm sorry we couldn't let you get cleaned up first." He picked up his cell phone. "Hey, yeah, can you bring in a change of clothes for Brian?" He nodded. "Yeah, we'll bag those and check them into Evidence. Okay, thanks." Irving returned his phone to his pocket. "We'll get you out of those clothes, but listen here, son. Those FBI folks are going to ask you questions about what happened with Sam. About why the hell you went to Hardy's store with Jason."

Brian's chin quivered. "I told you, I haven't done anything wrong. I didn't kill Jason. You have to believe me. Someone else was there. It had to have been Sam..."

Irving raised his hands. "Son. Son, just take a breath, all right? I need you to stay calm, as hard as that might be right now. Now, before I say anything further, you have the right to have an attorney present..."

"Oh, my God. Am I being charged?" Brian's voice raised an octave. "I'm under arrest?"

Irving checked his tone and took his own deep breath. "Look here. You have the right to be questioned with an attorney present, if you so wish. That attorney can advise you on further questioning. What I'm telling you now, son, is that if you got nothing to hide, then it's best you be straight with them. Be straight with all of us." He pulled back in his chair. "Do you wish to have an attorney present at this time?"

Brian swallowed the fear that knotted his gut. "No, sir. I didn't kill Jason. I'll do whatever I have to do to prove that. It's Sam you want to question. He's the killer. I know he is."

Irving stood again. "I'm going to send in Abrams, now, all right? You talk to him. I have to pay a visit to the Hardy home."

THE LATE AFTERNOON sun kept the relentless heat and humidity at its peak. No breeze blew. No clouds dotted the sky. It was only the sun that shone down on Kate as she started toward the perimeter. Surrey took the south side of the building.

Kate squinted at the sky, cursing at it under her breath, then peered down again at the asphalt. She carried on toward a narrow strip of pavement that continued down the side of the building and widened as it neared the back. A few pine trees lined the edge of the asphalt.

She'd shared a connection to virtually all the killers she'd come across in some form or another. That connection seemed impossible to shake. And now, years later, they consumed her, ate at her insides like cancer. But when she found that one thing. That one thing that clicked and made her certain of herself, it was all worth it. Would it be that way again, or had SSA Kate Reid lost her gift, as evidenced by a case that had so far confounded her? Every instinct seemed wrong. Had her gift, or curse, finally been extinguished? If so, what would she become?

Her footfalls now echoed in her ears. Irving's team had cleared out the curious and fearful people who had lingered and now, only the trees whispered.

"You were here," she began. "What did you leave for me to find?" The corner of her lip raised into a smile as she heard Nick's voice in her head. *"Finding the minutia is what you do best, Kate."* And as she considered those words he'd once said to her, she wondered aloud, "Will I find it now before someone else has to die?"

Kate had walked about 75 feet and stood several feet away from the back corner of the building. That was about half the length of the roughly 20,000-square-foot building. Large for a small town store, but small in comparison to those found in a big city.

Along the pavement, she noticed no fresh tire marks, no dirt tracks from a car that might've driven along a dirt road. Nothing appeared out of the ordinary. Until...

The wind picked up and a candy wrapper drifted along the side of the building. Kate walked over to it and with a gloved hand, picked it up. "Snickers." She examined the inside of the wrapper and narrowed her gaze. With her index finger, she pressed inside the wrapper and when she pulled it out, a small piece of chocolate stuck to the glove. "This is fresh. The chocolate's soft but not melted." And then she smiled. "I hope you left prints."

The candy wrapper wasn't proof of anything, except that someone had been here recently. "All right. What else you want to show me?" She carried on, walking parallel to the building. Her eyes searched every inch around her. Beyond the pavement and into the dried grass, she searched for tire ruts in the still-soft earth. And as she reached the end of the building, where she would join Surrey just around the corner, Kate stopped in her tracks.

The downspout from a rain gutter was attached to the building. Her chest filled with expectancy. Her gut screamed at her to check inside the opening. Kate squatted to examine the metal drainpipe. It appeared undamaged, save for a few knicks of paint that had fallen off. She reached inside and closed her eyes when her fingers touched something that had been wedged against the walls of the pipe. She knew. Kate knew exactly what she'd found and carefully loosened it from its position until it dislodged.

Still squatted low with one hand on the pipe she clutched for balance, the other hand held an object wrapped in blue shop towels. Kate stood again and unraveled the object, certain of what it was. Relief washed over her. "The knife."

Her head spun for a moment as adrenaline ran through her veins. "I found the damn knife." She heard steps ahead and spotted a lean shadow in front of a lowering sun.

"I thought I heard you over here." Surrey continued toward her. "What's going on?"

Kate wore a broad smile and held up her find. "It's the knife."

His lips parted and his brow raised. "Are you serious? The knife used to cut..."

"Unless someone else decided to wedge a hunting knife inside a drainpipe. It's been wiped clean, but we get luminol on there, and we'll find traces of blood." Kate still beamed. "This is the final piece of the puzzle."

"It sure as hell looks like it," he replied. "What made you look in there?"

She raised her shoulder. "Turns out, I still have the one thing I thought I lost."

23

T he evidence was in Kate's hands and on their return to the station, she and Surrey made their way to the officer behind the front desk. She tucked the wrapped knife under her arm. "Where's the lieutenant?"

"Agent Reid, Agent Surrey," he began. "I'm afraid he's gone to the Hardys to look for Sam."

"When did he leave?" Kate pressed on.

"Ten minutes ago, I reckon. Brian Keller's in an interview room and we put Randall Hardy in a holding cell. What do y'all have?"

"Proof," she replied. "We're going to use the lieutenant's office if that's all right with you."

"Yes, ma'am. Go on ahead." He gestured to the hall.

The two started back toward Irving's office and on arrival, Kate opened the door. "We'll have to call the ME ourselves. The autopsy reports are in here."

"You take a look, and I'll make the call." Surrey grabbed his phone.

Kate noticed the folders on Irving's desk and opened each one. "Looks like he received the Hoffman preliminary report as well." She eyed Surrey while he raised his index finger.

"Hang on." He returned to the call. "Dr. Rozier, Agent Surrey. We need a favor." He placed the call on speaker. "I'm with Agent Reid."

"Afternoon," Rozier replied. "Where's Lieutenant Irving?"

"He's following a lead," Kate replied. "Doctor, we found what we believe is the knife used on our victims. For the sake of time, can we send you a photograph of it for confirmation?"

"To compare the pattern of the knife's edge against the severed tissue?" Rozier replied. "Yes, I can do that."

"How long will it take?" Surrey pressed on.

"Send me as detailed an image as you can and give me an hour. Maybe less."

"The sooner, the better, Doctor," Kate replied. "I'll send the image now, and we'll wait for your call."

Surrey returned the phone to his pocket. "It won't tell us who the knife belongs to. That'll require we send it to our lab for DNA analysis, prints, all that."

Kate raised her index finger. "But it will confirm whether it was the same knife used on all the victims. The rest will fall into place."

IRVING GRAPPLED with the idea Sam Hardy could have killed his friends and the girl he seemed to care about the most. Maybe this was all a ploy by the young man's father to hide his illicit affair, though God knows why any one of those kids would've given two shits about it. Irving knew the power Randall Hardy wielded over his family. It was practically textbook. Of course, none of that could excuse murder, or the concealment of it by the rest of the family.

He climbed the front porch steps and prepared his plea to Carol Hardy. She was his last shot at finding Sam, and maybe she knew more than she wanted to admit. Irving knocked on the door and stepped back. "Mrs. Hardy, it's Howard," he called out.

He prepared to knock again when the door opened. Irving's eyes raked over the woman. Her makeup left black trails down her full cheeks. Her eyes were swollen, and her short dark hair was disheveled as though she'd only just awakened. "Jeez, Carol. Are you all right?"

Her lips trembled. "Where's my boy, Howard? Where is he?"

"I don't know." Irving closed his eyes a moment. "I was hoping he was here. May I come in?"

She stepped away from the door. "Randall's still at the police station?"

He walked inside and removed his hat. "Yes, ma'am. Carol, I don't know what to say about all this, but I need to find Sam, you understand? I have to talk to him."

Carol closed the door. "He didn't do anything, Howard. It's just not possible."

"It seems that way, yes, but the signs—the signs are there."

She started into the kitchen and turned on the coffee maker. "But you know my son. You know what he's like. He couldn't harm a fly."

"I wish I could just sit down with you a few minutes, but time's run out, Carol. If I don't find Sam, I have to get the county and state police involved to help me find him. I'm not sure what'll happen if I can't contain this. I do know Sam. And if someone other than me finds him, the results could be devastating."

She turned to face him. "I promise you, I don't know where he is, Howard. He left this morning, and I haven't seen him since. You took my husband. I can live with that. But don't take my son."

Irving glanced through the French doors at the back of the kitchen that led to the rear yard. In the early evening light, he peered out over the few acres of land that stretched back a ways. And there was that garage again, its door was still partially open. He looked back at Carol. "May I take a look around back?"

She returned with a coffee cup in her hand. "What for?"

"Given all that's happened, Carol, I'll have to get a search warrant for your property in any case. Now, if you want to help, the best thing you can do is allow me to just take a quick look around."

Carol appeared resigned. "All right, Howard. If that's what you need to do."

He started toward the back door and turned back. "Carol, is there anything you want to say to me?"

"Such as?" she asked.

"Anything at all that could shed light on this whole awful situation."

"I'm not sure what you're asking of me, Howard."

He cast down his gaze. "All right, Carol." Irving stepped outside into the hazy light and walked toward the garage that was set back from the front of the house. He'd spotted it earlier when he brought in Randall Hardy, but now, something bothered him.

Sam drove an old gray Chevy Trailblazer. Randall drove a newer model Ford half-ton truck, also gray. But he recalled that the senior Mr. Hardy tinkered with junkers on occasion, hence the big garage tucked back on the property. Noticing that garage earlier set off the reminder.

Officer Erin Calvert had been running on the search for a blue vehicle that would've sustained severe front-end damage after the

Hoffman crash. All they knew was the color of the car, no make or model yet, so the search continued.

But if all the signs pointed to young Sam Hardy, then it would make sense a blue car with significant damage would be inside that garage right now.

Irving approached the garage and stood in front of it. Fear of what lay inside clutched at his chest, nevertheless, he had a job to do. One, it seemed, he had failed at miserably, even going so far as to fire the FBI agents because he didn't think they knew their asses from their elbows. "Maybe that was me who didn't know." He walked toward the door and reached for the handle to raise it. The metal rollers slid along their tracks and the door rolled open.

Irving stepped inside. His lips trembled and his eyes stung at what had been revealed. He walked around to the front of the blue sedan. The bumper was gone, the headlights were smashed, and the hood had buckled. "Goddam it." The lieutenant retrieved his phone, raising it to his ear. "Erin, I found the blue car."

KATE CHECKED the time on her phone while she and Surrey waited in Irving's office. "He should be back here any minute."

Surrey paced the small office and set his sights on her. "What did he say about the knife when you talked to him?"

"Given what he found at the Hardys' house, I don't think he's that interested in it, to be honest. I think he believes this is it. Game over." She glanced through his office window. "He's pulling in now." Kate started toward the door and stepped out into the hall. She looked back at Surrey, who'd stopped in his tracks. "What?"

"You don't think this is game over, do you?"

"I'm reserving judgment." Kate walked on, heading into the lobby when she spotted Irving enter. "Lieutenant."

"Agent Reid, Surrey," Irving nodded. "Any word back from Dr. Rozier?"

"No, we're still waiting," Surrey replied. "What's your plan now?"

Irving waved for them to follow him back to his office. After they stepped inside, he closed the door. "All right, Randall Hardy had to have known about Sam and the car. I've got Officers Calvert and Abrams there now, waiting on the tow truck."

"What about Mrs. Hardy?" Kate asked. "She must've known something. She might know where Sam is."

"I've just been down that road. Mrs. Hardy was mum as to Sam's whereabouts," Irving replied. "As I said, I'll have my team there for a while. They'll keep eyes on the mother while we gather the evidence."

"In the meantime, we've got Randall Hardy in custody," Surrey cut in. "What do we do about Brian Keller? There's no way the ME has even processed Gatwick's body, which means we can't dismiss Keller, not until we know for a fact that Sam Hardy is our guy." He turned to Kate. "But you have reservations."

"You do?" Irving regarded her. "Such as?"

"Why would Randall Hardy burn down the library?" Kate shrugged. "I can almost understand if it was for some kind of diversion, but that's too weak. He would've known we'd come to him given the proximity of his store, alone. I'm having trouble swallowing the idea. And Pumphrey is still nowhere to be found. He offered a sample, then seemingly vanished," she added.

A knock sounded on the door.

"Come in," Irving called out.

"Sorry to interrupt," Officer Toomey said. "But uh, Chris Pumphrey is here and so are Jason Gatwick's parents."

The lieutenant shot up from his chair. "We'll be right there. Do not, under any circumstances, let Pumphrey leave."

CHRIS PUMPHREY STOOD from a lobby chair when he noticed the lieutenant and the FBI agents approach. "I got a call from Jason's parents. They told me what happened and that they were coming here. I didn't know what to do, so I grabbed a few of Jason's things, his iPad, laptop, a watch... Things I thought they would want, and came down."

Irving eyed the bag in Chris's hands. "That was good of you to do, son, but under the circumstances, what you're holding right now is evidence. This is a murder investigation. I'm gonna have to ask you to hand that over to me."

"Oh. Oh, I hadn't realized you... of course." He handed him the bag. "Here, take it. I didn't go through all his stuff, so if you want to come to the apartment, I can let you in."

Irving tilted his head. "The rest of Jason's things are as he left them?"

"Yes, sir."

The lieutenant turned to Jason's parents. "Mr. and Mrs. Gatwick, I'm very sorry for your loss. Thank you for coming down." He gestured back. "This is Agent Reid and Agent Surrey."

Jason's mother, Louise, stood from a chair and wiped her eyes. "I don't know why he was there. With all that's happened. All his friends. I don't know why he'd go with Brian like that."

Pumphrey noticed how frail she appeared when the woman turned to him.

"Had you spoken with Jason today?" she asked.

"Yes, ma'am, but just briefly this morning. He was going on shift after the library fire, and I was clocking out."

"He didn't tell you what he had planned for the day?" Mr. Gatwick asked.

"No, sir. Just work, I thought. It was a long night with the library fire and all." He noticed the lieutenant's stare and turned back to him.

Irving planted his hands on his hips. "We were wondering where you went off to today, son. Suppose you can fill us in?"

Irving joined the agents in the hall as they huddled together. "What do you know about that? Pumphrey turned up here."

Kate glanced back into the lobby. "This doesn't feel right. I'm telling you, I think Pumphrey is putting on a show. He's here playing the grieving friend, looking to comfort the parents. But something else is at play here."

Irving regarded her. "You're going to have to come up with something better than that, Agent Reid."

"Yeah, I get that." She looked on. "The doctor's time is up. I'm going to call him now and see what he has for us on the knife."

"I'll go talk to the parents," Irving replied. "Come get me when you can find a way to explain all this." He headed back into the lobby.

"You want to make the call, then let's make it." Surrey walked on toward the office near the back and held the door for Kate.

She continued inside and grabbed her phone. "Dr. Rozier, please. Yes, I'll hold." She placed the call on speaker as Surrey closed the door.

"This is Dr. Rozier."

"Yes, it's Agents Reid and Surrey, Doctor," Kate began. "I'm sorry to hound you like this, but we've been presented with a situation, and we've reached critical mass. What did you learn about the knife?"

"Hold on just a moment, please."

The sound of shuffling feet arose through the phone's speaker and a moment later, Rozier returned to the call. "I apologize, but I needed to get back to my desk. All right, I have gone through the three autopsies I've completed so far. Obviously, with the latest victim—"

"Understood, Doctor," Kate continued. "What did you find?"

"I did get a surprising result, actually, Agent Reid. The photo of the knife you sent was compared to the severed tissues as well as the remaining tissue in the victims' mouths. It appears the serrated edge of the knife in the photo matches the marks found on Heidi Sumner and Amber Hoffman."

Kate drew in her brow. "And Emma Katz?"

"I'm afraid it did not match. A different knife was used in that attack."

She placed her hand over her mouth and drew back her shoulders.

"So we have another killer out there, is that what you're saying, Doc?" Surrey asked.

"I suppose that's on you folks to figure out. I'm saying that two different knives were used on these three young women. As far as the newest victim, again, I have to process the body—"

"How soon?" Kate jumped in.

"Ma'am, it'll take hours. I'll do the best I can."

"Thank you, Doctor. We'll be waiting for your call." Surrey waited for Kate to hang up. "Jesus."

"It's Pumphrey," Kate said. "I don't know how yet, but he's the second unsub."

"That means you think he and Sam were working together?" Surrey pressed on. "What about Randall Hardy? The blue car found at the Hardy home? There are multiple variables to consider."

"I understand," Kate replied. "We'll send the knife to our lab for analysis tonight. For now..." she considered a plan. "We search Gatwick and Pumphrey's place. The kid brought in Gatwick's personal devices. Why?"

"To possibly avoid a search of their apartment?" Surrey asked. "Maybe he's buying time. If that's the case, we search it now while the kid is here."

"We still have Brian Keller. Do we let him off? What if I'm wrong?" Kate asked.

Surrey pulled back and eyed her. "Do you think you're wrong?"

She held his gaze. "No."

24

To let go of a possible suspect had been the biggest risk Kate had taken in this investigation and maybe in any investigation. And Surrey backed her up one hundred percent. Whether Irving agreed remained to be seen. This was his case, and the two had already butted heads on its direction.

Keller had decided to go to Hardy's store, he claimed, to find Sam or his father. The result was that his friend was killed. The possibility existed Keller worked with the unsub to bring Gatwick there. But the motive was lacking. This was where the risk lay. This was where Kate's gut could betray her.

She headed back into the hall with Surrey trailing and stopped cold when Irving stepped out of his office.

"Agent Reid, pardon. I didn't see you coming," he said.

"That's all right. We were coming to see you anyway." Kate peeked into his office and noticed Jason Gatwick's parents and Chris Pumphrey. She stepped back as the parents walked through the doorway and entered the hall where they stood.

Mr. Gatwick eyed Kate. "You're with the FBI?"

"Yes, sir, I am," she replied.

He turned down his lips and nodded. "Guess y'all are seriously overpaid then, huh? You let my boy die today, so you and your FBI colleague can go straight to hell." He reared back and spat in Kate's face.

She flinched as it struck her cheek.

"Damn it." Irving grabbed Mr. Gatwick by the shoulders. "That was unnecessary, sir." He led the man toward the lobby.

His wife stopped and looked at Kate while she wiped away the spittle with the back of her hand.

"Normally, ma'am, I'd be angry with my husband for being so crass, but I'm not entirely sure you didn't deserve that." She hurried to catch up to her husband.

"They're usually very nice people," Pumphrey said as he stepped out.

Kate turned her attention to him. "Sorry?"

"The Gatwicks. They're kind folks, but they're hurting right now. The whole town is."

"We've been trying to find you, Chris," Kate said.

"Well, I haven't gone anywhere, ma'am." He fixed his gaze on her. "Are you any closer to finding out who's been doing this? Who killed my roommate?"

"When did you say the parents called you?" she pressed on.

"I didn't, but they called me about an hour after Jason was taken to the county morgue. That's what the lieutenant told them, anyway."

Surrey cocked his head. "And the first thing you decided to do was to gather Jason's stuff?"

"His devices and stuff, yeah," Pumphrey replied. "I didn't know it could be considered evidence. I never would've touched it if I had."

Kate now recalled that Gatwick mentioned Emma hadn't been

fond of his roommate. "I heard you and Emma Katz didn't get along very well."

"Did Jason tell you that?" Pumphrey asked. "Because it wasn't me. Emma didn't like me. I thought she was fine. Jason liked her, so what the hell did I care?"

"In your statement to Irving, you said you hadn't seen Emma at Town Park that day," she continued.

"That's because I hadn't," he replied. "And if you'll recall, I was there with Jason when we found her. So, I'm not sure what you're getting at. Look, my roommate was just murdered. I came here to help his parents. What do you want from me, ma'am?"

Kate raised her eyes to meet his. "You weren't supposed to be on shift last night when the fire happened at the library."

"That's right. We were all called in. It was a 3-alarm. We needed everyone on deck." Pumphrey shifted his weight and licked his lips.

Kate touched a nerve; his body language revealed his agitation. Pumphrey was the only person with some relation to the 1835 murders. His whereabouts were unaccounted for leading up to the fire. But what threw her was that he'd voluntarily submitted a swab. And only Sam's DNA was found on Emma. There was more to him than she knew, but the pieces couldn't yet be put together. "I'm sure Lieutenant Irving would like to continue a conversation with you if you'd be all right sticking around for a while."

Pumphrey checked his Apple Watch. "Uh, yeah, I suppose I could. I hadn't planned on it, but if it will help find the person who murdered my friend and roommate, then of course."

∽

KELLER WAS FREED on the basis that the blue car had been found at the Hardy home and the fact Sam had taken Keller to the woods. Irving had agreed to the decision, and while he stayed back to further question Pumphrey, Kate and Surrey would search the apartment. And still, there had been no sign of Sam Hardy, even as every unit in Jansville searched for him.

Kate drove on toward the apartment Gatwick shared with Pumphrey as the sky finally turned dark. "I'm not sure what proof we'll find or whether it will make a difference as far as Sam Hardy is concerned. None of this lines up, and the only explanation is that we have two killers."

"One of the Hardys rammed that blue car into Amber Hoffman and eventually killed her. We have Sam Hardy dead to rights on Emma's murder thanks to his DNA. As far as the rest, let's hope we find the second knife." Surrey pointed ahead. "There's the complex on the right."

Kate turned in and parked at the front of Building C. She opened her door and stepped out. Surrey caught up to her and they climbed the stairs to the second-floor unit. With the keys Irving retrieved from Pumphrey, Kate unlocked the door.

Surrey flipped on the lights. "All right. Let's get started."

Kate continued into the narrow hall of the two-bedroom apartment and reached the first bedroom door. She turned on the light and placed gloves on her hands. Surrey continued down the hall to the other bedroom, but she leaned out. "We've reviewed Emma's phone records. Pumphrey's number never appeared."

Surrey looked back. "These kids communicate through apps now. Just because his number wasn't there, doesn't mean they weren't in contact."

"True." Kate noticed pictures on the nightstand. "This is Pumphrey's room." She walked over to examine them. One photo of his family. One of Pumphrey standing in uniform in front of a firetruck. She focused on Pumphrey. "You were there when she was found. Same as Gatwick." Kate ran through various scenarios that might explain how he could've returned to the top of the hill unseen by Gatwick or anyone. Of course, she hadn't known how long Emma wandered through the trees, suffering from her injuries. "Couldn't have been too long, but maybe long enough for you to get back into position?"

The question that screamed in her head was, 'Why?' Why had he killed her? What had she known? Maybe he'd hit on her, and she rejected him? Pumphrey wasn't part of the circle of friends. Regardless, he must've been around Emma somewhat while Gatwick dated her. Had there been feelings between them? But to murder her, and to do what had been done to her spoke to an uncontrollable anger. And then there was Sam Hardy.

Kate's head spun as she tried to make sense of how Pumphrey fit into this. She continued to scrutinize his bedroom, walking to his closet and opening the doors. "I don't know what the hell I think I'll find in here." She reached her hand to the top shelf and blindly felt along it when she hit something. Kate raised on her tiptoes and grabbed what felt like a sheet of paper.

She brought it down and saw it was a letter-sized envelope. Kate opened the flap to the envelope and retrieved its contents. The letterhead indicated it was from the University of Roanoke. "That's where Emma went." She read on.

"We regret to inform you that we are unable to offer you a spot in the Freshman class of 2024...."

"He got rejected." Kate walked into the hall. "Hey, I found something."

Surrey emerged from Gatwick's bedroom. "What is it?"

She held up the letter. "Pumphrey was rejected by the same university where Emma attended."

"Oh, that's interesting," Surrey replied. "And probably not a coincidence. But he's older."

"By two years, yes," Kate said. "He could still apply even if not straight out of high school. But the thing is, had he wanted to go there because Emma did?"

"That's a fair assumption." Surrey continued inside the bedroom. "Where did you find this?"

"On the closet shelf. See if you can find anything else up there."

Surrey stepped back and raised his gaze. "I'll grab a chair." He walked out and soon returned with a dining chair, setting it in front of the closet. "All right." He climbed on the chair and spotted the boxes. "We have a few shoe boxes up here. Let me see if I can reach them. Got 'em." Surrey stepped off the chair and set down the boxes.

Kate raised the lid on one of them and peered inside. "Flash drives." She shot him a look. "Who keeps flash drives in a shoe box in their closet?"

He returned a side-eye. "People who don't want them to be found."

IRVING DECIDED to let Pumphrey sweat it out a little while he worked to get information from Randall Hardy. However, after almost twenty minutes, he had grown tired of the man's lack of cooperation. "Mr. Hardy, we know about the affair with Heidi."

He shrugged. "As I've said, that hardly makes me a killer."

"It makes you the last person to have seen her alive. We have it on video," Irving replied. "And DNA was found on her. Now, placing you under arrest on a murder charge means we can insist on obtaining a sample from you with or without your cooperation. You understand that, I'm sure."

"First of all, Howard, I'm here answering your questions without an attorney present. I can end that at any time if you want to start threatening me."

He leaned over the table. "Then how about we cut the shit? The influence you have over your son suggests he would do anything you told him. You had to know about the wrecked car in your garage—"

"You think I told Sam to murder his friends? To cut out their tongues?" He scoffed. "You're insane, you know that? I had nothing to do with what happened."

"If you'd like to offer some clarity on the situation, I'm all ears," Irving replied.

Hardy rubbed his forehead. "I'm telling you, I didn't hurt Heidi, all right? Am I an asshole for cheating on my wife? Yeah. But I'm no killer. As far as the car goes, I don't go into that garage. If it was there and you know it was used to run Amber Hoffman off the road, well, then you'll have to talk to Sam about that."

WITH HER LAPTOP on the dining table in Gatwick's apartment, Kate inserted the flash drive while Surrey looked on with expectancy. "I'm starting to think Pumphrey had a thing for Emma." She waited for the files to load. "And if she rejected him, it could be a motive for murder."

"I agree, but why cut out her tongue?" Surrey asked. "And how the hell did Sam Hardy's DNA show up on her, and not Pumphrey's?"

"I haven't figured that out yet." Kate opened the folder and the screen populated with videos. "What the hell is all this?" She clicked on the file to open it.

The video played. Kate's lips parted and her face turned blank. "Oh my God."

"It's Gatwick's bedroom. Jeez, did he..." Surrey's face screwed up. "Is this when Gatwick and Katz were dating? The girl was barely out of high school."

"He watched them." Kate opened another file and pressed play. "Oh, no." She rubbed her brow. "He recorded them whenever she came over. My God. He was obsessed with her."

"But this was a year ago," Surrey added.

"And Pumphrey had tried to get accepted at her university. He wanted to follow her there." She turned to him. "Is it possible Emma found out about this?"

"That could've been the secret, but if she had, why not go to the police?"

"Maybe she wanted to confront him about it first. I wonder if he'd sent her emails and attached these files, threatening to upload them to the internet if she talked," Kate continued. "Then she comes home for the summer, he realizes she intends to say something—"

Surrey cocked his head. "At the very least, don't you think she would've said something to her parents? Her friends? Maybe even Jason Gatwick, since it involved him?"

"We'd have to know when this all came out. If she'd only just discovered it, then it makes sense she kept it to herself until she could figure out how to handle it," Kate replied. "Except she's dead now. And it had to have been a knife Pumphrey used to cut out her tongue."

"Seems a hell of a message, unless he assumed her friends knew what she'd planned."

Kate drew in her brow. "And only a week or so later, Heidi turns up dead."

"Which we know the crime was committed with a different knife, a different object used on the blow to the head." Surrey turned up his gaze as if searching for a logical answer. "So Pumphrey lays low, realizing he hadn't done it. The cops were busy looking at everyone else."

"And when the schoolteacher talks about the old murders, Pumphrey knows a connection to him could be easily made, so he sets the library on fire." Kate fixed her gaze on Surrey. "Randall Hardy tries to hide his affair, fearing Heidi told Emma. And we already know how he treated Emma. He exploits Sam's grief, knowing his son's vulnerabilities. His susceptibility to suggestion out of fear for his father."

"Holy shit." Surrey's face masked in disbelief. "We have to get back to the station."

As IRVING WALKED Pumphrey into the lobby, Kate pushed through the entrance and noticed them. "What's going on?"

Surrey walked in behind her. "We need to ask you some questions, Mr. Pumphrey."

Irving set his sights on Kate, appearing hopeful they found something. "He'd volunteered his time to answer our questions regarding Jason Gatwick, but if you have something else." He turned to Pumphrey. "You'd be open to giving us a few more minutes of your time, isn't that right, son?"

As it turned out, they'd arrived at the station just in time. Irving appeared left with no choice but to let the kid go. Now, she noticed a glimmer in his eye, as though he understood that they found something.

"I guess I could stay for a few minutes. But I'd like some time to mourn the loss of my friend. I'm sure you can understand," Pumphrey replied.

"We won't keep you for long," Surrey added.

Irving ushered Pumphrey back into the corridor. "I do apologize for this. It's just protocol. Go on in. I'll chat with them for a moment, so I know they aren't wasting your time." After Pumphrey entered the room, Irving closed the door and turned back to the agents. "Boy, you'd better have something good for me."

Kate opened her laptop bag and retrieved a Ziplock full of flash drives. "Pumphrey was watching Emma Katz and Jason Gatwick during their intimate moments in his bedroom."

Irving looked away. "Oh, Lord."

"We also found a rejection letter from the university where Emma attended," she added. "He'd tried to get accepted, I assume, to follow her there."

"And did you find a second knife?" Irving placed his hands on his hips. "We're going to need that to tie him to Emma's murder."

"Not yet, but we will," Surrey replied. "But you have enough to book him on charges. I'd venture to say Emma wasn't yet eighteen in those videos. It's enough to hold him."

He nodded. "That is true, so where does that leave us with Sam Hardy? I've spoken to Randall. He admits to nothing, as you'd expect. But I feel it in my bones that he led his son astray."

"Given the DNA results, the forensic evidence is there for the murder of Emma Katz. The car is enough for Amber Hoffman. We can tie Sam to the other murders once the knife is processed. I'm certain his DNA will show up on it, possibly fingerprints," Kate began. "The knife used on Emma is key here too. We keep the father in custody, as well as Pumphrey."

Irving appeared to ponder the situation. "Then all that leaves us with is to find Sam."

Kate eyed them. "And hopefully, that will lead us to lay the final pieces."

HEADLIGHTS REFLECTED the yellow lines on the dark highway. Walsh was on his way back to Jansville. While Kate and Surrey pushed through to see this case to its end, he would retrieve the knife, return to Quantico, and hand it over for analysis. His phone rattled in the center console of his SUV, and he answered the call. "Kate, what's happening on your end?"

"How far out are you?"

Walsh checked the road signs. "I'm practically there now. Why?"

"We're at the station and I need a favor," Kate replied.

"Shoot."

"Sam Hardy is still missing, and we need to find him. This is a kid who probably wouldn't venture too far from home. He's never been outside the town, at least, not on his own. Irving has a unit at his house and units patrolling the streets. They've checked the store, but it's been a while. We need to have someone there to keep watch. Can I ask you to do that until we can get there? You'll be looking for an older model gray Chevy Trailblazer?"

"Course, I can do that."

"Thank you."

"What about this knife? You want me to get it to the lab tonight, right?" he asked.

"That was the plan, but for now, we have to find this kid," Kate replied.

"All right. I'll be in touch." Walsh ended the call and noticed the sign for the grocery store. He killed his headlights and drove into the parking lot. At first glance, he didn't see any vehicles out front. The lights were on inside the store, and he noticed the police tape around the entrance.

Walsh continued toward the building but veered off to the side to park. He cut the engine and stepped out of his vehicle to walk the perimeter. He flipped off the holster strap for his sidearm and palmed the butt of his gun as he started on.

Lighting out here was scarce with only a couple of fixtures mounted on the building around the front. A couple on the side. And as he reached the back, it was completely dark. Walsh began to sweat almost immediately in the sultry night air.

Within minutes, he'd returned to the front of the store, where a car slowed just before the entrance. It came from the direction of town. The opposite way led out of Jansville. "Whoever you are, you must be coming from town."

And, as if nature held its breath, the cicadas silenced. The woodland creatures ceased to move, and the breeze died. Walsh kept his eyes fixed on the beams of light, waiting for them to shift their aim right at him. "Come on in, friend."

The car turned into the parking lot. Walsh squeezed his sidearm. It rolled on for a moment before the driver switched off the headlights. He took measured steps toward the side of the building while the car continued toward the front entrance. He still hadn't recognized the vehicle and it was impossible to see who sat behind the wheel.

When it finally stopped, Walsh halted in place just as he reached the front corner. He tucked back behind the building to remain unseen and waited only a moment before peeking around. "Looks like a Chevy to me," he whispered.

The driver's side door opened, and the interior light illuminated the cabin, but the shadows still obscured the face. One thing was certain, a man was inside. And as he stepped out, Walsh leaned around the corner for a better look.

When the man stepped onto the sidewalk that led to the entrance, the light at the front of the store shone on him and the vehicle. Walsh reared back as his eyes sharpened. "Here we go."

25

It took only minutes from the time Walsh called in the sighting to mobilize quickly and arrive at Hardy's store. Kate spotted the red sign in the distance and slowed to make the turn. "Walsh said Sam's Trailblazer was parked out front."

"I don't see anything yet..." Surrey looked on. "Hold up. Someone's there. I see the vehicle."

Kate flipped off her headlights and rolled into the parking lot. "Sam must've waited for the patrols to clear the area before coming back."

"I don't know how he managed to stay out of sight all day." Surrey unbuckled his seatbelt and placed his hand on the door handle. "Unless his mom was lying to Irving, and she knew where he was the entire time."

Kate thrust the gearshift into Park and stepped out. When Surrey joined her, she continued. "It's definitely Sam Hardy's Chevy. Let's find Levi first and make sure he's safe." She drew her gun and kept it down at her hip. "He said he was around the side of the building."

They veered right and Kate saw a shadow ahead. Levi?"

"Over here," he whispered.

When they reached him, Kate continued, "Did he go inside?"

"Yep. He's in there. What do you want to do?"

She eyed the building. "We go in."

Walsh started toward the main entrance. Kate fell in next to him with Surrey trailing only by a step or two. All kept eyes peeled and guns ready. As they reached the entrance, the doors opened.

"It's unlocked," Kate said. "He'll know someone's here. We go to the back. His dad's office."

They took their positions and walked through the store. The sound of soft rock filled the otherwise empty space. It felt just as it had before when Kate had spoken to Randall Hardy while she paid for a six-pack of beer. A few feet away, she thrust out her hand at them and mouthed, "Stop." A door opened and she peeked around the corner where Hardy's office was located.

Sam stepped out with a gun in his hand.

The agents raised their weapons when Kate called out, "Drop the gun, Sam!"

His eyes were swollen from tears. His face was red and sweat dampened his tousled brown hair. "I heard you come in." Sam's lips trembled. "I didn't mean to."

"What are you doing, Sam? Put down the gun," Kate said.

"My dad keeps this gun in the safe here. He always thinks the store will get robbed. That's why I'm here. I needed to get it."

"What for?" Kate continued.

Sam eyed the three federal agents with their guns trained on him. "I didn't do it. I didn't kill Emma. I could never hurt her."

Kate drew in her brow. "Sam, we found proof that you'd had contact with Emma before she died."

"I did." His eyes pleaded. "You don't understand. We went for a walk in the woods. We talked about all kinds of stuff. School, friends, and then she said she had to go. That she had to meet someone."

"Who?" Kate asked.

"I don't know," Sam replied.

"Put down the gun, Sam," Walsh cut in. "Now. Before you do something you'll regret."

He kept his eyes on Kate. "We stopped at the top of the hill. I wanted to tell her how much I missed her, but she kept talking about other stuff."

"Then what, Sam?" Surrey asked. "Did you hurt her then?"

"No, no of course not. I told you, I could never..." Tears streamed down his face. "I kissed her cheek and said that I cared about her, and I wanted the best life for her. She said thank you. I didn't see her after that."

"I don't understand why you didn't say anything about this?" Kate insisted.

"I was sad and angry. My dad said it was my fault. And when I told him that I knew about how he talked to Emma that day and that I knew he was with Heidi behind my mom's back, he got so mad at me."

"Sam, I'm giving you five seconds to put down that gun." Walsh stepped forward.

"Wait." Kate held out her hand. "Sam, did your dad kill your other friends? Amber, Heidi, and now Jason?"

He looked down. "No."

"Then who did?" she asked.

"Me." He raised the gun and pressed it under his chin.

"Whoa!" Surrey called out. "Hang on, Sam. Put it down, all right? Come on. You don't want to do this."

"I wanted to show Brian," Sam continued. "To try to explain how it all happened. How I thought they were all responsible for taking Emma from me. It was all of them. They did this."

"No, Sam, they didn't," Kate said. "Your dad convinced you it was them, though, didn't he?"

He shrugged. "Emma went away to school. I loved her, and then she was gone."

"Kate," Walsh called out.

She held out her hand. "I got this."

"I know what I did was wrong," Sam said. "But I got angry, just like my dad. And then when he saw I wrecked the car..."

"Sam, you don't know what you're saying right now, okay?" Kate cut in. "Why don't you give me the gun and we'll take you down to the station and you can talk to Lieutenant Irving. We'll get all of this figured out, I promise."

"You're a nice lady," Sam said. "I'm sorry, ma'am, but I can't go with you. I can't go back with any of you." He closed his eyes and raised his chin while he pulled back the safety.

Kate lunged forward. "Sam, no!"

The gun fired. Sam crumpled to the ground.

IRVING STOOD at the entrance to the station as the agents returned. "Where's Sam? You said you found him, and I haven't heard a thing in an hour."

Kate walked inside. Surrey and Walsh weren't far behind when she approached Irving. "Sam shot himself."

"What?" Irving's eyes expressed confusion. "How the hell did he get a gun? What are you telling me right now?" He swung around with his hands on his hips. "I can't believe it. It doesn't make sense."

"No, sir. None of it does," Surrey added. "We'll have to keep working to get definitive proof that Pumphrey murdered Emma, but what you have right now is a good start."

"And the other kids?" Irving shot back. "You're telling me Sam Hardy murdered all of them? And what, Randall Hardy is an innocent man?"

"I don't know about that," Surrey continued. "It's safe to say Randall Hardy had a great deal of influence over his son and he had his own secrets to keep. You have enough to put him away on charges of conspiracy to commit murder. Sam admitted his dad knew about the wrecked car. Randall Hardy was aware of his son's culpability."

Kate looked on. "All of this because Sam blamed everyone for Emma's death, in no small part thanks to his dad."

"He was an abused kid," Surrey cut in. "He struggled with social norms, with comprehending friendship and love. I'm not sure he fully understood what he'd done, even if he insisted he had. And that's the sad part about all of this. We couldn't have stopped Emma's murder, but if we'd been paying attention to Sam Hardy, we would've understood him better and maybe—"

"You can't think like that, Surrey," Walsh cut in. "We worked the case, the profile."

"And he didn't fit it," Kate said.

Walsh shoved his hands into his pockets. "No? I think you'll find he fit it exactly as you'd predicted."

"But I didn't predict him. Not until it was too late," Kate replied.

THE DRONE of the tires on the highway was the only sound in the car. Kate kept her sights fixed on the dark road ahead with only her headlights by which to see. "I didn't expect this."

Surrey turned to her. "I know you didn't. I don't think any of us did. It's hard to feel good about finishing a case when so many innocent kids died because of a young man who lacked a full understanding of his emotions."

"And a father who perpetuated it. He should've been given help," Kate said. "But I don't think Randall Hardy cared much about that."

"Doesn't seem the type," Surrey replied. "For what it's worth, we could've lost Brian Keller too, but we stopped Sam before it could happen."

"That kid is going to be messed up for the rest of his life," Kate added.

He peered through the passenger window. "At least he'll get to live one."

Kate glanced in the rearview mirror and caught sight of Walsh's SUV behind them. "Levi's timing couldn't have been better, huh?" Her phone rang and she answered the call. "Hi."

"Hey, are you heading back to DC?" Nick asked.

"I am. Jonathan's with me."

Surrey glanced at the phone. "Hey, Scarborough. How's it going?"

"Good, thanks. Not so great for you guys, though, huh?"

Kate returned a crooked smile to Surrey. "Could've gone better. Are you at home?"

"On my way, actually. So I'll see you in a few hours?"

"You bet. See you soon. Love you," Kate replied.

"Love you. Bye."

She ended the call, and the car went silent again. After a few minutes, Kate glanced at Surrey. "You know what I said on the boat that night?"

He turned to her. "On the Fourth?"

"Yeah, about how I was completely okay with Nick working with his ex-girlfriend and that it was no big deal."

"I remember." He chuckled and set his sights ahead. "Not so easy when it gets down to it, is it?"

"Not as easy as I thought it would be. But I'd never say that to him. Not that I feel like I'd be keeping a secret. I trust my husband, but you know when you work closely with someone, things happen. It did with Nick and me."

"And you think it could with him and this ex of his?" Surrey pressed on.

"Deep down, I suppose not, but there's always that voice in the back of your mind..." She returned a sideways glance. "I'm not usually the jealous type."

Surrey tapped his fingers on the armrest and nodded. "I will say this, Scarborough would be crazy to risk losing you."

26

Thirty-six hours had passed, and the results had finally arrived. It was time to confirm what Kate suspected, that Sam Hardy's DNA, prints, all of it would be on that knife used to cut out the tongues of his friends.

It was only when Chris Pumphrey was booked that Irving managed to get out of him the truth about his past relatives. It hadn't pointed to murder, but it had pointed to inspiration. And it was the reason Pumphrey burned down the library, as Kate suspected. When confronted with the videos, Irving got the confession. Pumphrey had cut out Emma's tongue to stop her from telling everyone that he'd violated her intimate relationship with Jason and that she'd rejected him. Hitting her in the head was done after the fact when she tried to escape.

Sam Hardy copied what had been done to Emma to make it appear it had been the same killer. No doubt, it was Randall Hardy's idea he planted in his son's head. Though, currently, no charges were pending against the elder Hardy.

Irving sent Kate a message earlier this morning that

Pumphrey's mother admitted to telling the kid when he was younger about his past relatives. And she also happened to recall a place where Chris would go hunting. Irving was headed there this morning and Kate expected that was where the second knife would be found.

As far as Carol Hardy, well, she was hardly blameless, but she finally stood up to her abuser, blaming Sam's troubles on Randall casting the boy aside his whole life. Never once attempting to get Sam the help that he needed, while she stood by and let the abuse continue.

Walsh peeked his head inside Kate's office. "Do you want to go downstairs with me and get the results?" He noticed the look on her face. "You okay?"

She pinched her brow. "Not really. I know we stopped all this, but so many kids died. And for what?"

Walsh continued inside. "Come on, Kate. You know better than this. You've been through this enough to know—"

"Yes, I have. And yet it never changes."

He pulled out a chair to sit. "Look, none of us could've predicted what happened in Jansville. It wasn't like anything I'd ever seen, and I know it wasn't like anything you'd experienced either."

"I'm used to catching the bad guys because they're bad. Sam?" She raised a shoulder. "He acted out of an anger he had no way to control."

"The kid still knew right from wrong," Walsh cut in. "Don't forget that. I'll grant you that he didn't process things as we do, maybe, but he murdered his friends. He cut out their tongues."

"He needed help." Kate stood from her desk. "It doesn't matter now. The case is over. The results are waiting for us downstairs."

Walsh led the way to the adjacent building and entered the forensics lab. Kate hadn't said a word and followed him inside.

When they reached the workstation, Walsh appeared to wait for Kate to speak, but she remained silent.

"Uh, hey, you have some results for us?" he asked.

"I do, Agent Walsh. Agent Reid, good to see you," the tech replied.

Kate nodded.

"Okay, I'll go back and get them for you. Hang on. I'll only be a minute."

After he disappeared, Walsh turned to her. "Maybe you should take the rest of the day off. Take some time to clear your head. Surrey and I can close this out and get with the lieutenant."

The tech headed back with a manilla envelope in his hand. "Here you go."

"Thanks." Walsh opened it and pulled out the report. He flipped the page to get to the summary and turned so Kate could read it. "Says here...yeah, here we are. Sam Hardy."

"Just as we thought. We should get this to Irving." She eyed the tech. "Thanks for rushing this through."

"Any time, Agent Reid. Good to see you."

Kate returned a cordial grin and spun around to leave. Walsh trailed her as they reached the corridor again. "If we'd had this knife sooner—"

"You can't 'what if' this away, Kate," Walsh replied. "We did what we could do and that's going to have to be enough."

She stopped cold and squared up to him. "I've spent my entire career at the Bureau listening to Nick tell me there was nothing more I could do. And now you're doing the same thing." She looked away. "Maybe I should listen to Jonathan."

"How so?" Walsh asked.

Kate walked on again. "Well, he says that I should be focused on ways to prevent these murders."

"We'd all like to prevent them, but it just isn't that easy," he replied.

"No, he didn't mean it like that," Kate added. "He meant it like I should be focused on finding ways to identify these people—killers—before they kill."

"He wants you to be a mind reader?"

She glanced at him. "Because of my background. Because of what I went through with Hendrickson, he thinks I can use that knowledge, among other resources, to find them before they kill."

"How would you go about that? It would be impossible to make that happen," Walsh said. "I don't get his meaning here."

"Maybe I don't fully understand it either, but I guess what I'm saying is that I have to put myself in their shoes."

"More than you already do?" he pressed on.

"Much more. My profiles are too generalized. I have to find a way to home in on the real reasons these people are doing the killing. Maybe Sam Hardy isn't the best example—or maybe he is, I don't know, but there is a common thread somewhere among these killers. That, Levi." Kate pointed a finger at him. "Is what I have to find."

He shrugged. "All right. Tell me how we go about that."

Kate revealed a crooked grin. "It starts at the beginning."

WALSH HAD BEEN RIGHT. Kate needed the day to clear her head. She'd been running on fumes and the exhaustion brought on a fog that clouded her thoughts.

She arrived home and unlocked the door, stepping inside the condo. In the mid-afternoon, a narrow shaft of light spilled into the living room from the partially opened curtains.

With Nick still at Headquarters, Kate grabbed her phone and made the call. "Hey, it's me. Are you busy?"

"Always, but I can spare a few minutes. Is everything okay?" he asked.

"Fine, yeah. Levi insisted I take time to clear my head, so I came home." Kate walked to the patio slider and stepped out onto the balcony, overlooking the bay. The air was cooler today and hadn't felt as damp. "I've been thinking about doing something that Jonathan suggested."

"Okay, and what's that?" Nick asked.

She looked out over the glistening waters. "If I want to be at the top of my game. If I want to stand any chance at truly getting into the minds of the people I go after, I'm going to need to learn more."

"I'm not sure I follow."

"I've based my profiles on the work of those who came before me. The likes of Quinn, you, and even Georgia. But the time's come for me to base them on what *I* know to be true. What *I* see inside these people. And the only way for me to do that is to sit down with them, get a sense of their personality from a perspective I've never had before."

"You want to talk to them—in person?" he asked.

"I do. Those I've imprisoned. Those the agents before me have imprisoned," Kate continued. "Hear me out. You know that most of them love to talk about their kills. Brag about them, even. Not all, but some. The ones who don't often speak of their kills in a detached manner, as though they hadn't committed the crimes."

"I'm aware."

She rested her elbows on the railing while the light breeze brushed against her face. "My goal is to walk through with them every kill so I can understand the emotions they experienced. The excitement, the remorse, if there was any. I have to understand their process, Nick. It's the only way I can even hope to identify a killing that has the possibility to become part of a string of killings. Markers exist, no matter how small. They leave them for us. And I have to identify them. This is how I start."

"And have you spoken to Fisher about this?"

"Not yet. I plan to draft a proposal. A plan of action." She noticed he'd grown quiet. "Nick?"

"Are you planning to do this alone?"

"I'm not sure there's any other way." Kate raised her chin to the sunlight. "I think this is the only way I survive the job, Nick. I feel like I've accomplished so little, that I've helped so few. And this last case," she closed her eyes. "If only I'd... I know I can be who I was meant to be, who Quinn insisted I would be. So, what do you think?"

"I don't know Surrey that well," Nick began. "But it seems to me that he's opened your eyes to a viewpoint, frankly, I'd never considered. It's a risk, Kate. You need to understand that. And it will change you."

Kate returned upright and stood firm. "That's what I'm counting on."

THE END

ABOUT THE AUTHOR

Robin Mahle has published more than 30 novels in the mystery/thriller genre. She also writes historical fiction as <u>Christine Chase.</u>

Her most recent series, the Detective Rebecca Ellis thrillers, are published by <u>Inkubator Books.</u>

It is Robin's fast-paced style of storytelling combined with tense action and thrilling twists that bring her readers back for more. So be sure sure to subscribe to her newsletter to keep up on all the latest releases, sales, and giveaways. Go to <u>robinmahle.com</u> and sign up today!

Robin lives in Coastal Virginia with her husband and two children.

If you enjoyed Ms. Mahle's work, please share your experience by leaving a review on <u>Amazon.</u>

ALSO BY ROBIN MAHLE

The Kate Reid FBI Thriller Series (17 books)

The Chef (stand-alone psych thriller)

The Man in My Attic (stand-alone psych thriller)

The Compound (standalone psych thriller)

The Remy Fontaine Fugitive Hunter Thrillers (4 books)

The Det. Rebecca Ellis Thrillers (5 books)

The Allison Hart PI Thrillers (5 Books)

The Lacy Merrick Thrillers (4 books)

**Visit robinmahle.com and sign up to receive Robin's Newsletter so you can stay up to date on her new releases, events, contests and even exclusive new material!